Thought I Knew You

Kate Moretti

Thought I Knew You
A Red Adept Publishing Book

Red Adept Publishing, LLC
2664 Timber Drive
Suite 157
Garner, NC 27529

http://RedAdeptPublishing.com/

Third Print Edition: June 2014
ISBN-10: 1940215293
ISBN-13: 978-1-940215-29-7

Cover and Formatting: Streetlight Graphics

DEDICATION

For Chip, who takes care of everything and everyone while I tap away. How'd I get so lucky?

ACKNOWLEDGMENTS

FIRST AND FOREMOST, WITHOUT CHIP, I wouldn't have had the time to write a letter, much less a novel. The man has rearranged his life for my new, all consuming "hobby" and his patience is astounding. Thanks in advance to my future grown children for not holding the hours of neglect during their young childhood against me. Thanks to my parents, Pat and Patti and my sister, Megan, for their understanding. Thanks to Becky Riddle for reading (and in some cases, re-reading) many drafts and letting me talk it through; to my various beta readers, most notably Elizabeth Buhmann for reading this manuscript in full almost as many times as I have and offering endless encouragement; to Clair Gibson for her very extensive edit to the rough draft; to my best girlfriends: BethAnn, Betsy, and Sharon for their feedback and just altogether being amazing fan club presidents; to Aunt Mary Jo, Uncle Jeff, and Molly, my biggest fans and personal publicists; to Elizabeth Vega Casey, grief counselor, for her advice and insight; to Authonomy for introducing me to a network of writers and without which I would not have found a home for my book; to my small, but reliable group of writer friends who have navigated these new waters with me (Melissa, Collin, Elizabeth, Ann, and Clair). Thanks to Michelle for challenging me to do better and Lynn for never letting me get away with anything—you both turned a rough manuscript into a book. Finally, thank you, Sarah DiCello, without whom I never would have finished it. You did it first and encouraged without competing. We'll always have reindeer fur.

CHAPTER 1

GREG AND CODY DISAPPEARED ON the same day.

One or two Fridays a month, Greg and I hired a babysitter for date night. The idea was to take some time for ourselves and reconnect. The reality was significantly less romantic. We typically ate at Pesto Charlie's due to some combination of availability and timing. I'd order whatever seafood was on special, and Greg would get Chicken Piccata—light on the sauce, of course. The food was always dependable, we never had to wait for a table, and with the low lighting and heady aroma of Italian spices, the restaurant was atmospheric enough to check *Date Night* off our to-do lists.

A few times, we tried other places, but either the food wasn't good, the service was poor, or we'd leave the restaurant late and miss the beginning of whatever movie we planned to see. Greg refused to go into a theater late. He called it rude and always clucked disapprovingly when others did so. So Pesto Charlie's became something of a tradition, albeit not a very exciting one. We'd get home between ten and ten thirty, pay the sitter twenty bucks, and go to bed. Sometimes we'd make love, but not every time. Even date night wasn't a guaranteed lay.

Greg was due back around one o'clock that Friday afternoon, having been on a business trip all week. He traveled for work more than I liked, but I'd stopped complaining about the monthly trips years ago and just accepted them as a part of life. Greg and I worked for the same company, Advent Pharmaceuticals. He was a professional trainer, not a weightlifting trainer, but adult education for the corporate set. He taught various courses on compliance, regulations, and the science behind Advent's drugs. He was based in Raritan, New Jersey, about ten miles from where we lived in Clinton, but often flew as far as Canada. Greg was good at his job; actually, Greg was good at almost everything.

I worked part time as a technical writer. My job was less demanding, allowing me to work from home and take care of the children. I just worked for extra money. *Something to do,* Greg had once joked at a dinner party, his arm draped across my shoulders. My face had burned at that, even though I had said the same thing a million times.

"Mommy, I think Cody got out." Hannah stood in the doorway between the hallway and the kitchen. Her earlier neat blond ponytail had fallen to the side, and she had some furtively acquired lipstick smeared on her cheek.

"What? Hannah, seriously, stay out of my purse, please." No matter how hard I tried, Hannah seemed determined to look a mess. *It's like an age requirement for four-year-olds.*

She pointed at the screen door. "Mommy, look!"

Sure enough, the screen swayed gently in the early October breeze. The opening between the mesh and the frame was jagged, as if it had been clawed. Had I let him out? I thought so. With the girls and the library, the memory of the morning blurred. I wasn't concerned. Cody would have been more aptly named Houdini. Our yard was large, several acres, with a small patch of woods in the back, perfect for chasing small animals and sometimes bringing them back as prizes, dropping them on the doorstep with a triumphant thump. Given that our closest neighbors were a quarter-mile away, Cody had the run of the place, but he always knew where home was.

"Sweetie, he'll be home. He's just out for an adventure." I poked my head out of the door and looked around the yard. "Cody! Come back, bud! It's dinner time!" It wasn't, but "dinner time" never failed to evoke a response.

I didn't see him, but he could have been anywhere. An old barn sat at the back of our property. I could imagine him there, tucked under the rarely used workbench, bathed in a shaft of light let in by the broken side door. I'd look in a bit, after the babysitter, Charlotte, came, but before we left for dinner. I let the screen door slam and checked the time. I was surprised to see that the clock showed three fifteen already. *Where was Greg anyway?*

I gathered two-year-old Leah from the playroom, her cheeks rouged from the same Hannah-pilfered lipstick, and plopped her in the high chair. After tossing some Goldfish crackers on her tray, I picked up the phone and dialed Greg's number. My call went directly to voicemail, so I left an irritated message. Frustrated, I tapped my fingers on the phone. Greg had likely forgotten our plans, his mind a million miles away, his wife last on his list. I stormed around the kitchen, slamming pots and pan lids, half-expecting him to appear behind me and say teasingly, "Feel better now?" like he generally does when I get cranky and start making noise.

I had to think a moment to remember the last time we spoke. Wednesday evening, he had called to say good night and to tell the girls he loved them. He didn't call last night, but that wasn't all that strange. I filled my time with kid-friendly activities, play dates, family, and friends, so we didn't talk every night. I could think of a few trips, particularly in the last few months, where the week would come and go before I realized we hadn't spoken at all.

"The bigger question, Hannah-banana, is where on earth is your daddy?"

At six, I called Charlotte and canceled.

Then, I called my mom. "Can you believe he didn't even call me? Should I be worried?"

"Nah, you never know when he's coming home," Mom reassured me. "Remember last month? His flight was delayed for a whole day."

"Yeah, but he called at least." I bit my bottom lip.

"Not until pretty late, though, right? He was stuck on the runway. It's probably the same now." I could envision her dismissively waving her hand in the air.

Her lightness eased something inside me, and I exhaled a breath I hadn't known I was holding. "I'll bet he forgot. It's so typical lately. I have no idea where his head is anymore."

"Well, if his plane was delayed, I'm sure he can't call. That whole 'don't use your cell phone while flying' rule."

Mom and Dad lived about ten minutes away in the same house where I grew up, and I talked to my mother no less than twice a day. She loved Greg and probably knew more about our life than a mother should, but she wasn't privy to the small details. She didn't know about Greg's recent distance or our inability to have a conversation lately, or our apparent—mutual—sex strike, which caused our bed to be the scene of a new Cold War. *Ups and downs, is all,* I kept thinking. *We all got 'em.*

But when we had talked on Wednesday, things seemed a little better. Greg wanted to go to a movie; we hadn't done that in a while. And he even suggested Mexican. His long silences, usually heavy with unsaid words, seemed lighter somehow. Almost easy. When I tried to end the call, I sensed an unusual hesitancy. Generally, Greg ended the conversation first, a sense of urgency coming through the line from the minute he said "hello," but Wednesday had been different. Or maybe that was just my hopeful thinking.

Leah started crying from her high chair.

"Ma, I gotta go. I'll call you tomorrow."

After six o'clock, I secured the girls in the playroom in front of the television before bed and hiked to the back of the yard, skirting the edge of the woods. Behind the woods was a steep hill, ending at some little-used railroad tracks.

"Cooooody!" I called him over and over again. I expected him to come bounding over the hill, carrying some treasure from the tracks. When he didn't materialize, I fought a sense of deep unease, of everything being slightly out of place, two voids in the house defying reason.

Worried about leaving the girls alone too long, I jogged back to the house. On the back porch, I turned once more to gaze out at the inky yard, a black, starless sky swallowing the earth that seemed to shift ever so slightly beneath my feet. Trying to convince myself that Cody would show up later, I went inside to wait for my husband.

I put the girls to bed with only a minor inquisition from Hannah about her missing daddy. I waved the question away with a cheerful façade. She let it slide, used to going days without seeing him. After calling Greg again and leaving yet another message, I curled up on the couch for some backlogged DVR. I skipped around, aiming for distraction as I fought the unease that settled in the pit of my stomach. Pulling the blanket up to my chin, I shivered from the end-of-season chill, wishing, suddenly, pitifully, that I had my husband to curl up on the couch with, even though it had been months since we'd done that. Briefly, I considered the irony, the way we'd avoided talking or touching in the evenings, but how when faced with a growing sense of anxiety, I longed for it. *When he gets home, we'll fix this.*

I was startled awake at one thirty in the morning. As I sat up on the couch, I remembered. *Greg. Was he home?* I checked the doors—both still locked. I checked our bedroom—no suitcase on the floor, no Greg on the bed. I checked the garage—no car. I was angry. One lousy phone call. *Hi, I'm stuck on a plane. Hi, I missed my flight.* I tried his cell phone and left a third message. After I hung up, worry bore down on me, heavy and oppressive.

Taking a deep breath, I logged onto our laptop, which had a permanent home on the kitchen island, and Googled United Airlines, the only airline Greg would fly. From the junk drawer, I pulled out the notebook where Greg always wrote down his flight numbers. The entry for October 1 read, "Flight UA1034." I typed in the flight number—"On Time." I called the toll-free number at the bottom of the webpage and asked if Greg Barnes had checked in for the flight. After confirming our address, I was put on hold.

"We have no record of Greg Barnes checking in on Friday. He did check in on Tuesday evening for his incoming flight from Newark to Rochester, and he picked up one bag at baggage claim." I heard a keyboard clicking. "No, I'm sorry, but it does not appear as though he boarded the return flight UA1034 on Friday morning. Can I help you with anything else?"

The question jarred me. *Sure. Can you help me find him?* I said, "No, thank you," and hung up the phone.

I sat at the island, drumming my fingers. Could he have missed his flight? I tried to think like Greg. If he had missed his flight, he would have rented a car. The drive would have only taken four hours, so he would have been home even before the kids' bedtime. That also didn't explain the dead phone.

Before I had time to think, I called the police station. A woman answered on the second ring, her tone clipped and official.

"Hunterdon County Police Department."

"Hi, this is strange, but my husband went on a business trip and was scheduled to be home at one o'clock yesterday afternoon, and he's still not back." After I said it, I realized how I sounded. *Pathetic.* "I can't get in touch with him; he's not answering his phone. This is really unlike him. I'm not sure what to do."

Silence.

"Hello?"

"Would you like to fill out a Missing Persons Report?" she asked, sounding bored.

I heard the sound of a clacking keyboard in the background. "I'm not sure. I mean, I'm sure there's an explanation, but I'm worried. He's usually much more... reliable." I paused, unsure of how to finish, unsure of anything.

"How long has he been gone?"

Not *missing*, I noted. *Gone as in left?* "He's been missing since one o'clock yesterday afternoon. I mean, he left on Tuesday..." I trailed off, and my words echoing back to me through the phone sounded helpless.

"Well, we *can* send someone out tonight to take a report, if you'd like. Typically, we won't initiate a missing person's report for an adult until he's missing for forty-eight hours and—"

"Forty-eight hours seems excessive," I interrupted, anxiety tight in my chest. Forty-eight hours was *two days*. Surely, he would be back before then.

"Ma'am, with all due respect, most husbands or wives who are reported missing choose to be missing. So yes, forty-eight hours is our procedure. By then, maybe he'll come home on his own." She no longer sounded bored. She sounded compassionate, and that infuriated me.

The finger of fear inched up my spine. "My husband is not *choosing* to be missing. It is very possible that something has happened to him." I felt panicky, nauseous. Zero to sixty. Less than ten minutes ago, I wasn't even worried.

"I'm sure it's possible, but in most cases, the spouse returns within a day or two with a very plausible explanation for their absence. You can call us back tomorrow or Monday, if you'd like to initiate a report or if there is a new development."

"Thank you," I said quietly. I felt it then—the certainty that I would be calling her back. I would not be getting any explanation, plausible or otherwise.

CHAPTER 2

SATURDAY MORNING, I FELT GROGGY and hung-over from lack of sleep. I sat at the kitchen table, drinking coffee from Greg's mug. With the DVD player on repeat, the girls stared blankly at the TV, and for once, I didn't care. The high-pitched tinny voices of Dora the Explorer and her friends pounded in my head, and I winced with each trill of cartoonish laughter.

When the phone rang at nine, I snatched it. "Hello."

"Hi, honey, the farmer's market is open today for the fall festival. Dad and I are taking a ride out. Do you want to come?" Mom asked. The normality of the question was a vaudeville act, dreamlike and surreal.

I inhaled deeply. "Mom, Greg didn't come home."

"What? Why not? Did he miss his flight?"

"I don't know. I can't get in touch with him." A sob caught in my throat. "I called the airline. His flight was on time, so I called the police..." I drifted, hesitant, lost.

"I'm sure there's some explanation for all this. I'm coming over. We'll figure this out."

I hung up and stared at the phone, willing it to ring and for Greg to be on the other end. *Have I got a story for you*, he'd say, laughing. Or more likely, *Goddamn airline, you won't believe this.*

"Mommy, why are you sad?" Hannah stood next to me, wide-eyed. Children had the ability to ask loaded questions in a way adults could never manage, with no subtext and no fear of the answer.

"I just miss Daddy, honey." I pulled her to me, inhaling the syrupy scent of her hair.

"When is he coming home?"

"Soon, sweetheart." I realized I was holding her too tightly and loosened the hug. "He's away working."

"Can I play with Annie today?" *I don't know. I don't know what we'll do today. I don't know what we'll do any day until he comes home.* "We'll see, Hannah."

I pulled out the notepad. I was a list maker.

1. Call Rochester hospitals.
2. Call Greg's hotel.
3. Call Rochester police.
4. Call Hunterdon County police.
5. Find Greg.

I enjoyed lists. Lining through completed items gave me a sense of satisfaction, and I couldn't wait to line through number five.

Leah and Hannah rattled around the house, whiny and bored.

"Mommy, can we go outside today? Are we going to the library?" Hannah asked.

"No, honey, I'm sorry. We're going to play inside. Mommy has a lot to do." I almost laughed at the absurdity of the phrase. *A lot to do.*

How would I figure out what happened to Greg and keep things normal for the girls? How did people function in real crisis situations with small children? It wasn't even a real crisis, just a missed flight and a dead cell phone battery. *Except, except...* Why couldn't he call from the hotel? Borrow a cell phone from a stranger? Nothing made sense.

I fed Leah and asked Hannah if she wanted to watch Cinderella. The time would give me an hour or more of thinking and planning. I plopped them back down in front of the television, Leah clutching her ever-present Uglydoll, and they zoned out.

I jumped when the doorbell rang. I ran to the door, my heart thudding. Just as I reached for the knob, I remembered Mom had said she was coming.

"I have a plan," Mom said. My mother was always a force, in her element during a crisis, strong and sure.

We divvied up my list. I gave her number one, as I needed to be the one to call his hotel. I passed the computer to her so she could look up the Rochester hospitals. I had Greg's notebook: departing flight number, returning flight number, hotel, date. Every single time. Greg the Metronome.

I dialed the hotel number. "Hi. My name is Claire Barnes. My husband Greg stayed there this week. He should have checked in on Tuesday and checked out early Friday morning. Would you be able to tell me if he did check in and out?"

"Yes, we can tell you that, Mrs. Barnes." I heard the clicking of a keyboard. "Yes, Greg Barnes did check in on Tuesday night. However, he did not check out on Friday morning."

My mouth went dry. *What's going on?* "Okay." I needed to talk to this faceless voice on the phone and force her to be human, not like the calls to the police station or the airline. I needed her to be on my side. I took a deep breath. "My husband was scheduled to return yesterday, and he didn't come home. He never boarded his plane. The police won't help me until tomorrow, at the earliest. Is there any way you can check his room? I don't know. Make sure he didn't have a heart attack up there or something? Please. I'm begging you."

"Oh, my goodness, sweetheart." She had a deep southern drawl, not Carolinas. Alabama, maybe. "I'm sure the manager would be happy to check the room. Can I call you back? What's your number?" I gave her my cell phone number, and we hung up.

I sat in the dining room and stared out the window. I counted to seven hundred and fifty nine before my phone rang. I checked the display. Ten minutes had passed. Before I answered, I just knew he was dead in his room. His father had had a weak heart and died at fifty-eight. The phone rang again. I picked up and mouthed hello;

the actual word stuck in the back of my throat. My stomach churned with fear.

"Mrs. Barnes? This is Carol Ann from the Fairmont in Rochester?" *Yes. I know who this is. Please, is my husband alive?* "Honey, I don't know if this is good or bad, but I swear, I don't believe he ever set foot in the room."

My mind raced. *He had checked in, but not used the room?*

"Honey, are you still there? Are you okay?"

"Yes. No. No, I'm not okay, but I'm here. So you're telling me he checked in on Tuesday, but you don't think he stayed there? How could you know that?"

"Well, we put little welcome cards in the locks of all the doors, you know? Our guests have to remove them to swipe their cards, but his is still in there. The bed doesn't seem to have been slept in, and the cleaning staff said they haven't cleaned it because it didn't need it. So either he never entered his room, or he wanted it to look that way." She coughed nervously.

An affair. She thinks Greg was having an affair. Why didn't I think of that? I laughed, a barking sound, like a seal. Greg with another woman? Of all the scenarios that had run through my head, another woman had never been one of them. Greg could barely make a move on me half the time. He was reserved that way. I had never seen him even look at another woman. He never went to strip clubs or commented about actresses. When I teased him about it, he asked, "Why would I look at other women when I can look at you anytime I want?" I used to think it was sweet. The thought, and the raw tenderness that accompanied it, brought tears to my eyes.

I hung up without another word and put my head down on the dining room table. Between thinking he was dead and then wondering if he could be sleeping with someone else, the tears came out of me like possibilities dripping onto the table. I wanted to collect them all, organize them into a list, and check them off one by one until only one was left, and then I would know what happened to my husband. I felt Mom's hand on my back, patting me like an infant.

"Graham," she spoke quietly into her cell phone. I couldn't hear Dad's response. "Come get the girls. We're going to have to call the police."

CHAPTER 3

TWO POLICE OFFICERS CAME TO take the missing persons report. Though it hadn't been forty-eight hours, they didn't so much as utter the words 'protocol' or 'procedure.' Both were kind, accommodating, and seemed slightly wary of me. I answered all of their questions: Greg had brown eyes and light brown hair flecked with gray; he was thirty-five years old, five-ten, one hundred ninety pounds; he had no birthmarks or tattoos. They asked where he was when I last saw him and where did I believe he disappeared from, as well as some bizarre questions like who were his family doctor and dentist—I realized later that dental records could be used to identify a body. I was also asked to list all vehicles he could be driving—one, an Acura RL. Compounding the surreal quality of the interview, one of the officers ushered Mom into the dining room, questioning us separately.

For the first time, reality began to dawn. Initiating the report would be irreversible. The thought gave me an uneasy sense of permanence. Then, it occurred to me that the officers were ensuring we had nothing to do with Greg's disappearance. That train of thought made me feel wildly out of control.

The detective interviewing me had kind hazel eyes and gray hair. He smiled comfortingly with every answer, and I gained confidence as we continued. After about ten minutes, Mom joined us in the living room. She put her hand on the back of my chair in a show of comfort and support. We gave them Greg's spare hairbrush and about fifteen photos from the past year. The officer asked a lot of questions about our marriage: were we happy, did we have a fight, what was Greg's relationship with the girls? After a few minutes, I realized he was trying to figure out if Greg ran away. When he finally finished, he put away his notebook and pen.

"Are adult men ever kidnapped?" I asked, controlled, not hysterical, not shaky anymore.

He sighed. "Sometimes, if he witnessed a crime, or possibly for money." He answered cautiously, obviously trying to walk the line between brutal truth and blatant lie. I must have given him the impression I could handle the truth, because he added, "Mrs. Barnes, I have to be completely honest with you. We will investigate this. We'll track down his last movements, where he was, who he saw, what he ate, and what he did. We may find him. We might figure this out. But *very* few adult men are kidnapped. Unless you have a million dollar trust fund you failed to mention?" I shook my head. "There's no motive in that. Money, that's it. With women and children, kidnappings are frequently religious or sexually based. Or with women kidnappers, sometimes children are taken because the woman wants a child. But for men? What would the motive be? So assuming he's alive, we have to explore the possibility that he may not want to be found. Do you understand what I'm trying to say, Mrs. Barnes?"

I nodded, too confused to talk. I *did* understand what he was saying, but I needed him to stop saying it.

The officers left with a promise to follow up sometime in the next day or so, after they had time to initiate the investigation. Mom sat next to me, not talking, with her hand on mine. Next to me, my cell phone trilled. I snatched it up with shaky hands and looked down at the caller ID. *Drew.* I didn't feel like explaining everything yet. I hit the silence button, and the call went to voicemail.

Mom asked, "Who was that?"

"Drew." I motioned to the phone and rubbed my forehead. "I didn't feel like talking about it."

"Are you okay?"

"Yes, but I think I need to be alone for a minute. I'm going out to

14

look for Cody."

Mom looked surprised. "Oh, my gosh! Where's Cody?"

I explained about the screen door.

She shook her head. "And he hasn't come back yet? That's so strange."

"I know," I said wryly. "Seriously, everyone who lives here is disappearing."

She gave me a small smile, waving me away. "I'll be here. Just go."

I walked outside and headed toward the barn. The leaves had begun to fall, and the yard was littered with various seedpods, strewn about like nature's confetti. I took a deep breath. The crisp air smelled of impending fall, the rotting organic perfume of a changing season.

Greg's favorite season was fall. He loved apple picking and the pumpkin patch at Halloween. Having children seemed to give Greg permission to indulge in the juvenile fun of Halloween. He was finally able to shake off his hard, serious exterior so he could run up and down the rows of the pumpkin patch, showing Hannah how to find the perfect pumpkin. The stem had to be strong enough to hold its weight, and the sides had to be round and the bottom flat. The shell had to be thick enough to withstand carving, but not so thick that it was too hard to carve. Then we'd take our pumpkins home, and Hannah and Leah would paint theirs while Greg would spend an hour carving a perfect face into a third, using patterns and a small knife kit. I remember marveling at the change in him, his smile wide and open-mouthed, his eyes crinkling behind rimless glasses when he laughed. The gray in his sandy hair reflected the sun, and his face seemed to transform, becoming soft and malleable, where before it had been all hard angles and edges.

I missed him. I missed the idea of him being there, and I was terrified the void was permanent. I began to resent the detective's implications. *Greg wouldn't leave this; I know that.* He was practical and methodical, and he loved his children more than life. *Could he leave me?* My heart wondered. *Maybe.*

We'd been less than perfect lately. Before he left, we had a fight—a secret I had not shared with the detectives. Something had been missing lately. We had a broken connection, not beyond repair, but temporary, part of the marital ebb and flow. The subject was raw, as we had clawed at it over and over again. Whenever I tried to bring it up, Greg withdrew, and I became angry, a pattern we never seemed to be able to break.

The day he left, he'd responded differently. "Why do you push this, Claire?" He lashed out, his voice raised as much as he ever yelled, which was to say not very loudly or forcefully. "You don't accept who I am. You don't let me just *be*. I'm always not enough somehow."

"Greg, that's not true, and you know it. I want to go back; that's all. I want us back the way we were a year ago. Something is going on. I have no idea what, but it eats at me. It keeps me up at night. When I lie in bed and look at your back, I want to shake you awake and ask, 'Why are you a million miles away? Where are you?'"

"Do you cross the line, Claire?" he asked quietly, his back to me. "The demarcation line in our bed, do you move to the other side? Why do you just stare at my back? Why is it always my burden?" He picked up his suitcase, turned, and out of habit, kissed my forehead. Emotionless, rote. He left for the airport. I hadn't seen him since.

In the dim light of the barn, the late afternoon sun shining through the slats in hazy beams, I cried. I cried because he was right. Greg was the fixer in our life, our go-to guy when everything went to pot. He'd addressed the termite problem last spring. When we had water in our basement over the summer because of three days of rain, he called a plumber to install a sump pump. Until then, I hadn't known what a sump pump was. He paid the bills, and a few weeks ago, when we had some illegitimate charges show up on our Visa, Greg called Visa and had them cancel our cards and get the charges removed. Those little things in life that I didn't know how to do, or wouldn't think to do, terrified me. How were we going to work as a family until he came home? We were fractured, a puzzle missing a piece, without him. He needed to be home. He needed to come home and fix it. *Fix us.*

"Cody? Come here, Cody! Come home, bud!" I searched the mostly empty barn, pausing to listen for the sound of his nails on the concrete floor. The barn was empty save for the neighbor's cat, which ran when he saw me, a black ball of fur, skittering away on little white feet.

Cody wasn't there. I wasn't surprised. Whether rational or not, I started to believe with unflinching certainty that Cody would not come home until Greg did.

CHAPTER 4

THE FIRST YEAR I WORKED at Advent, my manager sent me to a training class to understand compliance and the Code of Federal Regulations for drug manufacturing. I worked in the Quality Control Lab as an entry-level technician, and the training was part of orientation. At the time, basic orientation and compliance training were temporarily done offsite in Rochester so employees from New Jersey, Rochester, and Toronto could be trained at the same time.

I jumped at the chance to do the three-day training course and dragged Sarah, my college roommate, with me. We called it a mini-cation. She took four days off work, and we drove her ten-year-old Toyota the five and a half hours to Rochester. The first night there, we each drank a bottle of wine in our hotel room, silly and drunk on our freedom. I used my corporate American Express for everything—the room, our meals, gas, and the wine. We had a completely free vacation from our one-bedroom box of an apartment. We got the most expensive room I felt comfortable getting, which included a large Jacuzzi tub.

The next day, class started at nine, but being so nervous and green out of college, I arrived at the conference center at eight thirty. The instructor was already there, setting up the room in a large tabled "U." I hurried to a seat in the back corner and pulled a book from my bag, trying for invisibility. I had a pounding headache from the wine and a venti-sized Starbucks coffee to help me through it.

The instructor coughed, and I pretended not to hear him, avoiding eye contact. Tucked into my book, I heard people filter into the conference room and take seats around me. I realized quickly that almost everyone knew each other, as the greetings were filled with a jovial familiarity that included private jokes and nicknames. In addition, I seemed to be the youngest person in the room by no less than five years. *Oh, good. This should be a fun-filled three days.* I took out my notepad and pen, just for something to do, and then reddened when I realized that no one else seemed to be taking notes. Too self-conscious to put the pad away, I left it unopened in front of me.

"Hello, everyone. I'm Greg."

Half the room tittered. "Hi, Greg!"

The introduction was solely for me and possibly one other person. When Greg announced we were going to introduce ourselves, my mind went blank. For a moment, I forgot everything about myself, save for my name. *Why was I here? Where did I work?* I listened to everyone ahead of me and formulated my answer, repeating it like a mantra. *I'm Claire McGivens, and I work in Quality Control in Raritan, New Jersey.*

When my turn came, I said, "Hi, I'm Claire McG—" I raised my hand to self-consciously tuck my hair behind my ear, and in the process, elbowed my obnoxiously tall cup—*for heaven's sake, why is it so damn tall?*—spilling coffee all over the table in front of me. The lukewarm liquid traveled toward the lip of the table as I sat, paralyzed. Two classmates raced over with paper towels.

I mumbled, "Thank you," propelled into action by the coffee edging across the table, threatening to spill over onto my colleague's suit pants.

"I'm sorry. I'm so sorry," I repeated as people shifted their chairs back to let me clean. I realized then that the class was largely male, and I caught a few exchanged smirks and eyebrow raises. My face burning, I walked stiffly to throw away the soaked towels.

Greg touched my shoulder, his smile warm and inviting. "Thank you, Claire, for the ice-breaker." He held my gaze with an expression that was reassuring and unsettling at the same time.

The class laughed, not unkindly. I smiled, attempting to show I was a good sport, but would have gladly welcomed the proverbial swallowing of the earth.

I went back to my seat, kept my head down, and pretended to take notes. When I felt bolder, I snuck glances at Greg. He was tall and broad-shouldered with slightly thinning sandy-blond hair, black square glasses, and a trimmed goatee. He exuded confidence and had an easy manner in front of the group. He caught my eye once and surreptitiously winked. The move was so quick, I wasn't even certain the gesture was aimed at me. Still, my heartbeat quickened, and I ducked my head.

Greg was funny, compelling, and given the rather tedious subject, able to command attention in an impressive way. As the lecture continued, I watched him with interest, and when our eyes would meet, I felt the heat in my face. I learned a great deal more than I'd intended, and the day progressed quicker than I expected.

After class, I walked across the street, humming under my breath, almost forgetting about the coffee incident. Almost.

Sarah had planned to shop in downtown Rochester while I was away, and I couldn't wait to see her resulting cache. I let myself into the room, heard the soft *whoosh* of the shower, and flopped back onto the bed, mentally reconstructing the day. My mind skipped over the spilled coffee and instead settled on Greg's smile, his laugh, the little turn of his head as he may or may not have winked.

"Earth to Claire." Sarah stood in the bathroom doorway, towel drying her hair.

I grinned. "I'm here. I'm here. What'd you get today?"

After she showed me all her goods, we dressed for dinner. Sarah was infinitely trendy, while I always seemed to "look nice," but together, we didn't fail to attract attention.

We decided to stay at the hotel to eat. The restaurant downstairs had a gastro-pub feel to it, and the air was thick with the smell of corporate cologne. Men mingled in suits and loosened ties. Deep laughter echoed off the wooden walls.

"Well, now. These are no slim pickings." Sarah grinned wickedly.

We were halfway through our strong post-dinner martinis when a voice behind me said, "I hope you're more careful with your cocktails than you are with your morning coffee."

I turned to see Greg standing behind me, a Sam Adams in his hand. He had ditched the business casual in favor of jeans and a black polo shirt. His attire felt intimate, as though we weren't colleagues but friends, and heat flushed my face.

With a smile, he pulled a chair up to our table, while simultaneously extending his hand to Sarah. "I'm Greg."

With a wide smile, Sarah shook his hand. "I'm Sarah." Naturally, she commandeered the conversation. "Why are you here at the hotel? Don't you live in Rochester?"

I averted my eyes, intently studying the scarred oak table. My heart hammered in my chest. I felt uncharacteristically nervous and tongue-tied. Not that I was normally a flirt, but I could put together sentences. My mind was blank, and for the second time that day, I tried to remember my name.

"No," he replied with an easy smile. "Right now, I live in Pennsylvania. But I've been posted here temporarily while they get the New Jersey site training program back on track. Apparently, they're doing all East Coast training in Rochester, and all West Coast training in San Diego. Somehow, I feel cheated by my post, but I get a free efficiency apartment for six months, complete with kitchenette."

"Wow," Sarah cooed. "Big man on campus, then, eh?"

Greg reddened slightly and cast a look sideways at me. "Can I buy you ladies another drink?" He stood up, gesturing toward the bar.

We nodded, and when he walked away, Sarah said, "Claire, you should really go for it with him. He's so *cute*, in such a nerdy *you* kind of way."

"What? He could be married with three kids for all I know. I know nothing about him." I threw back the remainder of my martini, feeling the vodka heat bloom from my center. I felt nervous and giddy at once, despite my protests. I recalled his wink during class.

"Well, I feel a headache coming on." She put her hand up to her forehead for mock emphasis. "I really think I'm going to head back to our room and try to sleep off some of these martinis." She gathered her purse.

"Sarah, this is crazy. Please don't leave."

She just smiled, wiggling her fingers as well as her eyebrows, and slipped out before I could stop her.

Greg returned with two martini glasses. He cocked his head to the side with a tentative smile. "I generally don't scare women away that fast."

"Sarah claimed she had a headache. She's a misguided cupid. I apologize." For the second time in ten minutes, I felt my face grow hot. *God, just shut up. How much did I have to drink?* I rushed to change the subject. "Well, tell me about yourself. How did you become a trainer for Advent? How long is your post in Rochester? Are you married?" I felt scattered, running off at the mouth. His hand rested next to mine on the table, barely touching, and I studied his arms, thick and strong, and briefly wondered how they would feel around my waist.

He didn't answer immediately, and the silence seemed to last forever. Finally, he laughed. "No," he said, with a small smile, giving me a nudge with his elbow. "I'm not married."

Conversation flowed easily, and unlike a lot of the men I dated, he struck a nice balance between awkwardly quiet and excessively talkative. He laughed frequently and had a smile that reached his eyes, crinkling them at the corners. When he walked me back to my room at two in the morning, I was drunk and head over heels. When his mouth opened to mine, I knew I never wanted to kiss another man for the rest of my life. And when he invited me back to his deluxe suite, I never hesitated.

Later, I couldn't remember the subject matter from the other two days of class. More than once, he stumbled over his words or lost his place in the lecture, not so coincidentally after we made eye contact. That told me I had the same effect on him that he had on me. We spent the remaining two nights after class together, and poor Sarah's mini-cation was mostly spent alone in a hotel room. She never complained.

The morning we left, I couldn't find Greg to tell him goodbye, but Sarah and I spent the entire ride home analyzing my new love interest. I was giddy on hope, and with a little prompting, I looked up Greg's number in the company directory and called his office the day after we got home.

Until recently, I couldn't be sure that we'd gone a day without speaking in ten years.

CHAPTER 5

"I'm Detective Matt Reynolds." The man stood on my porch, wearing a wrinkled button-down shirt and a pair of equally wrinkled khakis. He held his credentials with the badge out for me to see.

When I made no move to look, he shifted his weight from one foot to the other, and wordlessly, I opened the door.

He stepped over the threshold. "I'm from the Hunterdon County Missing Persons Unit. I wanted to stop by to follow up with a status update."

What status update? Here's the status: Greg isn't home yet.

"Do you want something to drink?" I asked, turning to walk to the kitchen.

He followed me down the hallway. "Uh... no, thank you, Mrs. Barnes."

I detoured into the living room. "Please, call me Claire." I motioned for him to sit on the couch, while I sat in Greg's easy chair.

He lowered himself onto the middle cushion. "I'm going to be the lead investigator, and I promise you we will do everything we can to find your husband. Right now, we have no reason to believe he's dead. We queried all the morgues within a twenty-mile radius of Rochester for a John Doe matching his description. So far, there's no one. I'm leaving this afternoon for Rochester to discuss some of the details of the case with the local authorities there. We've had phone conversations with personnel at the hotel and the airline, and we've confirmed what you told us earlier. We do believe he landed in Rochester and checked into his hotel, but we don't think he ever stayed in his room. In addition, we can't locate his luggage."

He pulled a pen and a small notebook out of his shirt pocket. He clicked the pen once, twice, and seemed to be waiting for me. I nodded for him to continue.

"This is all we know right now. But I do have a few follow-up questions, if you feel up to it."

"Yes, of course. Anything." All the talking seemed superfluous, taking up precious time. I couldn't understand how talking to me would help them find Greg. I wanted to push him out the door, out into the real world where the clues would be.

"Mrs. Barnes... Claire, I need to ask you some tough questions, regarding your marriage, your life, things that may feel very personal. I don't believe you had anything to do with Greg's disappearance, but you may be able to tell me something about who did. And you might not even know it yourself, so it's very important that you don't hold back on me. Do you understand?"

I nodded again, frustrated at his careful pace. "Yes."

"I need to understand the state of your marriage."

Even though he had warned me, I was surprised at the candid statement, the abruptness of it. I inhaled deeply and closed my eyes, thinking about how to put into words what I avoided thinking about. How did I explain? We were like ships passing in the night. He went about his day, I went about mine, and if our days overlapped and we connected, great. But in the past three months, more often than not, we hadn't.

"Greg and I have a marriage. We have highs and lows, but we don't fight regularly." I paused, searching for words. "But we don't really... talk regularly either."

"Is this a recent development?"

"He was up late at night. Working, he said, and sometimes I would hear him on the phone. When I pressed him on it, he got frustrated, frequently telling me not to worry about it. I needed to understand him. He needed me to not need that." I stopped, staring at my hands, which were clenched in my lap. I took a deep breath, consciously relaxing them. "I don't even know if everything I'm saying is making sense."

Matt smiled. He had a kind smile and soft green eyes. I could see why he had become a detective. I instinctively wanted to tell him everything about my life, and I was quite sure he took a lot of confessions. I would have bet even hardened criminals trusted him.

"I understand, Claire. I was married once. It sounds familiar. It also doesn't sound unusual. I think most marriages have these times, and more often than not, they pass. Do you think things will get better, or do you have a sense of your marriage ending?"

"No, we'll pull out of it," I said quickly, trying to convince the detective. And myself. "A few years ago, Greg had a friend who passed away. He became reclusive and moody. The only people who could reach him were the girls. I realized that's how Greg deals with complicated, emotional situations. I think there's something similar going on because his behavior lately has been the same. But this time, the reason behind it is a mystery to me. It's been this way for close to a year, off and on, with the worst being the last four months or so. I expect to eventually know the reason behind his self-imposed exile. I was trying, but..."

Matt nodded.

Taking the gesture for encouragement, I continued. "I'd become impatient lately, pushing him, wanting to know what was in his head. I became insecure, needy. Did he still love me? I'm sure that pushed him further into himself. But I couldn't see that at the time. I can see it a little more clearly now."

Matt glanced down at his notebook. "Would Greg hurt himself?"

The question seemed preposterous. "No. I know I've admitted I don't know my husband very well right now, that there's something going on with him that I can't figure out. However, I know him deep down, the person that he is, fundamentally. He's the most stable, emotionally secure person I've ever met. When he has something

THOUGHT I KNEW YOU

difficult to deal with, he does withdraw. But he deals with it. That's the difference. Suicidal people aren't able to deal with their difficulties. In addition, he adores his kids. He would never, *ever* do that to them."

Matt nodded. "Tell me about Greg the father."

I relaxed into the chair, crossing my legs. *An easy one.* "Greg is the most hands-on father I know. He knows the girls inside and out. Hannah was colicky as a baby. She cried all the time, and only Greg could calm her. He's more patient than me. He's more fun than I am. When he takes the girls out for the day—which is one day a week, at least—he's completely focused on them. They go to the park, have a picnic in the yard, or play outside with a ball for hours. His relationship with them is completely different from mine. I'm always doing a million things at once, and the girls have to fit into my life. He makes the girls the focus of his day, and all the other tasks fit in around them. To that extent, he's a better parent than I am."

"Do you believe Greg could be having an affair?"

The question hit me hard. There was a difference between knowing the police were speculating and having one of them ask me outright. I wanted to answer him steadily and unemotionally. I studied the arm of Greg's chair, an old plaid recliner from eons ago, pilled from years of use, and resisted the urge to lean over and bury my face in the fabric. I imagined Greg sitting there, the gentle dip in the arm of the chair where he'd hold the television remote and mindlessly change the channels. I could faintly smell the remnants of his cologne, tiny pieces of Greg interwoven in the threads.

"I don't know. I don't think so. With who?" I shook my head. "It's not that he wouldn't do that to me, although I believe that, too. But it was too *out there* for him. Too far off the beaten path. Too deviant. Greg likes the order and structure of marriage, the routine. I don't think he could juggle, lie, and compartmentalize to the degree that you would need to in order to have an affair."

"Thank you, Claire. I think you were honest, and let's hope that this will help. I don't know how yet, but that's how it goes sometimes.

You collect information, and you don't know what will be the lead, what will break the case, but when you assemble it all, sometimes the answer is in the interviews." Before he left, he gathered the names of our friends, family, colleagues, and neighbors. He also asked for the name of Greg's manager and the phone number.

"One more thing, did Greg have a passport?" he asked, standing in the doorway.

"He used to. About five years ago, he had to travel to Canada, and I think he had one then. I have no idea if it's expired or not."

"We're going to put an alert on his passport, so we'll be notified if he leaves the country. We'll be in touch." He loped across the driveway to his car, and I shut the front door behind him.

"Mommy, who was that man?" Hannah stood between the kitchen and the living room uncertainly, swaying gently against the door frame, sleep from her afternoon nap heavy in her eyes.

I took a deep breath. Leah was sleeping, and the house was quiet. It was a good time to talk to her. "That man was a policeman."

"When is Daddy coming home?" she asked for the tenth time that day.

"Daddy is lost. Remember when you got lost in the grocery store?" She nodded seriously. "Daddy is lost like that right now, and we don't know where he is or when he's coming home."

"Why doesn't he use a map? A map can help Daddy get home!" She smiled brightly.

I laughed. "Maybe the policeman will help Daddy find a map," I said, kissing her head. "We'll figure it out. Okay, Hannah? Don't worry. Daddy and Mommy love you and Leah very, very much."

"Does Daddy have Cody with him?"

"I don't know, Han. I guess it's possible." The mystery of Cody baffled me almost as much as Greg's disappearance. I hadn't the energy to summon a full-on search for him, but fortunately, Dad had taken on the task. The neighborhood was plastered with missing posters, and I thought it ironic that more people probably knew that Cody was missing than Greg. My subconscious had linked the disappearances, and for a while, I considered that if Greg had run off, he'd taken Cody with him. Nothing about that made sense, but then again, the entire situation seemed to defy logic. Superstitious, I left Cody's dog bowls in place, nestled between the cabinets and the screen door. I even walked around his oversized tennis ball and Kong chew toy, leaving them in place until he—and Greg—came home. I felt an indescribable certainty that they would return together. That gave me hope, somehow.

Detective Reynolds had genuinely seemed to think our conversation would help. I also hoped that he would find something in his investigation of our family and friends. Conversely, I didn't believe Greg's disappearance was connected to anyone we knew.

Then what did I believe? I didn't know. That he had amnesia and was wandering around Rochester? That would be the most positive scenario. If I didn't believe there was an affair, or that he had left voluntarily, or that he had been kidnapped, then what did I believe had happened? I couldn't think about it; I couldn't focus on the why. I just asked myself the same question, a hundred times a day. *Where in the hell is Greg?*

CHAPTER 6

TOOK A SABBATICAL FROM WORK. I moved in slow motion. My heart and my feet felt heavy. I broke two glasses because I forgot I was holding them and simply let go. Hannah sometimes had to say "Mommy" three or four times before I would answer her.

Hannah knew something was wrong. The Pollyanna explanation she had gotten earlier in the week no longer held water after ten days. She was withdrawn and sad, repeatedly asking me when Daddy was coming home. Even Leah missed him, particularly long after she'd been asleep, crying out, "Daddy!" as his presence in her life had been reduced to a shadowy figure in her dreams. My chest ached for them.

On Sunday morning, someone knocked on the door. I stood immobilized, gripped by fear. That had become my normal response to the doorbell or the phone ringing. I was always convinced the moment had come, that I would learn my husband was dead. But an equal part of me believed that the moment had come for me to learn the truth, that Greg stood on the other side of the door or was on the other end of the line. The battle of my conflicting instincts resulted in paralysis. I couldn't will myself to action, and inevitably, the answering machine would click on, or Mom would answer the door.

"Mo-o-o-m!" Hannah called, a four-year-old going on seventeen. "Get the door. Someone's been knocking." Then, frustrated with my all-pervading hesitation over everything, she marched to the door.

"Hi, Squirt!" The deep male voice boomed down the hall. "Have you gotten taller? I feel like you are much, *much* taller than the last time I saw you!"

"Uncle Drew!" Hannah yelled.

A balloon of relief popped in my chest. What Greg couldn't fix, Drew could. Drew would bring Greg home. I ran down the hall and threw my arms around Drew's neck, nearly pushing Hannah into the wall. I sobbed as he held me, his body a wall of strength. I inhaled the scent of laundry detergent and a faint hint of cologne, his Drew-ness that felt like home to me.

"How did you know? Why are you here?" I blubbered into his shoulder.

"Your dad called me. I'm so sorry about what's going on. What can I do?"

I laughed the strange seal bark, as though I'd forgotten how to laugh, and when I tried, it came out unnatural and jarring.

"Please, please help." Truthfully, just having him there would help. I felt safer, not so vulnerable in my own home. "I'm sorry I didn't call you back. I just couldn't... I didn't want to talk about any of this..."

He waved away my apology, and I motioned for him to follow me into the kitchen.

When I was five, we moved into the house next door to Drew's family. Mom told me that the secret to making friends was to act as if you were having the time of your life. I rode my bike up and down the street, singing as loud as I could, convinced that I could lure the neighbor kids with my siren song of fun. After about an hour, all I had to show for it was a broken bike chain. While I was trying to fix the dislodged chain, six-year-old Drew appeared with what I thought was a small metal screw.

"It's a bike chain tool," he said matter-of-factly. He deftly pushed out the pin, snapped the two sides of the chain apart, and reconnected them, pushing the pin back into place while loosening the new connection.

"How do you know how to do that?" I asked.

He shrugged. "I fix all my own stuff, mostly 'cause I break so much, my dad won't fix anything for me anymore."

Drew's parents were older, and they passed away when Drew was in his early twenties, two years apart from each other. Mr. Elliot went first from a heart attack, and Drew claimed his mom died of a broken heart. They left him with a sizable inheritance, and since Drew was a *bona fide* genius, he quit his job to be a day trader. He saw the dot-com bubble about to burst and sold everything he had in 1999. In five years, he made enough to keep him afloat for the rest of his life.

With his newfound free time, he learned photography. He specialized in capturing images of the poor and indigent. Ironically, he recently sold a print collection for a few hundred thousand dollars. With that sale, he made a name for himself in the art world and has since fought off potential buyers with a stick.

The kids adored Drew. He was loud and raucous and everything that Greg and I were not. Next to Greg and my children, I loved Drew more than anyone else in my life.

"How long are you staying?" I asked. I needed a buffer between the girls and me, someone to absorb the silence and fill the spaces between my words, which were becoming few and very far between. Drew would fill the silent house with noise and laughter and voices again. I had to think to remember the last time I had seen him. A month ago? I wasn't sure, but it had been a little while. While not seeing each other wasn't unusual, we generally didn't go more than a week without catching up on the phone. I felt another pang of guilt for not returning his call last week.

"As long as you need me to."

Hannah whooped. "Leah! Uncle Drew is here and is staying with us *forever*!" She ran down the hall, her feet slapping the tile, the most animation we'd had in the house in days.

"See? Now you have to stay. Hannah said it, so it's unmitigated fact." I grinned.

"What's going on, Claire?" he asked, ignoring my attempt at levity. I filled him in on the facts as I knew them over a cup of coffee.

He shook his head. "It's just not like Greg. I mean, I know what the police say, but do you think Greg left?"

"No, I don't. If it was just me, maybe. But even that seems weird and out of character. We weren't great, but we weren't bad. We had a great day together three days before his trip. Even if he could leave me, which I still doubt, Greg loved those girls. He wouldn't just pick up and leave them. He's not heartless. He'd miss them like crazy, and never mind the part where that leaves them fatherless. That would break his heart."

Drew nodded. "Greg is a rules guy. Not me. I don't buy into the nine-to-five job. I don't own a house because I don't want to be nailed down. I don't want a mortgage or even a long lease. Greg isn't like that. He does what's expected of him, what needs to be done." He sighed. "I'm not saying this right. I know guys. I know guys like Greg. They make mistakes, sure, but they always do the right thing. There's an underlying sense of responsibility. Does that make sense?"

"More sense than anything anyone else has said," I said with relief.

Drew had put into words what I couldn't. He strengthened my belief that Greg could not have left us. He was right. Greg, above all, had a ridiculously strong sense of responsibility. He was never late on a bill or even a library book. He'd never received a parking ticket. He believed the speed limit was absolute, that rules were meant to be followed, not broken. Leaving his family would have been the most out of character act I could imagine. I felt a release, an exhaled breath of air.

"So now what?" Drew asked.

We sat in silence, thinking, tapping our coffee mugs.

Finally, Drew said, "I think we need to go to Rochester."

CHAPTER 7

I DID NOT TELL DETECTIVE REYNOLDS that Drew and I were going. I knew he would try very hard to stop us, and I feared that he could. Interference with an investigation was possibly a crime. Maybe he could call me a suspect in order to keep me in the state. I had no idea if that was realistic or if my fears were based on what I'd seen on television.

The next day, I asked Mom to stay with the girls while we went.

She agreed with raised eyebrows. "I think the police—"

"We'll take them for as long as you need, sweetheart." Dad hushed her concerns with a wave of his hand and pulled me into an infrequent hug. "Whatever you need us to do."

Drew and I packed the SUV with enough clothes and toiletries for four days. We didn't make a hotel reservation. I wanted to stay at the same hotel where Greg registered, but Drew convinced me it would be too macabre. I kissed the girls goodbye with a heavy heart. Instead of having a mother that was present in body, but not in mind, they wouldn't have a mother around at all. I turned my head when I hugged Hannah so she wouldn't see my tears.

"Are you going to bring Daddy and Cody back?" Hannah asked.

"I'm going to try, Hannah-banana." I felt a pang of guilt, knowing that even if I figured out what happened to Greg, Cody most likely wasn't with him.

"I love you," Hannah said.

"I love you more," I whispered. I kissed Leah, cupping her small head against my shoulder.

As Drew backed the SUV out of the driveway, I watched Mom

usher the kids into the house, probably singing brightly to keep their attention. They'd forget I was gone in no time at all. I had to believe that.

We rode in silence. I had no words in me—a recurring issue lately. I'd lost the ability to function in the real world, to make small talk with the grocery store clerk or the mailman. Some of the neighbors had heard about Greg's disappearance. Pastor Joe had come over earlier on Sunday to say he had prayed for us. I thanked him, but had nothing else to add. After a lengthy pause, he began to shift his weight uneasily, then asked if we needed anything before he left, hurrying down the walk.

I didn't know if my continued silence came from grief, fear, or anger, but I knew I radiated hostility. I felt completely ill at ease having a conversation at all, as if I might accidentally blurt, "Greg didn't leave us," during any conversation. I was so afraid of appearing desperate and reinforcing the image of a woman whose husband would pick up and leave without even a goodbye. Since desperation filled my thoughts, I kept them in, hidden from the world. Instead of projecting the image of a calm, pulled-together woman handling a crisis, I came off brittle, fragile, tenuous. I didn't care. I felt as Greg must have with all my incessant questioning–violated and shut off from the world, until my only choice was to turn inward. I reveled in sweet silence.

We stopped for gas in Binghamton, right over the New York state line.

After filling the tank, Drew climbed back in the car and clapped his hands with exaggerated brightness. "Okay, what's our game plan?"

I couldn't muster the same enthusiasm for the "game." I shrugged and stared out the window.

He let me sulk for another half-hour, but when we merged onto Route 81, he said, "Listen, Claire. Going to Rochester isn't the move of a timid or scared woman. If you really are looking for answers, you're going to have to talk. And you're going to have to be aggressive. Do you understand?"

I nodded. I didn't think I had it in me. I wasn't sure why we were going, or what we were doing. I leaned my head against the window. Outside, the highway zoomed beneath the car, while the bordering evergreens seemed to creep slowly, cementing the scenery with stable, unwavering anchors to the earth. Like Greg.

⁓᷐᷐᷐᷐⁓

We checked into the Chariot, across the street from the Fairmont, where Greg had stayed. I followed Drew into the lobby and hung back while he paid and chatted with the desk clerk. The woman smiled with dazzling teeth and checked us in with acrylic nails tapping efficiently on a computer keyboard. I should have interrupted—*Oh, no, I've got this, Drew*—but I couldn't. I had wanted him there, but irrationally, I resented his presence, his easy manner, his quick smile.

I needed a shower and a few minutes to myself. The rooms were adequate, with a queen-sized bed in each, a television, and internet hook-up, ideal for the business traveler. I couldn't have cared less, as long as mine was clean.

Under the hot spray of the shower, I realized Drew was right; I needed to be predatory. I searched for the anger I knew was buried under the hopelessness and silence. I needed to channel that fury into a force that would find my husband and the person responsible for splintering our lives. *And what if that person was Greg?* If he wasn't already dead, I vowed to kill him myself. By the time I dressed and blow-dried my hair, I felt determined. Or at least, I felt determined to fake determination until I was able to feel it.

I went into Drew's room through the adjoining door. "Let's go."

He was reading a complimentary magazine, lounging on the bed, and he started at my voice. "She speaks!"

"Very funny. Ha, ha. Now get up."

He saluted and followed me out of the hotel. Without needing to

36

discuss it, we headed to the Fairmont. I asked the clerk at the front desk if Carol Ann was working, and he nodded, then walked into the back room. He returned a minute later with a short, plump, fifty-ish woman in tow.

"Can I help you?" she asked in her familiar southern accent.

I took a deep breath. "Hi, Carol Ann. I'm the woman who called you a week or so ago regarding Greg Barnes."

"Oh, my goodness, honey! Yes, I remember." She lowered her voice conspiratorially. "You know, darlin', the police were here, and I spoke to them. I told them everything I know. But I guess since you're here, they haven't found him yet?"

I shook my head. "Can you go over exactly what you told the police?" I asked with a forced air of confidence. I wasn't expecting anything big out of Carol Ann, but hoped to possibly glean some small detail from a personal conversation with her. I leaned forward on the counter—*Let's chat like girlfriends.* I wanted her to *want* to help.

"I told them about our conversation and how Joe—he's the hotel manager—and I went up to the room to make sure your husband hadn't had a heart attack in there. When we went in, the place was spotless. I swear to you, honey, no one ever slept in there. I could just tell, you know?" She had adopted a nervous habit of ending all her sentences with a question. "Then they asked who was on duty when Mr. Barnes checked in—"

"Who was on duty?" I interrupted.

"That would have been Joe, the manager, who checked him in. The front desk clerk was on his dinner break." She gestured toward the man from earlier.

He nodded. "I'm Joe Templeton, Mrs. Barnes. I didn't remember him until the police showed me a picture."

I pulled out my stack of the same fifteen pictures the police had copied. I fanned them out in front of him.

He looked down and nodded. "Yes, that's the man I remember."

"Did you notice anything unusual about the check-in?" I asked.

Drew inched up behind me, and I shifted to give him room at the counter.

"It was a routine check-in. He had one bag. I offered to bring it up for him, but he said no thanks. He paid with a corporate credit card, not so unusual in this place, and he said he wanted to pay up front so he wouldn't have to check out later. That's typical. People want to go to their meetings and get..." His voice trailed off, and he looked at Carol Ann.

"Home." I finished for him and gave him a small smile. "That's okay, Mr. Templeton. They want to get home. Then what? Did you see him go to his room?"

"As I told the detective that was here, the office phone rang, and I had to run and get it. The desk clerk had stepped out to dinner. After he paid, I went into the back office. No one was in the lobby." He genuinely looked as though he wished he had seen if Greg walked toward the bank of elevators or out the front door.

A thought occurred to me. "What about surveillance?"

Joe shook his head. "We have one video camera on the front desk, and it keeps forty-eight hours of video and then tapes over itself. This is a corporate hotel in a corporate center. There's no crime here. The only reason we had the cameras installed was to watch the employees."

Carol Ann offered, "We had a situation a year or so back. The gentleman has since been fired, but that's why we have the cameras now."

"What time did the clerk come back? Maybe he saw Greg leaving on his way in?" I asked.

"I doubt it," Joe said. "Carlos went to the new Thai restaurant around the corner and returned through the side entrance, closest to the street. I'm really sorry, Mrs. Barnes. We said all this to the police. I really wish I had more information to give you."

My heart skipped. "Where is the Thai restaurant?"

Joe gave me directions.

"Thank you very much. I might be back with more questions," I added over my shoulder as I turned toward the door.

Drew had to jog to keep up. "Okay, Sherlock, what are you thinking?"

"Drew, Greg *loves* Thai, but I hate it. So he *always* eats it when he's away." I paused at the light, and even though the red hand flashed, I darted across the empty four-lane street, heading for the neon *Pad Thai* sign.

When we got to the other side, Drew grabbed my elbow. "Listen. You can't go in there guns blazing. You're not the cops. These people are probably immigrants. If you go in there, all hopped up on adrenaline and flashing pictures, you're going to scare them into silence. We need to finesse them. I can't believe I'm saying this, but you need to be sadder. Be the Claire I drove up here with and less your old self."

"I'll try," I promised, but my hands were shaking. I wasn't a cop, but I knew a lead when I had one. I also knew my husband. He had checked into the hotel around dinnertime, and there was a Thai restaurant within walking distance. He had eaten there. I could feel it. No one but me would know that.

When we pushed open the door, a bell chimed. The restaurant was empty, and pop music drifted softly out of the Muzak system. The intoxicating scent of fried seafood made my mouth water, despite the fact that I didn't like Thai food. A fifty-gallon aquarium filled with bright orange and white koi took up one wall. A thirty-ish Asian woman sat behind the counter on the opposite wall, reading a tabloid. She looked up, and I gave her as sad a smile as I could muster. She returned my smile with her own inexplicably sad one.

I wondered what time they opened for dinner and checked my watch—two fifteen. "Hi. My name is Claire Barnes. I'm looking for someone. Can you tell me who was working on the evening of September twenty-eighth?" I tried to look forlorn, but I was fearful that I had come on too strong. It was a cop question, not a sad woman missing her husband question.

The woman nodded. "I work every day," she said in stilted English. "Every day not Tuesday. We closed Tuesday."

"Do you just work the register, or are you a waitress, too?"

She shook her head as if she didn't quite understand. "I work tables, at register, in kitchen. This my father's restaurant."

I reached into my purse and pulled out five of the fifteen pictures of Greg. I shut my eyes for a moment. I needed her to say she had seen him. I fanned the pictures in front of her, as I had done with Joe at the hotel.

"Do you remember seeing this man?" I asked. "Take your time. Think about—"

"Yes. I seat him. He sat in this booth." She walked out from behind the counter and pointed at the booth right behind the register. "It was early. Only few table with people."

Excited, I started to thank her.

She added, "He was with woman."

CHAPTER 8

"THAT SON OF A BITCH!"

Drew put his arms around me and moved to shield me from the people on the sidewalk who had turned to look. "Look, you don't know anything yet. Dinner isn't an affair. Does he work with a woman? It really could have been innocent."

"If I believe that, then I'm a complete idiot. I've been so adamant that Greg didn't leave us, but he did, Drew. I really think he did." I put my hand over my mouth, feeling the bile rise in my throat. I sank to my knees in the middle of the sidewalk, not caring who might be looking.

Drew managed to get me back to the hotel and tuck me into bed. "Take a nap," he instructed.

I drifted in and out of a sleep interspersed with visions of Greg and spotty dreams, like a stuck filmstrip—Greg tied to a chair, blindfolded, loud and angry men with guns pointed at his head; Greg lying half-dead on the side of Route 96 somewhere; Greg in my hotel room pushing the hair off my face, shushing me, telling me everything would be okay. *Greg.*

When I woke up, the clock read six thirty. I looked toward the window. The dark gray sky with shafts of slanted light on the horizon gave no indication if it was dusk or dawn. My mind played back the day's events with the final realization of Greg's affair thudding in my chest. I thought of my girls, home with my mother while I chased...

Who? Invisible kidnappers? I was a fool, gullible and naïve. I knew what everyone else must have seen—a woman too desperate to believe her husband had left her, clinging to the fantasy of a mysterious "disappearance."

When I flung open the door between our adjoining rooms, Drew was lying on his bed, watching television. He jumped for the second time that day. "You've *got* to learn to knock." He grinned.

"Is it morning or night?"

"Night."

I was surprised. "Are you hungry?"

"Famished."

"Me, too, and I want to get very, very drunk."

"Claire..." He shrugged.

"Don't," I admonished. "Lecturing me about anything right now would be a very bad idea."

We left the hotel in search of a bar. I needed greasy food and beer. I still wanted to find Greg, but I wanted him to pay for what he had done to me and his kids. He needed to understand the consequences of his actions. Did he really think he could just walk away? If he was so miserable, why not just divorce me? Was it the money? I couldn't figure it out. Greg was never that selfish. He always put his family first. So why leave this way? What if he had cheated on me, and something horrible had happened to him? Would I care? Of course I would care; he was the father of my kids. My head was swimming with too many questions crashing into each other. I needed to stop thinking, and the fastest way I knew to do that was alcohol.

We found what we were looking for a few blocks away at McGraff's Pub. The air inside was cool and smelled faintly of stale beer and Pine-Sol. The restaurant was fairly empty, save for a few single patrons who sat at the bar, staring blankly at one of several flat screen televisions playing various football games. We chose a booth, and Drew sat across from me, unusually quiet. When the waitress came over, I ordered a cheeseburger and fries, then without thinking, a Sam Adams, which made me think of Greg. My mood swung wildly between melancholy and anger.

"I still need to find him," I said after Drew placed his order and the waitress left. I had finally found my words—most of them of the four-letter variety. On our drive down, I had been withdrawn and sad, lost in confusion, thinking of Greg as some kind of victim. With some solid evidence of an affair, I became the angry predator Drew had tried to draw out earlier. "But now, he better be terrified when I do."

Drew shook his head. "Listen. I want you to stop and think. We technically don't know any more than we did before we left to come down here. Dinner is just that—dinner. It could have been a colleague who happened to love Thai food. My point is, I'm okay with your anger because it's so much better than that lifeless, silent person you were before. But you need to focus if we're going to make some progress here. This is *not* a lecture."

"Really? Because it feels like one," I snapped, sitting back in the booth and staring past him. Greg used to call my silent treatment the Great Wall of Claire.

The overlapping sports games competed for attention, the announcers talking over each other in an enthusiastic rush. When our burgers and beers came, I gave up the brooding in favor of eating and drank four beers in succession. After the fourth, I asked for a shot of tequila.

Drew put his hand over mine. "Not a lecture, but legitimately a *terrible idea.*"

"I know. But I'm so damn tired of always having good ones." I grinned.

He motioned to the waitress, who was at the bar picking up my shot, and held up two fingers. Suddenly, it was a party. And not the pitying kind.

43

Drew wrapped his arm around my waist, holding me upright, our hips softly knocking as we walked. *Bump. Bump.* I swayed unsteadily with every step. The tequila tasted acidic, sharp, and stabbing in my chest.

"Do you think he's here?" I slurred. The street took on an unreal cast, and I squinted, blurring the glow of the street lamps together above my head.

"Here, as in Rochester?"

"Yeah, do you think we're gonna find him?" It seemed important suddenly that Drew not only be there, supporting me, but that he genuinely believe in our mission. *Our mission?* I laughed, a single guttural "HA!" *As if we're superheroes.*

Drew led me through the lobby and into the elevator. He pushed the button for the sixth floor. I watched the numbers above the door climb and winced at the *ding* when we reached our floor. The lights seemed too bright, the ding too loud, and the hallway swayed like a suspension bridge.

I fumbled with my card key, cursing at the unrelenting red light on the handle until Drew gently took the card. In a single movement, he slid it in, then out, and the green light blinked. I smirked. *Show off.*

In the room, I took off my shoes and tossed them on the floor. I dug out my pajamas—a T-shirt and mesh Princeton shorts—and with only a quick glance at Drew, pulled my shirt over my head, the hotel room air cold against my bare back. He had flopped on the bed and was studying the remote as I dressed. *Whatever. Where the hell is my hair tie?* I dug through my bag until I found a rubber band suitable for holding my long black hair away from my face.

"You're always taking care of me when I drink," I said, speaking slowly. *HA! I didn't even slur that one.*

"Well, then, stop drinking so much." He smiled and winked, patting the empty spot on the bed next to him.

I sat against the headboard, folding my legs underneath me, and cast a sideways glance at him. "Remember the prom?"

Drew shifted, pulling one leg up, ever so slightly angling away from me. He turned on the television and studied the guide. "Of course I remember the prom."

❦

We'd attended prom together for lack of other options. Drew had just broken up with his girlfriend—they were nearing his dreaded six-month mark—and I had stayed single most of my high school years.

I brought a flask and kept spiking my punch. Drew said he didn't need to drink, that he had just as much fun sober. By the end of the night, I was sufficiently drunk and led him to the rear of the school. My hair, once piled in ringlet curls on my head, had come unpinned during the dancing and was hanging haphazardly down my back. I wore a strapless light pink gown, a satin mistake that had become blotched with punch and rum. Drew's bowtie was draped around my neck, a badge of entitlement. His shirt was untucked and unbuttoned at the neck, the typical end-of-the-night mayhem of formal attire.

My face burned from the alcohol, and the air outside smelled ripe of summer and pheromones. I pushed him against the back wall of the school, aware then of the power I'd had over him, but the alcohol made me reckless, selfish, willing to risk our friendship. I leaned against him, feeling the entire length of his body against mine, and kissed his neck at the soft dip of flesh near his collarbone. I heard his intake of breath, and his hands ran down my back, pulling me into him.

"Claire." He kissed me. He tasted of sunshine and childhood, and conversely, seduction and sex.

He pushed me away. "Claire, you're drunk. I don't want this, not like this."

My anger came quick and hot. *Rejection, seriously?* I laughed. "Are you kidding? It's all you've ever wanted."

"I still do. But I want it... forever, not just for tonight, when you're drunk and can pretend this never happened."

"You get me now. It's your chance. *Now.* We get a hotel room like everyone else and make love on prom night like seniors are *supposed* to do. Or we don't. You choose." I stepped back, arms outstretched, like a game show host showing off a prize.

He turned his head to the side. "Claire, don't..."

I let my arms fall and shook my head. When he didn't move, I stormed away and left him against the wall.

"It would have been fun, you know." I laughed, then flipped back the covers. The action seemed dramatic, larger than life, because of the tequila. I felt humiliated all over again and didn't know why I'd brought up the memory. I rarely thought about it over the years, and we never spoke about it. *It's all you've ever wanted.* It was a cruel thing to say, and his stricken expression had stayed with me. Drew stretched out, crossing his feet at the ankles, and I burrowed beneath the blankets.

He looked over at me and, smiling, patted my head, Cindy Lou Who style. "Nah, we wouldn't have stayed friends, then."

When my head hit the pillow, I felt my eyes drift, sleep coming in waves, despite the spinning sensation in my head. I longed for sleep that was deep and dreamless, absent of images of Greg in danger. I reached out blindly and patted his arm. "Then I'm glad you said no." Before I had time to figure out if that was true, I passed out.

CHAPTER 9

MORNING WASN'T FRIENDLY. I SAT up, my head pulsing, and drank from the glass of water on the nightstand. I spotted a bottle of Advil beside the lamp and threw back two of them. Bless Drew.

He lay next to me on the queen-sized bed, sleeping on top of the covers, always the gentleman. He looked older than I remembered, still handsome with his dark hair and Roman nose. He was thinner, lankier. He had always been good to me, and I'd always taken advantage. I knew of some of his girlfriends, and I knew some of the breakups were painful, but he'd never called me in the middle of the night to talk, never showed up at my front door unannounced. I put my hand on his stubbled cheek.

He opened his eyes and broke into a wide grin. "You have got to feel *awful*."

"No, I'm okay." I kissed his forehead. "Thank you. I mean that. I don't know what I would have done on this trip without you. And thank you for the water and the Advil. That's so you."

"No problem." He stretched, yawning loudly. "So... what's today's plan?"

"Same as yesterday's—find Greg. I have ideas. Go get a shower and meet me back here?"

He saluted sleepily and trudged heavily into his room, shutting the door behind him.

We left the hotel an hour later, got a table at Starbucks, and formed some kind of game plan. My newfound kick-ass attitude was more comfortable with the game analogy than I'd been previously. We outlined a list of stops and walked the quarter-mile to Advent Rochester.

At the front desk, I flashed my Advent badge and asked to see Burt Rainer. Burt was the compliance contact at Rochester, and I knew he'd have a complete list of training classes and be able to talk about Greg's schedule. I asked Drew to take a seat and wait for me. I explained that everything in the company was badge access, and an outsider wasn't likely to be admitted past the lobby.

A few moments later, a tall, heavyset man in a navy blue suit came around the corner, puffing and red-faced from exertion. "Claire Barnes?"

"Hi, Burt." I extended my hand, and he took it. "We met a few years ago. I'm Greg's wife. I also work at Advent, but I'm based in Raritan."

A look of alarm crossed his face. "Hi, Claire. Of course I remember you." He motioned me down the hall and badged us into his office. He moved to sit behind his desk, and I chose one of the two chairs across from him.

He fiddled with a pen. "I heard something happened to Greg. The police were here, and I spoke to them, but I haven't heard any updates. What's going on?"

"Well, Greg is missing. No one from work has heard from him. I haven't heard from him, and the police can't find him." I took a deep breath. From what I remembered, Burt was a family man. "Burt, I have to be honest. I'm here because I'm driven to be. The police don't know I'm here. But honestly, if your wife went missing, wouldn't you feel compelled to go to the last place she'd been? I've already uncovered at least one detail the police didn't, based on the fact that I knew my husband. So, please, could you tell me what you told the police?"

He nodded. "I'd be happy to tell you the same thing I told Detective... Reynolds, was it?" I nodded. "Greg wasn't here for any official business. There was no training scheduled for that week. I have no idea why he was in town." He fidgeted, twirling his wedding ring around his finger.

I felt thrown down the rabbit hole. Again. I sat breathless, in stunned silence. Of all the responses I thought I would get, that was not one of them. I didn't scream or cry. With each blow, I became further removed from Greg, the husband I thought I knew so well. Each new heartbreaking fact hardened my armor.

"Are you okay?" he finally asked.

"Yes, I'm okay." Shockingly, it was true. I had a thought. "What about Toronto?" Advent had a small satellite site in Toronto, mostly just offices, no labs or manufacturing, but it had a regulatory section, which infrequently required Greg for training.

Burt looked thoughtful. "I haven't heard of anything, but I didn't think about that." He held up a finger and picked up his phone. He dialed and then waited a few seconds. "Hi, Jeannie. This is Burt. Can you check the training schedule for me about something?" He nodded. "Yep, the week of the twenty-sixth through the first of October. Did you guys have anything scheduled? How about the week before or after? Okay, thanks a bunch. Yep, I'll talk to you soon."

He hung up and shook his head. "No, there was nothing that week or the week before or after. That's not unusual. They only need annual training sessions, and I think they have qualified personnel onsite, even if they required an extra one." He looked thoughtful. "I'm really scratching my head here, trying to think of a reason why he would be in Rochester. We didn't even have any training scheduled for that week taught by anyone else."

"What about a meeting with someone?"

Burt shrugged. "When the police were here, I did a search of everyone's calendar for Greg's name. In addition, we pulled everyone who would have had reason to meet with him into the office, and the police interviewed them. Detective Reynolds said he was going to go back and interview Greg's manager and colleagues, but I haven't heard anything else."

I put my hand to my head, trying to steady my spinning thoughts.

"I'm sorry, Claire. I wish I had more. I know you said you uncovered a detail by coming here, so I'm glad it wasn't a wasted trip, but I do think you should go home and communicate with the detectives. I hope you figure all this out." He stood up then, a dismissal, a polite one, but still a dismissal. *Oh, your husband's missing? Well, that stinks. Listen, I have a ten o'clock, so can we reschedule this?* The corporate world turns.

I stood and shook his hand. "Thanks for meeting with me. I'll keep you updated. Please give me a call if something turns up." I pulled out a business card, jotted my cell phone number on the back, and handed it to him.

He took the card, flipped it over twice, studying the front and back, and slipped it into his shirt pocket. He coughed nervously and walked me to the door, promising to call if he learned anything.

In the lobby, I filled Drew in on the development. He finally looked shocked, the seeds of doubt about Greg's fidelity creeping into his eyes.

Husband lies about business trip, goes on fake business trip, checks into hotel for fake business trip, eats Thai with mystery woman, disappears. I was starting to see the writing on the wall, and it read, *Lying Cheating Bastard.*

After talking to Burt, I just wanted to leave. I felt so foolish, as half of what I found out, the police would already know. I needed to go home and meet with Detective Reynolds, who had probably found out about our adventure and wasn't thrilled with it. What had I been thinking, that I was going to ride up to Rochester and rescue Greg from invisible kidnappers? That I would find him when the police couldn't and magically bring him home?

I asked Drew to drive, and I resumed my window watching. I

actually felt sorry for him; this was some sad excuse for a road trip.

When I said as much, he laughed. "Oh well. I got something I needed out of this trip, too. You think I did this all for you? Pfffffttttt..." He waved his hand.

"What are you talking about?"

"I got to disappear for a few days," he said. "Pardon the expression. My disappearance is temporary, of course."

Ah... nothing is sacred. "From who?"

"Clients." He shrugged. "I have my agent and potential clients cold-calling me to find out when I'm releasing more prints. You know what I called the last one? *Irony.*"

I laughed. A real laugh and it felt good. "Why *Irony?*"

"Because it contains nine photographs I took of complete poverty, not in Ethiopia or some third world country, but in New York City. It's disgusting, and the guy who eventually bought it paid three hundred and twenty-five thousand dollars. He hangs the whole collection in his foyer, which I swear would hold your house. So there you go. That's irony, right?"

I was awed by the figure, but tried not to let it show. "If you're so disgusted by it, why do you do it?"

"Because what else am I going to do? I love photography, and I love making money on it. I hate that people will pay that amount of money for photographs of poverty, though. It seems criminal. I mean, that guy should have just donated three grand to charity. But he told his rich friends, and now, everyone wants pictures of poor people. It's so twisted."

"The world *is* twisted," I agreed.

"You know the worst part? I gave more than half of that away. I gave it to the people whose pictures I had taken. I condemn the rich for paying that much for art, but then I give only half of it away? I should just give it all away, but I don't." He shook his head.

I gaped at him. "You gave that much away? That's amazing. Nobody else would do that. Why would you put yourself down for that?"

"It doesn't matter anyway. The point is, I came here for you and your crisis in part, but really, I came for me. So thank *you*."

My heart swelled with love. It didn't matter if his story was true or not. I knew he had told me to help me feel as if I wasn't using him, though we both knew I was. I also knew he told me some of it to distract me from my own plight for the first time in about two weeks. That alone was worth the trip.

Five hours later, when we pulled into my driveway, Detective Matt Reynolds stood on the porch waiting for me.

CHAPTER 10

"NO, YOU'RE RIGHT. I'M NOT happy with it." Detective Reynolds sat in my living room, in Greg's easy chair. Drew and I sat on the couch, chastened children in my own home. "Here's why. We don't know Greg at all. For all we know, he was involved in something criminal and is now at the bottom of the Delaware River. Or more likely, the Genessee River."

I must have made a face because the detective gave me a stern look. "Mrs. Barnes, excuse me if I don't mince words, but you openly admitted you didn't know your husband well at the time of his disappearance. So you go to Rochester and start asking questions. What if someone finds out and decides you should take a swim with your husband? It's not out of the realm of possibility. Let us do our job. I repeat. Let. Us. Do. Our. Job."

"I understand," I said. "But *you* have to understand. Wouldn't you be drawn to the last place your wife was seen alive? I don't know if Greg is dead in a ditch somewhere or hiding out in the Dominican Republic with his mistress. I have no idea. Although I did find something that you didn't, so it wasn't a wasted trip."

"Okay, we'll retrace your steps. But please don't do that again. I promise we'll do all we can to find your husband. Now, please, let's run through what you did, who you talked to, and what you found out."

Drew and I recounted the events of the last two days.

When I told Detective Reynolds about confirming with Burt Rainer that there was no scheduled training class for that week, he nodded. "We knew that, but we didn't check with Toronto. So, that was good thinking." He wrote something down in his notebook.

I told him about *Pad Thai*, and he looked surprised. "We'll have to go back and formally interview the hostess, but we were planning on going back up there next week anyway."

"But I don't know what I'm supposed to *do*. I'm driven to do something. I need to be part of this, to find resolution."

The detective shook his head. "Claire..." He reached over and put his hand on mine. "You can't be part of this. We will update you as often as we can. We have Greg's car. It was at the airport, where we expected it. It's been at the station for a few days. It had to be searched and processed. You can come get it at some point, or I can drive it over."

"I don't want to drive it." I closed my eyes. I pictured the driver's side with the seat fully extended for Greg's long legs and his glasses, which he wore only to drive, in the glove compartment. All the mirrors were positioned for his eyes, and adjusting them so that I could drive would feel like another erasure, another small exorcism of Greg from our lives. Greg's car had a wonderful smell, like leather, cologne, vanilla air freshener, and Greg, all mixed together in an intoxicating cocktail. I knew there was no way I'd be able to drive that car.

"I'll pick it up," Drew said.

For a moment, I had forgotten Drew was there. I thanked him and turned back to the detective. "What else have you found out?"

Detective Reynolds opened his notebook. "Sometime after he landed in Rochester, he withdrew a thousand dollars from the ATM. Is that usual? Did he usually carry that much cash?"

I was taken aback. "Greg never really carried cash. I used to tell him all the time to take out more than twenty bucks at a shot because the surcharges are so high, but he never did. He used his debit card for everything. So, no, that's not like him at all." *That sounds as though he was planning something.*

Detective Reynolds wrote in his notebook. "We did get a hold of his corporate cell phone, corporate credit card records, and with your permission, we'd like to review your personal credit records, Claire."

I nodded. I wanted to add, *Could you tell me what's in them?* But I bit back the words.

"One other thing. We found a few calls to a nine-oh-eight area code that didn't match up with any number we knew. We traced the number, and it came back to a Go phone, one of those pay-as-you-go things. Some of the calls lasted an hour or more in the early morning hours. Any thoughts on who he was talking to?"

The realization hit me, low and solid in my core, churning my stomach. "Greg hasn't been sleeping much at night. He wanders the house at all hours. I never know when he comes to bed or when he wakes up. I always considered it part of whatever he was going through lately." I closed my eyes. I felt so stupid. It was a feeling I was getting used to. My life was a mockery. To have Greg living a drastically different self-contained life that I knew nothing about felt like a raw betrayal.

Detective Reynolds continued hesitantly, "We also looked at your cell phone records. The last time Greg used either his credit cards or his cell phone was Tuesday morning. In fact, we can't find anything to prove he was alive after Tuesday at seven p.m., which is when he withdrew the cash from the ATM."

I inhaled sharply. "Do you think he's dead?"

Detective Reynolds shook his head. "I don't think we can say that yet. He had a thousand dollars. You can go for a while on that kind of money, even longer if you have someplace to stay. Does he know anyone else that you can think of in the Rochester area? Think hard. He stayed there for six months when you first met, right? He must have made friends. Is there anyone he kept in touch with?"

I searched my memory, but came up blank. "No, he never talked about anyone he knew up there."

"What about his itineraries? Did he leave you with information when he left?" I got up and retrieved the travel notebook where Greg always documented his trips. The detective stood to leave, tapping the notebook on the cover. "If you go anywhere else, Claire, let me know. I'll keep you posted, okay?" We shook hands, and he left.

I felt bone-weary. I needed to see my kids. Drew wrapped his arms around me from behind and kissed my head. I relaxed into him briefly, but my thoughts wandered to Hannah and Leah. I needed to see them, to touch them, be with them. Either because he sensed that, or simply because he was tired, Drew retreated upstairs to take a nap.

I drove to my parents' house to pick up the girls. When I got there, they ran to me and clung to my legs.

"It's been a rough few days, Claire," Mom said.

I closed my eyes. I needed to talk to Hannah. But what could I say?

"I'm glad you came back, Mommy," Hannah said.

"I'll always come back, Hannah-banana," I said without thinking.

"Not like Daddy," she said, still holding my leg.

I picked her up and looked in her eyes. "Listen, Hannah, I want you to understand. Daddy didn't leave us. You didn't do anything wrong. Daddy loves us, and we love him. He just can't find his way home right now." I glanced at my mom over Hannah's head. She shrugged, shaking her head. She couldn't help me; no one could. There were no instruction manuals on how to talk to a four-year-old about her missing parent.

I held Hannah and inhaled the scent of her hair—berry shampoo and remnants of babyhood. She was growing into a child faster than I could handle. I prayed that I would do and say the right things, that I could guide her through the crisis, regardless of the outcome, as unscathed as possible. I wished they'd have as little fear as possible, as little uncertainty as possible, and hoped my desire to protect their small hearts would be enough. That my love would, somehow, be enough.

"Mommy, don't be sad." Hannah touched my cheek, a gesture absorbed from four years of observation, grown up beyond her years. "Daddy still loves us. You said so, right?"

I nodded, unable to answer. I held Hannah in one arm and Leah in the other, and gave Mom a kiss on the cheek. *Thank you,* I mouthed, quietly buckling them in the car. I drove into the setting sun, to the home that didn't feel like a home anymore.

CHAPTER 11

WHEN I PICKED HANNAH UP from school on Friday, her teacher pulled me aside. She had a long blond ponytail and wore jeans that hung too low on her hips for a preschool teacher. I had seen more than one dad ogle her during pick up, and I remember thinking, *Not Greg, thank God.* What a joke that had become. I motioned to another teacher in the school-age room, and she took Hannah's hand, guiding her gently into the neighboring classroom.

"Mrs. Barnes, I wanted to tell you, today we interviewed the children. You know, what are your mommy's and daddy's names? Your favorite food, your favorite toy, and so on. When we asked Hannah what her daddy did for a living, she said he was lost and that he took her dog with him." She paused then, looking at the ceiling, not knowing where to go. "I think, um... maybe you should talk to her about her dad?"

I clenched my fists at my sides and concentrated on not slapping her. "Miss Katie, what do *you* suggest I tell her? Besides the truth? That yes, her daddy is missing. I'm wondering what *you*, not being a mother, not having *any* life experience *whatsoever,* would tell your four-year-old. That her daddy left her? That's possible. That he's been murdered? That's possible. Please. Advise me. I'd *love* to know what they're teaching in the community college early childhood education classes these days about how to appropriately make a *fucking* four-year-old understand that her daddy might not be coming home, but maybe he will. Who the *hell* knows?"

I grabbed Hannah, who stood wide-eyed in the doorway, and left Miss Katie gaping with her mouth open. I could see the tears shimmering in her eyes and a very, *very* small part of me felt completely terrible. But most of me felt fantastic.

"Mommy," Hannah said, "you said a really bad word."

I sighed. I seemed to fail miserably at keeping the poor kid from being terrified at every turn. I kissed her head. "Yes, I did, Hannah-banana, and it wasn't nice." I gave her a big smile. "It's our secret, okay? So, what do you want for dinner? Anything you want. Ice cream? Pizza? You pick, *aaaaannnnnyyyy* dinner you want," I sing-songed.

Hannah thought for a second. "Can I have broccoli?"

I laughed and ruffled her hair. "Sure. You can definitely have broccoli if that's what you want. You're so weird, kiddo!"

When we got home, the four of us had dinner, a playact of a suburban family. Drew asked Hannah about school. Leah threw food, and Hannah scolded her. We watched *The Little Mermaid*, which Drew kept pretending he'd never seen, dramatically exclaiming over every scene, extracting giggles galore from Hannah. I gave the girls a bath and tucked them into bed. Low chords of sleep music drifted from their bedrooms, overlapping in a disorganized orchestra, the eerie result being both dissonant and harmonious at the same time.

Drew and I sat in the living room on opposite ends of the couch. I curled my feet underneath me and rested my head on the back of the sofa, feeling flattened by the day, the past few weeks. Drew laughed, coughing into his glass of wine when I relayed the preschool incident.

"I have no control over my mouth anymore," I said. "I feel horrible, that poor girl."

"That *poor girl* was a bit insensitive." He shrugged. "But then, isn't everyone at that age? Hmm, on second thought, how cute did you say she was?"

I hit him with a pillow. "Not funny."

"Look, seriously. I think genuinely kind-hearted people will forgive your occasional outbursts and overlook any inappropriate behavior for the moment."

I put my head in my hands. I felt tears pricking my eyelids. "This is how it is now. I'm laughing and normal, then I'm swearing and yelling, then I'm crying. I have the emotional range and self-control of Leah."

Drew reached over and put his hand on my back.

The wine made my head spin. "I really don't know what we'd be doing without you, Drew."

When I lifted my head, his face was inches from mine. His blue eyes, framed in dark lashes, held a love and intensity that I wanted to wrap myself in. I studied his face, olive skin and dark hair. He gently rubbed his thumb along my jaw. I closed my eyes, reveling in the touch of another person. Missing Greg. Loving Drew. I laid my head on his shoulder. He rubbed my back, his touch warm through the cotton of my shirt, that of an old friend. Or an old lover.

A shiver went through me, and I fought the desire to turn my head and kiss the tender spot between his collarbone and shoulder, where I'd kissed once before, years ago, and been crushingly rejected. *A person isn't meant to live without the touch of another person.* Before Greg left, how long had it been since we'd made love? Two months? Maybe.

A wave of longing went through me, and I brought his hand up to my lips and kissed his palm.

He let out a small gasp. "Claire." His voice was raspy. I'd heard it before, and I knew what he would say next. *We can't.*

Drew and I always had missed opportunities, blown chances. Fear, ego, and good common sense, those were our enemies.

Slowly, he withdrew his hand. His eyes were dark with desire, clouded with conflict, as he searched mine.

I closed my eyes, inhaling the scent of freshly washed laundry and something else distinctly male, distinctly Drew, like musk and sandalwood.

"Drew," I said, clutching his wrist as he gently rubbed his thumb over my lips, which naturally parted, the longing low in my belly.

He closed his eyes, his breathing ragged. "I know. Me, too." He leaned forward, touching his forehead to mine. "But you know we can't. Not now, not like this."

His words echoed back to me from fifteen years earlier, a memory of the prom, the sensation of his collarbone under my mouth, the humiliation that had followed then. Deep down, I knew using Drew to physically exorcise my pain and grief would damage beyond repair the one relationship keeping me from falling apart.

Greg had been missing for one month. All the women in the Mommy circles knew what had happened. Most people were kind and offered words of comfort, but when I ran into Nicole Lambert in Super Fresh, instead of her usual bubbly, "Hi, how are ya," she cast her eyes down and pretended not to see me.

I tried to understand. If Greg had died, then people could say, "I'm sorry for your loss," and move on. There would be a viewing or a funeral, closure not just for me, but for the community. The women could offer condolences, then go home and kiss their husbands, make love, and reaffirm that it couldn't happen to them. But the uncertainty, not to mention lack of an appropriate Hallmark card, made women question themselves. Did Greg leave us? And if he did, because we had seemed so happy, could their husbands leave them? But my problem was not their problem and since there was no way to officially acknowledge my pain, many people chose the option of unofficially pretending it wasn't there. Because of the anger I carried at all times, I didn't care about the discomfort of others. I reveled in it. I was a vampire, and other people's discomfort was my sustenance.

"Hi, Nicole," I said loudly.

She nodded curtly at me and quickly pushed her cart past the milk she surely needed for her three children.

The only person who didn't avoid me like the plague was Sarah, who called several times a week, sometimes to relay some bubbly gossip about her life, a distraction I welcomed. Other times, she'd just call to check-in and accept my moods however she found me. I found myself looking forward to her calls. She treated me like a person. *Like I was normal.*

Drew stayed another week. He helped me adjust to everyday life, giving the right amount of distraction to aid in the transition. I got out of the bed every morning because small hungry bellies didn't care if I wanted to pull the covers over my head and hide for the day, or the week. I tried to resume our routine of kid activities.

At night, after I put the girls to bed, I'd sit in Greg's chair, a physical and sensory barrier between Drew and me, while Drew would take the far corner of the couch. We'd talk and laugh easily, as though our near miss had never happened. Briefly, I wondered if the air between us would shift, but it didn't. Perhaps it was purely accustomed to the years of pulsing electricity, high-voltage moments intermingled with the steady line of friendship. An electrocardiogram of our relationship.

Before he left, he pulled me into a longer than normal hug. Part of me wanted to cling to him. *Stay. Stay and fill the hole in the house.* Impractical, of course. Probably also unhealthy.

"Are you going to be okay? Alone?"

I assured him we would be fine and promised to call. As he drove away, I waited on the front steps, hoping he'd come back. I knew he couldn't, but I stood paralyzed, unable to face the emptiness of the sleeping house, truly alone for the first time in my life.

CHAPTER 12

AMAZINGLY ENOUGH, MY BODY CONTINUED to function even when my heart felt eviscerated. I could breathe. I could talk. I made dinner, did laundry, ran the vacuum. However, I didn't think. I couldn't feel.

Numbness overtook me, and I went through the days on autopilot. With Drew gone, the house resumed its hollow quality. Voices bounced off the walls like pool balls reverberating in the seemingly empty rooms. I grew impatient with the girls.

I noticed a change in Hannah's behavior. She became selfish. Leah could no longer play with her toys. She would yell, "No, Leah. I *said* you can't *touch that!*" And Leah would cry. I would bang my hand on the counter out of frustration. I blamed Greg's absence, but my reactions were also damaging, and I didn't know how to change them. The days just progressed with the conclusion of hours, and end to end, those hours comprised the days.

I tried to take the girls to the library, toddler gym, and the playground. I wrote a semi-sincere apology note to Miss Katie. But mostly, those first few lonely weeks were colored by anger, intense, unmitigated fury. I slammed pots and pans in the kitchen, as if the cacophony would summon Greg home, if only to display annoyance at the racket and my need to slam things. At night, what kept me awake were the memories, specifically the good ones. I reconstructed happy events in our lives, looking for clues that would reveal the current ending.

On our first New Jersey date, after Greg returned from Rochester, we went to a distant cousin's wedding, where I met Greg's entire extended family. Greg drank too much champagne, an unusual occurrence as I later discovered, and I had to drive his car home. His car was manual transmission, and I had no idea how to drive it. I think I stayed in third gear the entire time, with the engine rev drowning out any conversation, while we giggled like kids. Greg tried to show me how to shift, but I kept grinding the gears. When we got to his apartment, he invited me to stay. I hesitated because it was our first real date, but I didn't have a car, and I wasn't about to try to drive Greg's without the aid of passenger seat instruction. He led me into his bedroom and gave me a stack of clean towels and a chaste kiss on the cheek good night.

When I asked him what he was doing, he looked shocked. "I'll sleep on the couch." He looked at the floor and rubbed the back of his neck.

I pulled him toward me by his tie and covered his mouth with mine. "I think you should reconsider." I led him onto his bed.

Another memory flashed of Greg with newborn Hannah in the hospital, holding her and looking at her face. He traced her nose and mouth with his finger, making sure she was real.

"I can't believe we made her," he said with tears in his eyes. "How did I ever do anything so perfect?"

Everything you do is perfect. But somehow, you're the only one who can't see that.

And another: Greg had been in the delivery room, my cheerleader, my champion. When the nurses took Hannah to clean and weigh her, he whispered in my ear, "You are so amazing, Claire Barnes. And I will love you until the day I die."

Lying in my empty marital bed, all I could think was, *Is today that day? Was October first that day?*

And another: Our first night in our new home, the one we bought together, we lay together on a mattress on the floor because we were too tired to put the bed together. We'd been married for two years, house shopping for one. Greg was particular; I was not. I considered any house we bought to be our starter home. Greg, fantastic with money, wanted to make sure the property had resale value. We talked for hours about all the improvements we could make, how we would make the house our home, fit for our family.

Greg confessed that he never believed he'd have anything in life. His father had died when he was five and his mother died shortly after we married. He had no brothers or sisters. He always believed he'd go through life alone, struggling the way his mother had. She had made ends meet, but not without worry and not with any joy, just fighting the demands and strain of everyday life. He confessed everything he'd ever feared: that he wouldn't marry, and then when he did, that he would fail as a husband, as a provider. I came to understand that the need to provide for his family was his sole driving purpose, and so ingrained in him, it trumped all else. We talked for hours, like newlyweds, and I promised we wouldn't fail, that together, failing wasn't a possibility. I tried to make him understand that there was more than one meter stick to measure success—happiness, fulfillment, laughter, joy—and that simply making a mortgage payment every month shouldn't be a life goal. To Greg, providing was all that mattered. Wherever Greg had gone, what was his meter stick? Did he think of himself as a failure? I couldn't reconcile the image of Greg as I remembered him with Missing Greg, lounging on an island with another woman.

I wore Greg's sweatshirts every day; only wrapped in Greg could I function again. Before, I would dress with care. I would take time with my hair, even apply some makeup, just to go to the library or the toddler gym. It used to be important that I looked composed, envied by other, more frazzled moms. But because coiffed hair and makeup looked clownish with oversized sweatshirts and yoga pants, I quit bothering. Since I also wouldn't wash them, they took on an odd odor after the first month. I didn't care. I felt swallowed by sadness.

Behind the sadness was a simmering anger. The anger would

boil over unexpectedly. I must have started cursing more without realizing it because I would hear Hannah in the playroom, trying to put together a puzzle, and frustrated with the pieces, she'd say, "Oh, shit," or "Damn it." I made a mental note to watch my mouth, but since I had no control over my verbal tirades, either the language I used or who I directed it at, my efforts were kind of useless. *Everything* felt useless.

Mom brought me a book titled *On Grief and Grieving* that was about grief having five stages. I started to read it, hoping that once I understood my emotions, I would be able to resolve them, or at least work toward pretending to be normal again. But the book talked about death, divorce, and infertility. There was no chapter on lost husbands. Everyone in the book had a label: a widower, a divorcee, an orphan. I was label-less.

The book explained the stages of grief, but my heartache was more than building blocks to be piled one on top of the other until I could bridge the gap between my two lives. My existence was a complicated tapestry: red for anger, blue for intense sadness, green for happiness. Yes, happiness existed, not much, but some, particularly in the early morning, in the place between sleep and awake when I'd think Greg was lying next to me in bed, and imagine us talking softly, deciding who would get up first and who should get coffee in bed on Sundays. Then Leah would cry, awake and wanting out of her crib. When I opened my eyes to the bare sheets, cool in the early morning light, I'd weave a thick, ugly braid of red and blue into my blanket of sorrow.

I searched each memory for signs. Was Greg unhappy? Did he really up and leave us? That one day a few months ago, he had said he didn't mind if I took the day off and went shopping while he stayed with the girls; was he really angry instead? How about the time I washed a few of his white work shirts with one of Hannah's red T-shirts and turned his pink? Had that been the final straw? For his birthday last year, I'd gotten him an expensive watch he claimed to want. When he opened it, he looked almost disappointed. Why?

No memory was safe from my scrutiny. I went through photo albums, studying Greg's face, his expressions, running my hands over the plastic-protected pictures. When he scowled at the camera last year on the Outer Banks because I insisted on taking a picture of him covered in zinc oxide, was that disdain in his eyes? I had waved off his protests, showing him the picture. *You just look so ridiculous! Like one of those old men with the white noses!* He picked me up, threw me over his shoulder, and marched down to the ocean. *It's not white, it's blue!* he yelled, mockingly shaking his fist from the shore after he tossed me into the water. When I came up for air, he stood with Hannah and Leah, all three of them laughing. Had he been genuine that day, or had I missed the signs all along? Those were my fears, that I'd missed the signs all along. That our happily ever after was a sham was the fear that would settle in my stomach, twisting my insides.

I felt sick all the time and even trudged into the CVS one day while the girls were at Mom and Dad's to buy a pregnancy test. *Wouldn't that be a bitch?* It had been a few months, but stranger things had happened. The nausea was so reminiscent of my pregnancy with Hannah. When I studied the readout, my hands shaking, and saw the one pink line instead of two, I collapsed on the toilet with relief. And then, inexplicably, overwhelming sadness.

I began to think of my life as divided: my before life, with Greg, and my after life, without him. The deep chasm that separated those two lives was my current purgatory, as deep and dark as it was wide. I didn't believe I'd feel so lost forever, and I frequently hoped that my life afterward would be sunnier, and maybe I'd legitimately laugh again one day. But Leah, Hannah, and I passed our days at the bottom of a black gorge, blindly feeling for the rope that would save us.

My parents called every day. My mom came over at least three times a week, sometimes more. She would come in the door, a flurry of movement, such a stark contrast to the stillness of our lives that I would cringe. She had bags of activities, small toys, or stickers for the girls and always a bottle of wine for me. She had apparently skipped the chapter in the grief book on the dangers of self-medication. Some days, she would take the kids to the park if it wasn't too cold, or to the aquarium or on some other outing where they could be the loud, unruly kids they should be, but selfishly, I limited those days. I needed Leah and Hannah. Without them, I was alone with my despair and had no reason to get off the couch or out of bed.

At night, after my mom would bring the kids home and help me put them to bed, I would drink wine until my vision wavered. I'd call Sarah, drunk and rambling, and day or night, she'd stay on the phone as long as I needed. She lived in California and asked more than once if she could come visit, but I kept denying her. She had a life—dating, drinking, single—a life I longed for some nights. I loved my girls; they were my life's meaning, especially now. But the anonymity of a single life, of meeting men in bars and not knowing their names or their secrets, of not carrying someone else's burden, sounded heavenly. But I couldn't have Sarah with me, another person to witness my sorrow, to look at me with pitying eyes. I didn't want her to ask if she could do something, maybe some laundry. She didn't need to witness the dishes that piled in the sink or the long stretches between vacuumings. She might actually notice and cringe when Leah found Goldfish crackers on the floor and ate one.

CHAPTER 13

TEN DAYS BEFORE CHRISTMAS, THE house was still not decorated. I hadn't put up a tree or done any Christmas shopping. I couldn't seem to find the motivation to face the crowds, the malls with their hauntingly happy music, or the laughter of families as they waited in line for their children to sit on Santa's lap.

Dad showed up with a small four-foot Christmas tree in tow. The tree was the smallest we'd ever had, and my first instinct was to scorn the gesture.

"Your mother said you needed a tree," he grunted. He carefully laid out a piece of plywood and set up the tree stand. The tree looked silly in the usual corner, like a pretend tree. *For a make-believe Christmas.* Before he left, he stood in front of me, shifting from one foot to the other and finally reached out, putting his large hand on my head, as though I were Cody. "The girls need a Christmas, is all."

"I know, Dad."

"You're on your own to decorate it." He looked over at the wilting, skinny tree and then back at me. His eyes looked wet and sad. We'd never had much conversation outside of *how's the car running,* and the sudden reaching out felt stridently out of place.

I kissed his cheek. "Thanks."

He left with a final grunt and another pat on my head, hunched and lumbering down the walk to his car.

My mother came later and picked up the girls. She took them back to her house to bake cookies like "everyone else." "You *are* going to get them presents, right?" Mom asked.

I gave her a withering glare. "What am I? A terrible person? Of course. That's a stupid question."

"Please wear something normal and go to the mall. Spend this on presents." Mom countered my spitefulness with patience, and I felt a small pang of guilt.

I gaped when she handed me three crisp one-hundred-dollar bills. She put up her hand, as if I would try to argue. I had no idea of the condition of my finances, but they couldn't have been good. Still unable to make myself go into the study and figure out Greg's system, I had paid the November bills with the checks I carried in my purse. I had no idea if they would clear or not.

For the first time in over a month, I went to my closet and pulled on one of my own shirts. It hung on me, draping over bony shoulders and sunken breasts. The diet of the grieving—the latest fad. I got out my straight iron and pulled my dark hair through the hot plates. I applied some mascara, foundation, and lip gloss. My reflection in the mirror appeared almost ordinary, like my previous self, but skinnier, sadder, with bigger eyes. I tried to will my lips into a smile, baring my teeth. The expression looked grotesque, a wolf in sheep's clothing.

I steered the van into the mall parking lot and surveyed the crowd, heavy for a Wednesday, but Christmas shoppers didn't differentiate. I felt a dull ache under my breastbone, dreading the music and the shoppers, which would both be irritating and cheerful. I forced myself out of the car, for my kids. They needed a Christmas. For that matter, they needed a mother. *They needed a father.* The walk from the car to the front of the mall seemed interminably long. When I opened the large glass door, I was assaulted by the smell of soft pretzels and cinnamon, and the sounds of Christmas music and Santa. *There are five fucking entrances in this mall, and seriously, I pick the Santa one?*

I kept my head down and made a beeline to Toys R Us at the far end of the mall. I had no idea what to buy. I certainly hadn't been paying attention to television commercials. I walked the aisles, pushing an empty cart, trapped by indecision. Electronics? Too old.

Polly Pocket? Too overdone. We had about a hundred. Dolls? Too babyish. Disney princesses? Hannah was past that phase. I needed help. I needed Greg. Every day, I thought that at least once.

In the bike aisle, I was struck with a memory. Months ago, Hannah had asked Greg if she could have a two-wheeler for Christmas because Annie down the street got one for her birthday. Greg and I made eye contact over Hannah's head with the same thought that we each had on a regular basis. *Our baby is growing up.* Our conversation later that night after the girls went to bed was one of the last times I felt us connect. We talked for an hour, about our lives, the girls growing up too fast, what we thought they would be like when they were teenagers. We laughed. We each had a glass of wine, and for once, the television remained dark.

I felt a ray of hope. A pinhole in my balloon of despair was letting in a small, yet unmistakable beam of light. If I could make Christmas extraordinary, fill our house with laughter and voices and magic, maybe we'd start the climb out of our black gorge of sorrow. I was so tired of feeling tired, of feeling helpless and hopeless. I looked around at the people in the store—mothers, fathers, aunts, uncles, and grandparents—all vying for the best present, the favorite present, anything to extract the brilliant smile of a child. I could be one of them, if only for a moment.

"Can I help you?"

I turned to a young man of maybe eighteen and tried on a smile. He smiled back.

"I want a pink bicycle. Not Barbie or Dora or anything like that. Just pink and sparkly with streamers on the handlebars and a bell."

He laughed and brought me around the aisle. He pointed at a bike in the rack that fit my description.

Pushing my luck, I continued, "What about a tricycle? Do you have anything similar?"

He showed me all the tricycles, and I spotted a pink one. No streamers, but it did have a bell. "I'll take one of each."

"Do you want me to ring it up?" he asked.

"No, I'm not done yet." I felt jittery... *excited.* To have any emotion but despair felt alien, but wonderful. I had spent about half of the three hundred that Mom had given me. I returned to the aisles that mere moments before had seemed overwhelming.

Barbies! Hannah had no Barbie dolls; I put three boxes in my cart. Then as an afterthought, I grabbed a Ken. *Someone around here should have a man.* I rounded the corner to the dress-up aisle. Into the cart went two dresses, one for each of my daughters. Shoes to match? Surely. I selected a new doll for Leah, as she only had hand-me-downs, and also picked out a canopy doll bed, complete with bedspread and pillow shams. I bought them each electronic reading systems, with a few books. I found markers, crayons, paints, coloring books, Play-Doh, and two pads of paper, along with a purple bucket to hold it all. By the time I was done, my cart was filled to the brim, not including the two bikes waiting at the register.

The total rang up to five hundred and seventy-five dollars, more than I had ever spent on Christmas for the two of them. A very small part of me was appalled, but more than that, I was excited. At the last minute, I threw in three rolls of wrapping paper and some ribbon, then ran my credit card to cover the difference. I was filling the void Greg had left in our lives with material possessions, and while some would argue it wasn't healthy or was only temporary, I didn't care. For the moment, I felt alive, human, and normal. And maybe my high would be contagious. *Maybe* some of that Christmas magic would rub off on the girls, and for one day, we would all be happy again.

However high on shopping I was, I knew my moods were fickle, and that by Christmas, I could very well be back underwater, drowning in sorrow, and all my efforts today would be for naught. But one person could help. He could buoy my capricious moods and keep the spirit of Christmas afloat despite the weight of sadness heavy in the air. I got in the car, started the engine to get the heat going, and pulled my cell phone out of my purse to dial a number I knew by heart.

"Hi, it's me," I said when he picked up. "Got any plans for Christmas?"

⁘⁘⁘

I stood in the guest bedroom, surveying the white sheets tucked under the mattress with folded precision. I'd never cared much about the state of the room for Drew, but it had somehow started to matter. I opened my grandmother's handmade quilt— zigzag triangles of green and red on creamy white—and shook it out, letting it fall to rest squarely on the bed.

I thought of the Christmas four years ago when Drew had visited. Hannah was a newborn, red and colicky, and I was exhausted all the time. I'd invited him every year, and he'd always said no. But for some reason, that year, he agreed. When I opened the door, he handed me a bottle of red wine.

Greg stood behind me in the hall. "She can't drink red anymore. Since the baby," he commented, tilting his head to the side, in a way only I knew was condescending.

I rolled my eyes. He was right. My face burned bright at the first sip, a reaction to sulfites, I'd read. I didn't care, though. Not that night.

"It's fine." I took the wine and went into the kitchen, retrieving two glasses from the cabinet. I set them on the counter and reached into the drawer for the corkscrew. Greg made a deliberate coughing noise in my direction and reached up to retrieve a third glass, raising his eyebrows at me with a small smile.

Drew stood over Hannah's portable cradle, which we had set up in the living room, studying her. She was in a rare state of contented sleep. I crept up behind him and passed him a glass, cradling my own in my other hand.

"She's so small," he whispered.

"I know. She's cranky, though. Wait 'til you see."

73

"Nah. Uncle Drew is here. You wait. She'll be a different kid; she'll be so happy to see me."

I nudged him with my elbow.

He nudged me back. "I can't believe you're a mom, now."

"Right? I'm in charge of another person. God help us."

"Oh, stop. You're the most responsible person I know. You'll be fine. Uncle Drew is going to have to show her how to have fun, though."

Hannah twitched and then settled back into sleep with a soft baby moan. When I looked up, Drew was watching me, and our eyes caught, trapped by the shared sensation of a door closing. He gave me a small, sad smile.

"What?" I asked.

"Nothing." He shook his head, ran his hand along the side of the cradle, then straightened and rubbed his hands together. "What's for dinner? I'm starving!"

Drew and I cooked in a routine performed on sensory memory, having made dinners together for years, throughout college and beyond, whenever we'd gotten together. He always chopped onions. I always made the sauce. We had our strengths and our traditions.

Greg comforted Hannah as she screamed. The respite of concentrating on something other than Hannah, her needs, her comfort—or lack thereof—provided a balm for my remaining baby blues.

Drew nurtured a variety of mushrooms in butter, slapping my hand away as I tried to pick. Over Chicken Marsala, we reverted back to conversations about people from our childhood and from high school. At first, I tried to include Greg, but as I drank, I forgot. Greg shrank further and further into himself, tending to Hannah and finally getting up to put her to bed. We moved to the living room, where Drew and I reminisced about his parents—his mom's homemade blueberry pie and his dad's insistence that before Drew could get his license, he had to replace all the tires on the car.

"I miss them," Drew said, letting his head rest against the

couch cushion.

I assumed the same position and watched him. "Me, too. Remember your mom's confused sayings? Brightest bulb in the drawer?"

"*Yes!* Oh, my God. Pitch white." We howled.

Greg appeared in the doorway, his expression unreadable. I stood up, aware somehow that I had gone a bit too far, but grateful for Greg's willingness to put himself last, even if for only one night. Glancing at the kitchen, where the dishes were piled on the counter, I inwardly groaned.

"Drew and I will take care of it, honey. Go on up," Greg said, his voice light.

I watched him skeptically, looking for signs. Was he jealous? Angry? He didn't seem so. "Are you sure? I can do it tomorrow..."

"Go to bed. We'll start, and as far as we get, we get. Then, we can pick it up tomorrow."

Knowing I only had about two hours of sleep before I was up again for a feeding, I walked down the hall. Shielded by the staircase, I paused in the hallway, listening. *What would they talk about? Me?* I stood silent and still, but heard only the sounds of glasses clanking as they made their way into the dishwasher.

I started up the steps, and then stopped when I heard Greg's voice. "I wonder how long you've been in love with my wife."

My heart hammered. *Why would he say that?* And then a new thought, *What would Drew's answer be?* I leaned forward, keeping out of sight as much as I could.

Greg spoke again, a register lower. "... married *me*... sometimes... don't know why, but she did..."

I tried to imagine Drew, what he would say. I waited for his reply, but heard nothing except the clattering of silverware.

I was paralyzed by humiliation. For Greg. For myself. For Drew. *Was Greg right?* All Drew had ever done was reject me. *Was I that transparent?* I crept up the steps.

As I waited in bed, staring into the dark, Greg's words raced through my mind. Did he really think Drew was in love with me? If so, why had he never said anything to me? Why would he just fade in and out of the room, leaving Drew and me to catch up, talk, laugh? It didn't make sense.

I heard the door creak open, and a few minutes later, Greg slid into bed beside me. I lay very still, pretending to be asleep. He moved across the bed, deftly sliding one arm under me as his other hand cupped my breast. His lips met my neck, and he pulled me into his body, a solid bulk form where I always felt sexy.

In the back of my mind, I tried to make sense of the conversation, fairly confident that Drew hadn't confirmed Greg's suspicions. *Jealousy, surely, right?* As his hand slid down, pushing off my pajama bottoms, my mind lost the ability to reason. In that moment, Greg's questioning felt primal. And with his mouth leaving a hot trail of need down to my core, I no longer cared. He covered my body with his, in all its familiarity, made all the more tantalizing by the sides of my husband I perhaps didn't know.

The next morning, I almost believed that I had dreamt the entire thing.

CHAPTER 14

ETECTIVE REYNOLDS SHIFTED IN GREG'S chair, waiting patiently for me to catch up.

My mind reeled, backpedaling, looking for an escape. "Four times?" I repeated.

The detective nodded slowly.

"Four times in the past year, Greg has lied about where he's been."

He added another nod, confirming my summary. Superfluous really. Receiving affirmation wouldn't make my words *feel* real.

He cleared his throat. "Greg took eighteen trips last year. That's actually quite a lot. We can confirm that fourteen of them are legitimate. We compared his itineraries with his manager's training schedule. So the four trips that he lied about were February tenth, May twenty-second, July sixteenth, and then this one, September twenty-seventh."

The trips were a blur to me, one long business trip—more accurately, the same trip repeated once, twice a month. I remembered only one, February tenth. We had a fight about it.

Really? Valentine's Day? What kind of company commands travel on Valentine's Day?

Claire, understand, Valentine's Day isn't actually a national holiday.

Well, then, your company should stop calling themselves the "Family Company" because they clearly don't care about divorce rates.

You're so dramatic. It's one year, one time.

If he'd lied, he did it because he wanted to be somewhere else on Valentine's Day. My hand over my mouth, I ran to the downstairs bathroom, retching my disbelief and hatred into the bowl. *If only I could actually do that.* I washed my hands and studied my reflection in the mirror. My complexion was pale and sallow, with bruised circles under my eyes from sleeplessness. I spotted wrinkles around my mouth and eyes that had not been there three months ago. I rinsed my face and my mouth and returned to the living room.

"I'm sorry," I said.

Detective Reynolds nodded once, looking down at his notepad. "So the first two trips, we believe he was in San Diego, where he claimed to be, but there were no scheduled trainings on those dates. But for the last two, we found nothing. No credit cards, no cell phone records, nothing. All we have is five hundred dollars taken from the ATM in Newark each time and then no traceable activity for his scheduled three to four days until he boarded the planes to return home."

"Where were the mystery trainings scheduled?" I knew the answer before he said it.

"Rochester."

The room seemed to expand then contract until I could see only his eyes—compassionate and pitying.

I'd put Hannah and Leah in bed for the night and felt no obligation to hide my emotions. I let Detective Reynolds back into Greg's study for the third time in two months so he could look for "supporting evidence." I had yet to set foot in that room. I asked that he please shut the door when he left and tell me if he took anything.

He returned with a leather-bound journal that I recognized as Greg's. "Is this okay? I'll make copies and bring it back."

I nodded mutely.

Once he was gone, I stood with my head against the door, gazing at the floor. When I felt a soft knock a few minutes later, I thought Detective Reynolds had forgotten something, so I opened the door without hesitation.

Drew stood on the other side, duffel bag slung over his shoulder. "You look awful, Claire. What's happened?"

He dropped his bag and pulled me into an embrace.

"I can't keep up with all the lies." My voice was muffled against him and he kissed the top of my head. I cried into his chest, leaving wet circles on his white T-shirt. "I can't even remember them all."

"What's the latest?"

I quickly recapped everything Detective Reynolds had said as I led him to the living room. We sat on opposite ends of the couch. Drew looked as baffled as I felt. "Here's what I can't figure out. Even if he was having an affair, where *is* he? I mean, right now?"

I shook my head. I had asked myself that question a thousand times. "If he left me, wouldn't he have used his credit cards or *something*? I've been checking our statements. It's like he's changed his identity. But that's crazy. Why would he go through with that? How is that easier than a divorce? He would have no access to any of his money."

"Unless..." Drew looked uncomfortable. I gave him a *go on* look. "Are you absolutely sure you know about all his bank accounts?"

"No, I'm not sure at all. I didn't deal with the money. Greg did. In fact, I haven't even gone into his study to figure out how to pay our bills. I'm writing checks on a wing and a prayer." I leaned my head back on the couch pillows, too exhausted to think about it anymore. I was wrung out, my mind blank, a visceral defense.

We sat that way for a while, in silence. Finally, Drew pulled me back against him, and in the security of his arms, I fell asleep for the first time in days.

❧

I woke up the next morning with Drew's arm still wrapped around my shoulder and my head resting against his chest. I sat up, blinking from the sunlight streaming through the windows, bright and painful. I turned to watch him snoring softly. I extricated myself and covered him with a blanket, knowing he had about twenty minutes of solid sleep left before the girls woke up.

Under the shower's hot spray, I reviewed the previous evening's turn of events. I made a mental list of all the evidence supporting Greg's affair and decided I could no longer play dumb about Greg's life—*our life*—before he had disappeared. Or maybe, before he had *left*.

I let the tears fall freely, safe from the children's scrutiny that never seemed to miss a thing. *Mommy, why are you sad? Were you crying?*

I pounded the shower wall with my fist and sank to the bottom of the stall. *How? How could you do this to us? Just leave us? Let me think you were dead?* Greg was alive. I knew that as certainly as I knew the grass was green. *Did you think I wouldn't let you go? Did you think I would make you stay? Are you free from guilt now? We weren't perfect, but I would have tried, goddamn it. I would have done anything. If you'd asked, I would have even let you go, just so Hannah and Leah wouldn't have had to.* I put my head down on my arms, and water sprayed over my back, bathing out the sorrow, leaving behind the wrath. *I'm done being a victim. And if you're not dead, you better hope to hell I never find you, Greg Barnes. Because I will follow you to the ends of the earth. I will make you look our children in the eyes when you tell them how you found it within you to leave us forever.*

I was toweling off in the bedroom when I heard the thumping of little feet. I looked up, and Hannah was standing at the foot of my bed, Leah in her shadow. Her smile told me I had made the right decision by inviting Drew for Christmas.

"Uncle Drew is here," she whispered as if revealing a secret.

I arched my eyebrows at her. "Really?"

She nodded, solemn and serious. "Can he stay for Christmas,

Mommy? Please?"

I fought a smile. "Well, you can't ever put someone out on Christmas."

Uncertain if that was a yes or a no, Hannah stood one foot in our room, one foot in the hallway, shifting her weight back and forth with impatience.

I put her out of her misery. "Yes. Yes, of course, Uncle Drew is here for Christmas."

And she was gone, down the steps as fast as her little feet could carry her, Leah close behind. "Uncle Drew! Uncle Drew! She said yes! You can stay!"

I heard his whooping all the way upstairs. I laughed. For the first time in months, I felt confident I'd done something right. Drew was the distraction we all needed to get through the first Christmas without Greg. *The first of many.* I quelled the thought as I joined my family.

The week passed quickly. I found that with Drew there, the air in the house was lighter somehow. I had energy, and I looked somewhat presentable. I went back to the mall and put a little more on my credit cards. I found the presence of mind to stop at Pet Center on the way home. Walking the aisles, looking for the perfect gift, I found it in the shape of a rubber, hollowed-out bone, an indestructible chew toy that could be filled with peanut butter. Buying Cody a gift had a fruitless feel to it, a deep-seated hopelessness that threatened to sap my previous energy. When I got home, I wrapped the toy in red foil paper and stuck it in Cody's stocking, feeling with relative certainty that he wouldn't ever get to enjoy it. Inexplicably, I never thought to shop for Greg.

I had Mom and Dad over for dinner one night so they could spend some time with Drew. Dad and Drew talked about football; Mom and

I talked about other family members or the girls. We were a pseudo-family. *Tonight, the role of Husband will be played by an understudy. We apologize for the inconvenience.*

Having Drew stay with us felt peculiar and right, if such a combination existed. After the girls went to bed in the evenings, Drew and I talked, drank wine or beer, and laughed. The conversation always eventually worked its way back to Greg. We'd bounce ideas off of each other, a macabre version of *Where in the World is Carmen Sandiego.* Drew came up with a theory that Greg had witnessed a crime and was in the witness protection program. I favored a Cayman Islands scenario. Had I been talking to anyone else, I wouldn't have been able to be so flippant. Somehow, anger and resolve had paved the way for other, more rational thought. An emotional Zamboni, I felt tenuously normal. We had no more near-intimate moments; Drew was simply there, my rock and much needed comic relief.

Christmas Eve dawned gray with heavy clouds drooping to the ground in a soupy fog. Although the temperature was low enough to hold out hope for a white Christmas, the easy feeling of the week slipped away, sadness edging its way back in. It was Christmas, for God's sake; the girls needed their father, not a stand-in.

I banished the thought and bustled around the kitchen, preparing ham, potatoes, corn, and a green bean casserole—all the fixings of a proper Christmas dinner. While the girls napped, I wrapped presents in my room. Drew had gone out, destination unknown. I was just putting away the wrapping paper and scissors when I heard the door to the bedroom inch open, and there stood Hannah, small and uncertain, afternoon sleep still in her eyes, linen lines creased her face.

"I miss Daddy," she said.

I opened my arms and folded her head into my shoulder. "Oh, sweetheart, I miss him too," I said, blinking back tears. "Do you want to tell me about it?"

She shook her head.

I thought if I could get her to talk, it might help. "What do you miss the most, Hannah?"

She thought about it for a while. "The way he would chase me, and also his potatoes."

"Oh, I *really* miss his potatoes!" I exclaimed. Greg thoroughly believed that every meal needed potatoes, and he had a hundred ways to make them.

"What else do you miss?" she asked.

"Remember when he taught you how to hit a wiffle ball?" She nodded, her eyes misted with tears. "Or how about when he would carry you around on his shoulders and you'd have to duck through all the doorways?"

"He'd call me, like I was lost!"

We both laughed then. I hugged her to me. "Hannah, you have to believe me that your daddy loves you, no matter where he is or what he's doing."

"Is he in Heaven?"

I was taken aback. "What do you know about Heaven?" I asked casually. Heaven wasn't a new concept—we'd gone to church—but I had no idea what she'd gleaned from her mornings at Sunday School. She was *four*.

"Annie said her grandpa went to Heaven and she doesn't get to see him anymore, but she knows that he can see her. And she said that maybe my daddy was there, too." She smiled. "Annie's grandpa loved baseball like Daddy, so maybe they're playing baseball together."

"Hannah, I think your daddy would love to play baseball with Annie's grandpa." I kissed her head. I made a mental note to call a child psychologist after the New Year. I needed guidance. How could I prevent my children from carrying tragedy around for the rest of their lives? How could I ensure that losing their father would just be something that happened to them, rather than reshape who they would have become? I didn't know. I realized then that my children's future was irreversibly altered; the women they would have become no longer existed. My heart ached.

That night, I got the girls ready for bed in their Christmas pajamas. Greg had always read *The Night Before Christmas*. It seemed unfair to have Drew do it, so I settled on the couch and tucked the girls under each arm. I opened the book, hoping I could do it justice. I must have passed the test because they were each half asleep when I finished. Drew carried Hannah to her room, while I tucked Leah into bed.

After filling the living room with my Christmas extravaganza, we gazed at the tree. How many Christmases had Greg and I done the exact same thing?

Drew took the chair; I sat on the couch. He had been careful with me all week. Not to get too close. Not wanting to get caught up in something we'd regret. The undercurrent had been there as long as I could remember, and our timing was always terrible.

"Remember that Christmas you came, right after Hannah was born?" I asked suddenly. We never talked about that Christmas. *I wonder how long you've been in love with my wife.* I'd heard only that one line, a portion of the conversation. What else had been said? I never knew. In the years since, Drew's visits frequently fell while Greg traveled, as I subconsciously kept them apart. The revelation came so clear in the muted colorful glow of the tree lights. I had partitioned my life, made myself a bridge for the gap between the two people I loved the most.

Drew nodded, averting his eyes. His face was impassive, but his eyes flickered imperceptibly.

"What happened with you and Greg?" I could never have asked Drew before; the question seemed too violating, a betrayal of Greg. *I don't much care if I betray Greg at this point.*

Drew shook his head. "Let it go, Claire. This helps no one."

"It helps me. Right now, I feel like it's possible I never knew my husband as well as I thought I did. I'm second-guessing all sorts of things so that I can put together the puzzle. You have a very small piece of this puzzle. I need it, Drew. Please."

He took a deep breath. "He was insecure about our relationship—mine and yours, that is—and he confronted me about it."

"What did you say?"

"I didn't say anything."

"What do you mean?"

"I literally said nothing. I didn't deny anything; I didn't confirm anything. I just remained silent. He was resolute, Claire, adamant in what he was going to believe. I didn't answer, and he went upstairs."

I thought back to that night, heat flushing my cheeks. Something had shifted after that. I had tried in a roundabout way to question Greg, who feigned ignorance and scoffed as though I were imagining things. I couldn't tell him I'd been eavesdropping like a child and heard part of the conversation on the stairs. Before that night, I had never seen Greg jealous. I had never witnessed insecurity in him at all. He seemed above all that, brash in his knowledge that I loved only him. Or so I thought. I even deluded myself into believing our lovemaking that night had been about us. But in hindsight, the sex was completely territorial. He should have just lifted his leg to urinate on me.

I laughed out loud at the thought. Drew looked up in surprise, raising his eyebrows.

"I heard part of it," I blurted. "I was on the stairs."

"Ahh, Claire..." Drew stared into his wine glass, swirling the red like a witch doctor looking for answers in a bubbling cauldron.

The silence stretched out between us, taut like wrapped canvas. His face was hidden in shadow, unreadable for so many reasons. I felt nakedly vulnerable and wished I could reach out and pull the words back. Regardless of what Drew said next, they would always be there between us, the suggestion of Drew's tightly guarded feelings, that up until now, I had perhaps not even acknowledged to myself.

Drew reclined the chair with an audible creak, stretching out his long legs and crossing them at the ankles. In his supine position, eyes on the ceiling, his face went from unreadable to invisible. "Remember the day we played hide and seek?"

I could see only his feet, which gave the atmosphere an aura of a confessional cloaked in such darkness. "We did that all the—" I stopped. He was referring to a specific day. "My first kiss. A first kiss for each of us, I assume. We were ten, so probably a safe bet."

I'd done a good job of hiding. I played a trick on him, surreptitiously moving to spots he'd already checked. He looked for twenty minutes and began to sound panicked as he called for me, while I lay flat against a long fallen tree, the organic scent of dirt and leaves surrounding me. Then, he stopped calling, and I heard only the resounding silence, the occasional call of a bird, and a woodpecker incessantly *tap-tap-tapping* in the distance. I stood and crept through the woods. I found him at the edge of my yard, sitting on the rock wall with his head in his hands. I tiptoed up behind him and grabbed his shoulders. When he whipped around, his mouth was open as if about to speak, but instead, he leaned forward and pressed his lips to mine in a chaste childhood kiss that both intrigued and disgusted me. Vaguely aware of the underlying power of being female, I had laughed and run away.

The memory, dusted off from the catacombs of my mind, felt surreal, as though it had happened to someone else. *Is that how long you've been in love with me?* I didn't have the courage to ask.

"I've fallen out of love with you a hundred times since that day," he said from the darkness of the chair. "Sometimes by choice, a forced break. Sometimes, especially in college, because you were just so damn infuriating and I was so sick to death of you."

I tried to remember college: hazy nights of drinking, crackling chemistry when I visited, coy advances I'd later retract. *All in good fun.* I'd been sure of that. I recalled my piercing jealousy when he'd answer the door, girlfriend in tow, and the drunken fight that would ensue later. Those fuzzy recollections seemed so silly as an adult. I felt embarrassed by my nonchalance, the ease at which I'd dismissed those days.

"I wasn't nice back then, I guess," I said finally. "I didn't know, really."

"There's a difference between not knowing and not wanting to know." His tone was soft, unaccusing, and I wished I could see his face. "This is pointless, you know? We've had years to talk about all this and never did. So why now?"

Even I couldn't miss the answer, so blatant and obvious. *Because I chose to.* Unable to bear the truth in that, I stood and crossed the room. I stopped in front of his chair, and he held my gaze with a small smile, sad and wry at once.

He reached out and grabbed my hand. "It's water under the bridge, Claire-bear."

But my bridge was crumbling.

CHAPTER 15

CHRISTMAS DAY, WE HAD MOMENTS of melancholy, but the celebration was mostly joyous. Drew did that—well, along with the overabundance of material things. *Bikes will make kids forget what ails them.* I had taken the easy way out, but what other options did I have? I promised myself that the next year would be easier, and we wouldn't need all the overindulgence.

Mom and Dad came for dinner, and I served my pre-prepared elaborate spread. Everyone stuffed themselves sick, and even Leah said her belly hurt after the meal. I felt warm, loose-limbed, and content.

I thought of Greg often, but only in small vignettes—Greg in the kitchen on past Christmases, announcing the carving of the "Roast Beast," his surprising ability to give fantastic and thoughtful Christmas presents. He always had at least one gift that I never knew about, even for the girls.

After I put the kids to bed, I pulled out a small wrapped box and placed it on Drew's lap.

He grinned. "A present!" He tore into his gift. I had gotten him a macro lens for his camera. He'd mentioned in passing that he wanted to get into macro photography. "Wow, these things are like five hundred bucks! Why would you do this? That's great. Thank you, Claire-bear."

I shrugged. "Call it my Christmas of buying everyone's affection."

He held up his finger, then went to his bag. He returned with a square velvet box.

"You didn't have to," I said.

He rolled his eyes, and I opened the lid. A white gold bracelet was nestled inside, formed like a three-strand braid, smooth on the inside. At each end was a solid ball.

"This is beautiful, Drew. Where did you get it?"

He waved his hand as if my question didn't matter. He turned the bracelet so I could see the engraving. *All the strength you need is inside of you.* My eyes welled with tears. As usual, Drew had said and done the perfect thing.

He took the bracelet and, sliding it on my wrist, said, "A braided rope is over a hundred times stronger than each strand individually. And it's ten times stronger than steel. No one strand bears all the weight." He held my hand, and I understood his message.

I am never alone. I closed my eyes. "Thank you," was all I could manage.

The day after Christmas, Drew packed his duffel and headed back to the city. Hannah and Leah went to my parents' house for the afternoon, and I rambled around the house, cleaning up from the holiday. Rain pattered off the bay window in the living room, blurring the outside world, creating a protected cocoon inside the house.

Feeling bold from my Christmas success and strong from my bracelet, I went upstairs and cautiously opened the door to Greg's study. I was assaulted by the smell—leather, Greg's cologne, a corporate citrusy scent, and man.

I sat down at his desk with no idea where to start and looked around as though in the room for the first time. Bookshelves lined the walls behind the desk, which was in the middle of the floor, like an office at a law firm, not a home office. The computer, surprisingly dust-free, sat in one corner of the desk next to a half-inch stack of bills and paperwork, neat and cornered. I could see him in the chair, squaring the corners and tapping the bottom of the stack on the desk. Getting his affairs in order? The corners of each of the September-dated bills were stamped "PIF." *Paid in Full.*

I opened the top drawer. A black address book lay on top. I thumbed through it: miscellaneous notes, business cards, phone numbers—all household-related and vaguely familiar. Nothing jumped out at me. *What was I looking for?* I laid the book on the stack of bills.

The brown notebook Detective Reynolds had taken a few weeks ago rested on top of a separate stack of papers. He'd returned it the week before Christmas, and still unable to face the study, I'd asked him to put it back. I gingerly picked up the notebook, as if it were contaminated, and fanned through the pages. It contained personal notes, a jotted journal of a man on the go: pieces of a thought, some functional, some endearing; a list of songs to add to his MP3 player; a "To-Do" list that included "exercise more, lower cholesterol, be a better husband"; a stanza from a song or a poem. I felt like a voyeur. Except when he left it all behind, did he have the right to privacy anymore?

Call Karen at Omni S.D. The note was jotted sideways, as if the book had been held at an angle, perhaps while he was on the phone, holding it between his ear and his chin, searching for something to write on. *S.D. San Diego? Two of the four times, we believe he was in San Diego.* I hit the power button on the computer. Having not been booted up in two months, the machine took a few minutes to come to life. Once the familiar desktop appeared, I opened the web browser and Googled "Omni San Diego." Omni San Diego Hotel appeared at the top of the searches.

I ran downstairs and found the piece of paper I had used to document the dates. Back upstairs, I picked up the phone and dialed the number on the screen before I could think myself out of it.

"Omni San Diego Hotel. This is John. How may I help you?"

"Hi, my name is Claire Barnes. I have a credit card statement saying that my husband Greg Barnes stayed at the Omni on May twenty-second, but he swore he stayed at the..." I referred to the screen and picked the next hotel down the list "... the Chariot." I forced a laugh. "I'm sorry. He travels practically weekly for work. It's impossible for us to keep all this straight, so we just now realized the discrepancy. Can you look to see if a Greg Barnes checked in on May twenty-second?"

"Let me check that for you, Mrs. Barnes." The man's tone was crisply official. After a moment, he came back on the line. "Mrs. Barnes, would you be okay with verifying your home address?" I rattled off our home address. "Yes, we have a Greg Barnes listed here on that date."

I thanked him, hung up, and called Detective Reynolds. When he picked up, I ran through my discovery. "Do you think it means anything?" I asked.

"We've checked a lot of this already, but nothing's popped." The loud crinkling of shuffling papers came through the phone. "Hold on, okay?" When he came back on the line three minutes later, he seemed interested. "Yep, we show a corporate credit card charge on May twenty-second for the Omni. In February, he stayed at... hmm... the Grand Del Mar, it looks like." He let out a low whistle. "That's a five-star hotel. Surely his company wouldn't pay for that."

"No. But they have a special 'cheating on your spouse' policy that allows you to use your corporate credit card for personal expenses, and they take it out of your paycheck."

"Wouldn't the spouse realize the paycheck was about four hundred dollars short?"

"I wouldn't. I don't manage the money. I *used* to like it that way. I'm rethinking that."

Detective Reynolds cleared his throat. "Okay, so we know where he stayed in San Diego. We knew that before, from his credit card statements. But what does that get us?"

"Nothing, I guess." I slumped in the chair. "Who is Karen? Maybe she's our mystery woman?"

"We're considering it. We've pulled the guest lists for all the times Greg stayed at the Omni, and there were a few Karens, but none that would fit our mystery woman. They all were there with families or other people, and none of them knew Greg." He was quiet for a moment. "But that doesn't really mean anything. I'd be skeptical that she was even registered, much less had her own room."

True. If Greg were cheating on me, he wouldn't have paid for two rooms. We chatted for a few more minutes about the holiday and hung up.

I opened the bottom drawer of the desk. I desperately needed to understand our finances. I pulled a handful of the files and fanned them on the desk. Each file had a label: ING, First Bank, and then one labeled "Inheritance." The last one commanded my attention. The first page, dated the previous January, looked like a standard bank statement. The sequential pages dated all the way back to May 2001. The statements had Greg's and my name in the top left-hand corners. In the description column, several transactions were recorded, with interest added and at what percent. When my gaze traveled to the bottom right-hand column, I blinked to see if I had misread the number. The figure next to "Total" was $657,997.23.

I couldn't comprehend that number. Did that mean six hundred and fifty seven *thousand dollars?* How was that possible? Was that ours? I grabbed the file for ING and scanned the contents. The Total column there was less impressive, only about eight thousand dollars and change. I did the same for First Bank and was relieved to discover that, as of September, we had enough in our checking account to cover the checks I'd been haphazardly writing, although I desperately needed to go lighter on my credit card. I doubted what we had in checking would cover what I'd charged over the last two months. *We. We didn't have anything in checking.* We did have a moderate savings account, both of our names typed officially at the top of the statement.

Satisfied, I piled the paperwork and pushed it off to the side. Then, another thought occurred to me. Did I have access to our accounts if Greg was only missing and not confirmed to be dead or alive? I went back to the "Inheritance" file and spread all the statements out on the desk. After about an hour of studying, I figured out that sometime in 2001, after the death of his mother, Greg inherited a little over a half-million dollars. He had put the money, untouched, in a joint account that I never knew we had. But Greg's mother had been broke. *He* had told me she was broke.

He had grown up poor and had paid for his own education. While in college, he'd received very little help from his mother. Poverty had singlehandedly driven him to achieve, molded the person he became. To receive a large inheritance after her death would have been a slap in the face. *Why didn't I know? Why didn't he talk to me, both for the financial aspect and the emotional impact it must have had?*

He never spoke about his mother and said very little about his childhood. The fact that my name was on the account surprised me. But then somehow... it didn't. Putting my name there was very much *him.* He would have wanted me to be taken care of, and sharing everything with his wife was natural for him. *But I suppose not the fact that the account existed, or how he felt about it.* Like many other things, Greg was a wonderful on-paper husband and father, but he reserved a large piece of himself for himself only, as if he thought being a husband and father meant the *act* of being a husband and a father, not necessarily the emotional commitment that went with it. Greg the Provider.

I couldn't reconcile the Greg I thought I knew with the Greg who would abandon his family. Either way, I was pretty sure that if my name was on the account, then that money was also mine. I put my hand on my head to stop the room from spinning.

Suddenly, I felt rich.

CHAPTER 16

WE ARE GOING TO A *Sunday picnic for a birthday party for Hannah's friend, Annie, who is turning four. We occasionally socialize with Annie's parents, Steve and Melinda, but Steve and Greg have very different personalities, so we aren't that close. I spend the morning making potato salad for the picnic.*

When we get there, Greg is quiet, sullen. I ask him what's wrong, and he says nothing. We go through that several times. There is something, I know, but I also know he will not tell me. He never does, and I leave it alone, then it passes. There are only two other couples there. They know each other, but we don't know them. Melinda introduces them as friends of theirs from church—their names leave my memory as soon as she says them; it's a fatal social flaw of mine. One of the couples has a baby. I stop to admire the baby and make small talk. Greg stands behind me, withdrawn. The husband tries to chat, but Greg is short with him and somewhat rude.

We walk away after a while, and I snap, "If you're going to be rude to people, we can leave."

He shrugs. "Okay, then, let's leave." He seems serious.

"Greg, we can't leave. We just got here. This is Annie's birthday party, and she's Hannah's best friend."

"Then why did you say we can leave?"

"Because I thought you would say no." I falter then, unsure if this argument is my fault. I see Hannah and Annie playing on the swing set and Leah walking unsteadily around the playground mulch to get to the baby slide. I keep one eye on Leah and turn to gaze at Greg. His jaw is working, his teeth clenched. He won't return my look.

"Greg, look at me," I say softly.

He turns, but says nothing.

"What's going on?" I ask.

"You don't let me be me." He folds his arms across his chest, and we stand facing off. "I'm always not good enough, somehow not enough. I had a headache this morning, but I'm not talking, or making potato salad, or doing what you think I should be doing, so it's constantly, 'What's wrong?'"

"But you didn't tell me you had a headache," I protest, sure that it would have been a different morning. Pretty sure.

"It wouldn't matter," he says, looking away. "When I do tell you, you roll your eyes."

"Do you really want to leave?" I ask, meaning it for a moment.

He shakes his head, laughs, and walks away. I walk to the playground area to tend to the girls. A mother with a toddler is there. We chat, laugh, and introduce our kids. I forget about the argument, about Greg.

A while later, the picnic has picked up, and Melinda's yard is filled with people. I search the crowd, find Steve, and give him a small wave. Hannah spills juice on her dress, so I head to the kitchen to retrieve a paper towel. To my surprise, Greg is there. He and Melinda are sitting together at the kitchen island, their knees touching. Each has a glass of wine. They are looking at pictures in an album. Greg is laughing in a way he has not laughed with me in a long time, his head bent close to hers. I stop short, and they look up, startled.

Greg coughs. "Melinda was showing me pictures of their vacation in Hawaii." But his eyes are looking at my chin.

I cock my head to the side. Melinda slides off the barstool, unsteady. A bit too much to drink? Possibly. I am cemented to the floor. Greg comes over and puts his arm around me, kissing my forehead. Slipping out of his grasp, I step over to the sink, retrieve a paper towel, and move past him, back outside to clean up Hannah's juice. I look back into the house through the French doors, and Greg and Melinda are talking. He looks uneasy now, his body angled toward the door as if to inch away. Melinda leans in closer to him. She puts a hand on his arm and gestures with her wine glass. Greg looks surprised, and then laughs, his head tipped back, mouth open.

He glances out at me, but I look away. I think of how beautiful Melinda is, with her long blond hair and gym-toned body. A size four to my size ten. She has a small waist and long legs. One of the playground moms once suggested that she may have breast implants. When I look back at them again, she's standing so close to Greg that one of those implants is touching his arm.

I pick up Leah and tell Hannah, "Let's get going. Time to leave now, sweetie." I try to be cheery, but the flirtation stings. I poke my head inside the door. "I think we need to get going. Leah seems cranky."

Greg looks surprised. Ignoring him, I turn and walk toward the car. He jogs after me and tries to take the diaper bag from my shoulder. He's smiling now. His headache has been cured. We drive home in silence. He knows I'm angry, but won't give me the satisfaction of talking about it.

When we get home, I put Leah down for a nap and settle Hannah in front of Cinderella. I find Greg sitting on the couch in the living room, watching ESPN.

I move to stand in front of him. "I want you to talk to me like that, look at me like that. Laugh with me like that." I wince at how pathetic I sound.

He says nothing.

I take the remote, turn off the TV, and sit next to him. "Why do you stonewall me?"

"Why do you nag me?" he shoots back.

I am momentarily stung silent. "I'm not nagging you. You were flirting. With Melinda. The way you were with her, you haven't been with me in a long time."

"She was friendly. We were talking. She is flirtatious; I'll give you that. But it felt... nice. You're always trying to make me into a different person. 'Greg, you should be happier.' 'Greg, doesn't this movie make you sad?' 'Greg, be more social,' and now, 'Greg, be less social.'" He shakes his head. "Melinda was happy talking to me, Greg, exactly the way I am."

I fold my arms. "I want to talk to you the way you are. But you don't actually talk to me."

He reaches out and touches my hand, his thumb caressing my palm. Despite my anger, a thrill goes through me. He hasn't touched me in months. His hand slides up my arm and strokes my hair. It feels delicious. I tilt my head back and close my eyes. He kisses my neck, softly, leaning in toward me. His body is warm against mine. He is aroused. By me or Melinda?

"Mommy, I'm hungry." Hannah is standing in the doorway of the living room.

Greg jumps as if caught doing something wrong. I give him a wry smile. Later, I mouth. The evening passes, dinner, bath, bedtime. Slowly, Greg retreats back into himself. The moment has dissipated. I try to draw him out, be more 'Melinda-ish.' It doesn't work. By the time I come back downstairs after putting the girls to bed, he's asleep on the couch. Frustrated, I go upstairs. Alone.

At two, I hear him walking around downstairs—his nightly wandering. I think I hear his voice, but I can't tell if I'm dreaming. I drift back to sleep. When I wake up in the morning, he has left for work. It's Monday. Tomorrow, he will leave for a business trip to San Diego.

CHAPTER 17

ONE THOUGHT PLAGUED MY MIND regardless of what I was doing, and I could not break free from it. *Is Greg in San Diego?* I'd stayed up all night more than once, looking for the link between San Diego, California, and Rochester, New York. I couldn't find one, except for the fact that Advent sites were in both places. His secret life, as I'd come to refer to it, had to be linked to his job.

I began seeing a therapist, a bespectacled fifty-something woman whose office was more like a day spa with sandscapes and trickling fountains. She played *Enya* softly in the background, and her office had woven tapestries hanging from wooden dowels on the wall. The place was calming, and I found myself thinking of it in moments of despair. She advised me to channel my fixation constructively into my children and reminded me to let the police focus on finding Greg.

After five months, the police hadn't found any major clues as to Greg's whereabouts. Detective Reynolds still followed his breadcrumbs, but his updating visits were less frequent. The FBI became peripherally involved, but because no one could be sure Greg wasn't missing of his own volition, they wouldn't fund a task force to aid the Hunterdon County police department. Greg's picture appeared on the FBI's missing person's website, and Detective Reynolds had permission to use FBI resources should he find information leading to Greg. But Greg had vanished, gone without a trace.

Most of the time, I was resigned to the fact that Greg would never return. I didn't believe he was dead. Although logically, I had no way to know, I somehow thought I would feel it. On the other hand, Greg and

I had been so disconnected prior to his disappearance that insisting I would somehow "know" if he died sounded senseless.

I resumed my life, to some extent. We went back to church and attended story time at the library. Hannah returned to preschool full time, which meant her scheduled three days a week, as opposed to the sporadic times I remembered to take her in the first three months after Greg's disappearance. I frequently felt like an observer of my life, rather than someone actually partaking in it. I read to the children and periodically played the piano and sang. But I watched things around me happen and felt nothing.

I had yet to touch the inheritance. I didn't need the money yet, and I fluctuated between repulsion and wanting to spend the whole thing on something lavish that Greg would have despised. Sometimes after the girls went to bed, I'd trawl online travel sites for exotic locales—Madrid, Paris, and the Turks and Caicos. I spent hours looking at expensive jewelry I'd never wear—large diamonds with sapphire accents, necklaces, and earrings. *To where? The supermarket?*

I didn't have the courage to return to work. I was still on unpaid leave, and I felt no guilt from dipping into our savings account. My boss would periodically call to check in, and I would make the concerted effort to sound sadder and more listless than I was until the silence stretched out across the line, and out of pity or laziness—I was never sure which—she would agree to another month. *Can I just fax you the leave paperwork?*

Greg's manager called to tell me that, unfortunately, the company was going to have to terminate Greg's employment. For the first four months, Greg's pay had continued to be deposited—I supposed from vacation time, personal time, and sick time, and then the kindness of his management—but understandably, that couldn't go on forever. I had some financial fear, but not much. I contemplated paying off the house with the inheritance money, but knew I really needed to see a financial advisor.

In the meantime, I shape-shifted into a suburban stay-at-home mom. The real me was hollow, checked out, unavailable.

Five months had passed, and I decided I needed a vacation. I didn't consciously choose to go to San Diego to look for Greg. But knowing he had been there and lied about it, I needed to see for myself where he had stayed, where he had eaten. The trip was different from my Rochester one, where I had been convinced I would find him and bring him home. Going to California was an act of closure. I simply had to say that I had tried.

I called to tell Sarah, who squealed with delight. She lived north of Los Angeles, but happily agreed to meet me in San Diego for three nights and four days. I felt excited as I packed. My excitement was stifled, like the sound of a band playing in the basement. I could feel the steady thumping of the beat, hear the high notes, but the melody and lyrics were lost. I used Greg's frequent flyer miles to get my ticket, first-class upgrade included.

Mom and Dad agreed to babysit at our house to lessen the impact to the girls. Hannah was doing better with the adjustment to life without Greg, under the circumstances. She'd had some bedwetting incidents, but they didn't last. She missed her daddy and frequently asked for Cody. I had no explanation to give her for Cody other than "He ran away." But we talked regularly, and she was able to express herself.

Leah, on the other hand, was having a tougher time. She still asked for Daddy, and being only two, didn't understand any given explanation—though there wasn't one anyway. She cried often and started waking up nightly, wailing for hours on end, high-pitched and painful. I sat in her room, the lights dimmed low, rocking her gently like a newborn, overwhelmed by my solitary responsibilities. Night after night. I was worn out, and my vacation would at least provide me a full night's sleep, which I hadn't had in months.

I kissed the girls goodbye with a twinge of guilt. But I also hoped that years later, they wouldn't remember me leaving. Hopefully, when they were older and looked back on their tough time, they would remember me for getting them through it—as flawed a human as I was. I also recognized that as a mother, there wasn't a time, tragedy or not, that I could leave my kids without feeling a twinge of guilt. It came with the territory.

I fell asleep soon after takeoff and awoke with a start to the plane touching down on the tarmac. Instead of feeling refreshed, I felt exhausted.

Sarah waited in baggage claim. She jumped up and down, clapping, when she saw me. She was dressed head to toe in white over a golden tan, looking ever the Beach Boys' California girl, with her blond hair cascading in waves down her back. We embraced, and I felt tears in my eyes. I hadn't seen her in over a year. With her in front of me, all the reasons I'd pushed her away the last few months seemed silly.

She held me at arm's length. "You look awful!" But she was smiling.

"Thanks a lot. You know, I've been through a tragedy here."

"Yeah, but do you sleep? At all? You look so tired!"

"If you tell someone they look tired, you mean they look *old*," I protested.

"Well, you finally lost those twenty pounds you've been talking about for years. How does that feel?"

"Oh, Sarah, I've hardly noticed it. Isn't that the shit of it? I can't even enjoy being in a size smaller jeans. I'd take every pound back and then some to erase the last six months." I pulled my red-wheeled suitcase off the conveyer belt.

"How do you look exactly the same?" I asked, shaking my head. "You don't age; you don't get fat. Have you had Botox?"

She laughed. "No, no Botox, I swear!"

She linked her arm through mine as we walked into the brilliant sun and led me to her car, a midnight blue BMW convertible. *Seriously? Good thing our friendship doesn't have a competitive edge to it.* I let the warm California sun beat down on my shoulders as she drove. The seventy-degree weather felt rejuvenating compared to the cold gray of March in New Jersey.

"What do you want to do while we're here, Claire?" Sarah asked.

I shrugged. I didn't have a plan. I didn't know what I wanted.

"Do you want to sightsee?"

"I think so. I think I want this to be a vacation with the understanding that I have to go to the places where I know Greg stayed. And I might need a day to be on my own, following my hunches. Does that sound crazy?"

Sarah shook her head. "Sounds good to me. I did some searching, and I came up with a few things we could do. The zoo, and there's a railroad winery tour. Gray whales migrate in the winter off the coast, so a whale watching tour is supposed to be amazing right now. And maybe a spa day. What sounds good to you?"

I waved my hand in a distracted *I don't care* motion. I couldn't concentrate. It was three-thirty in the afternoon, and all I wanted to do was start my hunt for Greg. I realized that was unfair to Sarah. "What about this? Let's go to the hotel, and I can drop you off. You relax. I'll take your car, if you'll let me, and go do my Greg things. Then, I'll come back and get you around seven for dinner."

Sarah shook her head. "No way. I'm coming with you. If you ever do actually find him, I need to be there."

"Ok, fine, but I get to kill him." I grinned.

We headed north on I-5 North to Greg's Valentine's Day hotel, the Grand Del Mar. I tipped my head back on the seat rest and looked up at the sky, blue and cloudless. *Did Greg look at this exact same sky? Maybe mere miles from me?*

I was unprepared for the lavish spread of the Grand Del Mar. A red adobe Spanish-style roof baked in the sun, and forty-foot palm trees lined the driveway, swaying in the gentle breeze. Elaborate stone fountains decorated the entryway. The luxury hotel was out of my league, out of *our* league. We'd stayed at a Hilton on our honeymoon.

A valet opened my car door. I felt self-conscious and out of place, as if I had come naked to the presidential inauguration.

Sarah gaped at the building. "What exactly are we doing here?"

she stage-whispered.

"Honestly, I have no idea." I touched the fifteen pictures of Greg in my purse and felt ridiculous. The Grand Del Mar was not a convention center hotel, and there would be no naïve southern belle at the front desk. The concierge would be a skilled trade master. We walked inside where a tall, frosty woman greeted us.

I stepped up to the counter. "I'm not sure if you can help me. But can you tell me if this man has stayed here recently?" I fanned the pictures in front of her.

She barely looked at them. "Ma'am, our guests greatly value their privacy, and I cannot tell you if anyone has stayed here or is currently staying here."

I nodded as if I agreed with her. "I realize that, but this is my husband, and I'm not sure if he is alive. Is there any way you can look at the pictures and tell me if you have seen him in the last six months?"

She glanced down at the pictures, then picked one up, looking at it thoughtfully, her birdlike features intent on the photo. "Truthfully, I don't think so. He doesn't look familiar, but again, we have hundreds of guests a month. I'm sorry." She handed the photo back to me. She did genuinely look sorry.

I took a shot in the dark. "Can you tell me if a Greg Barnes has been registered here in the last six months?" I asked, knowing what the answer would be.

She shook her head. "I'm sorry. We cannot reveal the names of our guests." She backed away from the counter to answer the phone. A dismissal. Over her shoulder, she said, "Feel free to look around. In public areas, of course."

"Of course." Sarah and I walked around the lavish lobby. I couldn't believe Greg had stayed there. A room probably ran three or four hundred dollars a night. Greg, forever frugal, balked at a four-hundred-dollar car payment. Would he really spend so much on his mistress? If so, then he was two different people.

I scanned a row of pamphlets on a table in the corner. One caught my eye. *Golf with the pros on a Tom Fazio designed course.* I looked across the lobby, out the large bank of windows and doors, and into the generous gardens beyond. Green as far as I could see. Images flashed in my mind like tumblers clicking into place: a single white golf tee in the pocket of his work khakis, elaborate cursive, *The Grand*, as in Grand Del Mar.

Greg didn't golf, at least not well, or often. At the time, I had dismissed the golf tee, thinking maybe someone had given it to him, or he had picked it up off the ground and meant to throw it away, the way someone might pick up a discarded wrapper, conscientious of littering. When was that? June, perhaps? I did remember that the day had been a hot one.

Absently, I walked out onto the patio overlooking the golf course. "He was definitely here. And I think he played golf here."

Sarah trailed after me. "Greg didn't golf," she said automatically, with the confidence of someone who knew her friend's husband well through the eyes of her friend.

I glanced at her. "Does this look like a place that lets a beginner whack around a ball for a few bucks a round?" She shook her head. "I think he did golf. I think Greg did a lot of things I didn't know about."

"This makes no sense," she said.

Nothing made sense anymore.

CHAPTER 18

WE STAYED AT THE HARD Rock Hotel. Sarah had insisted that I needed a serious injection of fun. The nightly rate was steeper than I would have liked, but I happily took it out of the inheritance fund. I harbored no guilt, particularly after seeing the splendor of his accommodations with his mistress. The interior of the hotel was slick and urban. Counters were underlit with electric blue, and the far wall behind the check-in desks was painted to look like a rock concert crowd. Thin men in black turtlenecks and tight black pants checked us in.

When we got to our room, I flung open the mini-fridge.

"Careful!" Sarah warned. "These places charge you for opening the door."

Ignoring her warning, I pulled out an airline-sized bottle of Crown Royal and downed it in one gulp. I flopped backward on the bed, splayed like a starfish, wanting to sleep for days and weeks and months and wake up when I reached the bottom of the rabbit hole, when all the facts had been assimilated for me, and I could stop feeling unwillingly whipped around by circumstance.

Lying on the opposite bed, Sarah stared at the ceiling. "How's Drew?"

I sighed. "He's happy to let me use him, and it's what I continue to do, I guess."

Sarah had a crush on Drew, not a serious one, but the way she had a crush on everyone. She loved men. She loved Greg, and she loved Drew. She always joked that it must be so great to have two husbands. In retrospect, the joke must have needled Greg. Probably because it was true.

She playfully hit me in the face with a pillow and pointed toward the shower. "Get up. We're going out to eat." She wagged a finger at me. "Look, you wanted me to come to bring you some fun. So that's what I'm going to do. You know what restaurant is in this hotel? Nobu! Where movie stars hang out!"

"Sarah, there are no movie stars in San Diego. You're in the wrong city."

Unsatisfied with my crabbiness, she pushed me into the bathroom. I turned the water on, letting the steam fog the mirrors. Though the bedside table read six o'clock, my body still thought nine. However, I wasn't too tired to appreciate the lush bathroom amenities. With the marble countertops and an oversized shower tiled in deep variegated slate, it might not have been The Grand Del Mar, but it was the nicest hotel I'd ever stayed in.

"Hey!" Sarah called from the other side of the door. "Do you know the Black Eyed Peas designed a room in this hotel?"

I smiled in spite of myself, shaking my head. The shower felt wonderful, hot and strong. Uninterrupted. After drying off, I chose a simple black wrap dress from my suitcase, my new size eight. I may have been overwhelmed by my life, but I looked fantastic, the best I'd looked in years. I felt a stab of longing. For Greg? Or Drew? I didn't know. For a man who loved me. I wished suddenly that I was not there in a fabulously trendy hotel with Sarah, but with Drew. My thoughts were marbles, shaking in a jar, ricocheting off one another: one marble for missing Greg, one for hating him, one for wanting Drew, one for wanting to pull the blankets over my head and sleep forever.

Sarah whistled when I emerged from the bathroom. "Woman, you look amazing!"

After a quick blow dry of my hair and some basic makeup, I not only looked normal, but possibly pretty great. Looking good helped my psyche. My melancholy faded, replaced by a fluttering in my belly that I vaguely remembered as excitement.

I admired Sarah's nonchalance in choosing her clothes. She got ready in less than ten minutes, looking thrown together, yet wonderful in a way I could never pull off. She piled her hair atop her head in a trendy, messy bun and wore a white strapless sheath dress that made her seem positively willowy.

We headed downstairs to Nobu, and because it was Wednesday, we were able to walk in without reservations. We didn't see any celebrities, and Sarah pouted. After dinner, we decided to have a drink in the hotel bar, which was surprisingly crowded. Apparently, we were staying at the only hotel I'd ever been to where the lobby bar was a chic place to hang out. Black tables and chairs with electric blue under-lighting dotted the room. The bar in the back held liquor bottles illuminated by neon lights, sparkling like costume jewelry.

I noticed the stares of men, and instead of my usual dismissal, I smiled encouragingly, returning their gazes. I nudged Sarah and nodded toward the corner, where two men sat at a table, both tall and good-looking.

She looked at me, astonished. *Yes, I notice men, too.* She glanced back at the table and gave the guys a small wave. I felt a bubble of excitement. *Oh, my God. I'm having fun. How long has it been?* We each got a martini, extra dirty with extra olives, and sat at one of the two top tables closest to the bar.

"Claire, you're different." She sucked the olives off her martini pick.

"I know. Losing a husband has that effect," I said.

"No, not just that. You're reckless; you're angry. I mean, not right now, but in general..."

"Yes, I'm both. I can't explain it. I think it's part of the grieving process. I'm in therapy now. Isn't that crazy?"

"Crazy would be *not* being in therapy in your situation." She shrugged. "But you're strong. I mean, you've always been a strong person, but you've erected this shell. I can't explain it."

"Oh, I think you're doing a good job. Of explaining it, I mean. I feel like I have this armor now. I can't rely on anyone; I even keep Drew at arm's length. I haven't called him since Christmas."

"That was over two months ago! When was the last time you went a month without talking to Drew in your life?"

"Never." I sighed. "I know it's strange. I'm just trying to get through this first year. I don't know what I'm doing, and I'm terrified of screwing up my kids."

"It's half over," she pointed out. "I think you're doing a great job of keeping it together. For the girls, anyway." She slammed her hand down on the table. "Where the fuck is Greg?"

I laughed. "I must ask that a hundred times a day." I told her about Christmas and showed her Drew's bracelet.

"He's in love with you, Claire. I hope when all this is said and done and you're in the position to move on that you do it with him."

"Do you think I picked the wrong guy? From the beginning, I mean." I twirled the olive pick in my glass, not positive I wanted to know her answer.

She wiped the sweat from her glass. "No, in the beginning and even for a long while after, you and Greg were good. You seemed compatible, easy, complementary. He was introverted; you were outgoing. He was so in love with you. Then... he changed. Last time I saw you two together, there was definitely something off."

I searched my memory for the last time Greg and I had seen Sarah. February of last year, she came to visit for a week, the first half while Greg was away. I didn't remember anything specific, but she was probably right. We'd been "off" for a while before that.

"Is there room at the table for two more?" a baritone asked from behind me.

I turned to see one of the two men from the corner table. He was tall, maybe six-foot-two, with glossy black hair and a dark complexion. His lanky form reminded me of Drew, except he was clean-shaven with the bluest eyes I'd ever seen.

He extended his hand. "I'm Will, and this is Owen." He jerked a thumb at the second man, who hovered shyly behind him.

Owen was the same height as Will, with dark hair and dark eyes. Both men were dressed in jeans and black shirts, stylish in a way that Greg never was and Drew never tried to be. I thought of Greg's khaki pants—*pleated for God's sake*—and Drew's raggedy jeans. They sat at our table and motioned for the bartender to bring another round. Very slick.

I felt stifled with nerves. Which was fine with Sarah, she was off and running. Within a half-hour, I knew both were single, where they worked, where they lived—they were locals—why they were at the bar—they just liked to hang out there. I gave very little about myself, but the darker one with the blue eyes—*Will, was it?*—inched his seat closer until his knee was resting on my thigh.

Is this what people do? The alcohol made me paranoid and jumpy, not the effect I'd hoped for. I studied Sarah, trying to pick up cues on how to be normal. She laughed, asked all the right questions, responded to the hard questions with coy answers, and flattered without being obvious. I watched her, amazed. Like a Russian ballet, every move was calculated, graceful, and perfectly executed. She had both men eating out of the palm of her hand. I hadn't seen Sarah in her element in years. She'd had some practice. As the hours passed, and we all got drunk, she became more affectionate, mostly with Owen.

Will attempted conversation with me, and I could articulate most of the time, but nothing like Sarah. I didn't have the training to compete with her. Every move I made somehow felt wrong, and I became incredibly self-conscious.

Not deterred, Will trailed his hand down my back and leaned over to whisper, "Do you want to get out of here?"

I didn't know people really said that. I smiled nervously. "Look, Will, I do." I put my hand on his arm, which felt warm and alive beneath my fingertips. I tingled with anticipation, such a newly fantastic feeling, but it all felt wrong at that moment. "Believe me, I do. And I know you don't want to hear this, but I'm going through something

right now, and I... I can't." I heard Drew's voice in my mind: *We can't.*
"Listen, are you guys going to be around tomorrow night?"

"We live only a few blocks away."

"We should get together then."

"Have you been to Float yet? It's upstairs. That's actually where
we usually go after a few drinks here," Will explained. "It's on the
roof of the hotel."

We exchanged numbers, storing them in our phones.

"Call me tomorrow night, and we'll meet up, okay?" He gave me a
chaste kiss on the cheek and a brilliant smile.

I got up to leave the table, tapping Sarah on the arm. *I'm going up,*
I motioned with my hand. *Are you going to be okay?* I mouthed.

She waved me away, obviously annoyed at my mothering. Sarah
went clubbing weekly in L.A. I waved at Will, who looked somewhat
confused about which way to go. Sarah leaned close to Owen, and I
had no idea if she was whispering to him or kissing him. I knew Will
would be a definite third wheel. I felt like the worst wingman ever.
But I needed my bed. When I got up to the room, I crashed facedown,
still in my dress, and didn't wake up until nine the next morning.

Sarah managed to wake up and shower before I rolled out of bed.

"What time did you get in?" I asked incredulously.

"Three-ish. Do you want to do the whale watch today?" She
perched on the edge of the bed to watch the weather channel on mute.

"Um. I don't know. Sure. Can I wake up first?" Yawning, I
swung my legs over the side of the bed. Sun streamed in through
the windows. The crisp white sheets with lime-green coverlets
and modern furniture, all lines and angles, gave the room a fresh,
contemporary appeal.

"Oh, how was Owen?" I asked sleepily, trudging to the bathroom.

She gave me a Cheshire cat grin. "Exactly what I needed. He has a fabulous apartment."

I stopped in my tracks. "You went to his apartment?"

She made a disgusted noise. "Stop being a mother. For once."

I shrugged and padded into the bathroom. I took another long, hot shower without any interruptions. No one needed anything from me. No one was waiting for me when I exited to tell me that Leah had spilled her milk, or stole her doll, or ripped a page in her book. I took my time getting ready, wanting to look good for the second day in a row. The vacation was performing its rejuvenation magic. I felt lighter, freer.

We barely made it to the dock in time and boarded the already crowded boat. We took a spot along the railing and prepared for our three-hour boat ride. Not a boat person, I was expecting to feel seasick.

About an hour out, we saw a group of three gray whales and one baby calf, and any concern I had over seasickness vanished. They swam close to the boat, so that we were lightly sprayed by the V-shaped blow. The largest one, "an old mama," surfaced right at our rail and stayed even with the boat.

Our tour guide announced that almost all gray whales go blind in their right eyes eventually. The whale's blind right eye gazed unseeingly at me, mottled with white milky spots in black glass. Her gray-speckled skin was cracked and bore battle scars, thick and jaggedly torn flesh that had healed, reopened, and rehealed, the cost of protecting her babies in the harsh open ocean. *You have been through some serious stuff in your life,* I thought, *a defensive mother, traveling alone with her offspring, shielding her calf from the perils of the month-long journey.*

Feeling sentimentally connected, I knelt down at the rail until I could almost run my hand along her barnacled surface. She veered left and gave a short blow *goodbye* as she rejoined her pack, the spray misting the boat. I watched the mammals fade into the horizon until I could no longer differentiate between the whales and the waves.

A megaphoned voice broke into my reverie. "Ladies and gentleman, that was somewhat remarkable. Typically, the gray whales will come up to the boat because they're curious about the people, but they do not frequently swim with it, as they are afraid of getting hit by the propellers. That one also came significantly closer to the boat than we usually see. So I hope you enjoyed that unusual event!"

There was a din in the crowd as people took pictures, exclaimed, and pointed. The rest of our trip was uneventful; we saw dolphins playing, but nothing came close to the mottled old whale. We docked just in time, as Sarah and I were both feeling mildly nauseous from the ride.

Exiting the boat onto the pier, I caught a flash of sandy hair with a touch of gray. Bile rose in my throat. The man's back was broad shouldered, and his walk was confident, almost a swagger. *The walk of a man who almost got away with it?* I grabbed Sarah's arm and wordlessly pointed. The man seemed to move faster, away from the pier and toward Harbor Drive. He was dressed in a red windbreaker and jeans and was holding hands with a woman. I motioned to Sarah to wait, that I'd be right back.

I stayed about twenty feet behind the couple as they crossed Harbor Drive, walking east on West Broadway. They stopped at a crosswalk, where he checked both directions, and from twenty feet away, I caught his profile. *Is it him?* I wasn't sure. I followed them for three blocks as they talked and laughed, but I couldn't make out the words. Once, the man put his arm around the woman and pulled her to him in a walking hug. I felt dizzy and paralyzed with fear, but knew I had to follow the couple to a possibly disastrous conclusion.

They stopped at Starbucks, and I stayed on the opposite corner. I didn't want him to see me before I saw him. I couldn't remember if Greg liked Starbucks. But what did that matter? Obviously, I didn't know the real Greg anyway. When they emerged, heads bent low as they whispered to each other, I ducked back behind the corner to avoid being seen. When they turned right, I trailed behind them to a cell phone store. They clearly lived in the city. They were comfortable. They knew where Starbucks was and needed to grab a coffee before one of them got their cell phone repaired. Together. Had we ever done anything like that? I couldn't remember. Those were the languid afternoons of childless couples.

I snuck up to the front door of the cell phone store and hovered off to the side, so I could still peek through the door. They stood at the counter for a while. When they turned to leave, I moved in front of the left door. They exited the right, and I stepped in front of them, blocking their path.

"Did you think I wouldn't follow you?" I asked more forcefully than I had intended. I hadn't even looked at his face; I couldn't.

"I'm sorry. What?" His voice was a register deeper, alarmed but kind. I looked up. Green eyes instead of brown. His large nose, slightly crooked, had probably once been broken.

Greg's nose has never been broken. "I'm... I'm sorry," I stammered, stumbling backward.

CHAPTER 19

"I FEEL LIKE SUCH A FOOL." I sat with my head in my hands, staring at the concrete floor of our hotel room balcony. Sarah topped off my glass from the bottle of Pinot Grigio she'd plunked on ice. I finished it off in two long gulps. "I'm apparently seeing him in crowds now. Am I crazy?"

Sarah was nonchalant about the whole event. "No, I think it's being in this city. You want to find him."

"Of course I want to find him. But you know what the weirdest part is?" The ground several floors below us seemed to waver, and I concentrated on the horizon, steadying my vision. I vaguely remember having heard that staring at an immovable point will stop sickness. I wasn't sure if that would help being drunk, though. Maybe the tip was for seasickness. "I was convinced it was him. About a block into the chase, I really thought it was him. All these thoughts were going through my head. What I would say? Would I be angry? Would I act angry? What would I do? Would he come home with me?" I took a deep breath. "Did I *want* him to come home with me?"

"Would you?" Sarah asked.

"No." I closed my eyes and pinched the bridge of my nose. "There will never be Greg and Claire again. I realized that today. I could never get over this. I could never love him again. Trust him again. While I was following who I thought was Greg, not once did I feel sad. Or hopeful. It wasn't like it was in Rochester. In New York, I was convinced I would somehow rescue him. I'm so fucking delusional."

"But what about the girls?" Sarah asked, never one to shy away from the tough questions. "Could you do it for them?"

Could I? Could I bring Greg home and pretend to be a family again? *Love him?* I pictured him in our room, in our bed, and waited for the heaviness in my gut. The sadness of missing Greg didn't come. The alcohol may have played a contributing role, but the only emotion I could put my finger on was anger. White-hot rage simmered behind my eyes, putting pressure on my skull. I shook my head. "No. I could have handled the cheating, or maybe the lying, and even maybe him just leaving me. But this? To put me through this? To put *them* through this, the unknown? No. Any love I had for Greg has been destroyed by his lies."

"So what are you going to do now? Are you going to keep looking for him?"

"I can't. I have to move on. This is making me crazy. Following him around the country. Retracing his steps. Looking for clues in his study, in our bank account and credit card bills. There *are* no clues. He doesn't *want* to be found."

"So you believe he ran away?"

"Do you?" I countered.

She didn't answer, but gazed over the railing at the intersection below.

I took a swig of wine. "Either that or he's dead. But that's so Hollywood movie because he would have had to have been killed in a way that either his body was never found or he was completely unrecognizable. Any unidentified man would be investigated and eventually come back to the missing Greg Barnes. Then, there'd be dental records comparison."

"Watching a lot of *Law and Order* with your spare time now?"

"Oh, mostly just listening to Matt Reynolds, your friendly neighborhood homicide detective."

"Hmm." Sarah smiled thinly. "Is *he* single?"

I swatted at her. "I'm starving. Let's go eat."

We ate at Sevilla, a sleek tapas bar that doubled as a flamenco nightclub. Sarah introduced me to culture, stripped of *Sesame Street* and *Barney*. We drank Sangria martinis. Unlike the previous night, the alcohol had a loosening effect. Warmth tingled in my arms and legs, and I suppressed the desire to get on the dance floor all through dinner. Possibly the day's events were contributing to my rowdiness.

"I've never seen you like this." Sarah shook her head. "I can't believe I'm saying this, but you should slow down."

"Who's the *mom* now?" I had no idea how to salsa. Loud Spanish music, glittering with castanets, thrummed in my ears. I tried to pull Sarah to her feet, but she resisted. I walked onto the dance floor alone. The other people ranged from professional flamenco dancers to simply talented dark-haired men and women. But there were no other Irish Catholics with two left feet. I immersed myself into the throng of hard bodies gyrating to the hypnotic music. I tried to focus on a woman near me and mimic her movements. After a few moments, I thought I looked pretty good.

"Where did you learn to salsa?" Sarah shouted from behind me.

I shrugged and pointed. "I didn't. I'm following her!"

"Could have fooled me! You don't look bad when you loosen up, Claire." Sarah mimicked my moves, and before long, we were both sweating.

I felt a man's hand slip around my waist. He pulled me to him, his lean body against my back. We moved to the music. Sensual and pulsating. He spun me around, and I caught a glimpse of his face: handsome, a tad older, dark skin, dark hair. I followed his lead, concentrating on my feet. He tightened his grip, and I lost my footing. He felt muscular in a way Greg never did—lean arms, firm chest, hard thighs. A dancer? Were there straight professional salsa dancers? I felt breathless. Most noticeably, I felt alive. The heady mixture of his cologne, sweat, and soap made my head spin. When the song ended, he kissed my hand, gave a little wave, and dissolved into the crowd. I turned to look for Sarah.

"Where's your friend?" she teased.

I shrugged, and we made our way back to the table.

"Let's go," I said, reaching into my purse for my cell phone.

She knitted her eyebrows. "Where?"

"Where else?" I replied, giving her a small shrug and a wry smile. "Float."

We found Will and Owen right where they said they'd be. They looked happy to see us, and I studied Will with new eyes, with new purpose. I saw the evening for what it would be before it happened. Will appraised me, smiling, probably sensing a different attitude. I was not the reserved, nervous, distracted Claire he had met the previous night. I flirted, fingertips resting lightly on his arm, and laughed at his jokes. As I drank more, I became bolder and touched his thigh, then his cheek. I leaned in to whisper in his ear and played with his hair.

He responded by softly trailing a hand down my arm, then my back. He kissed my bare neck, his lips pausing in the soft hollow of my collarbone, and I shuddered with barely contained anticipation. My insides twisted momentarily with guilt, not about Greg as a person, but for the vow I was going to break. And I *was* going to break it; I was sure of that. I'd known that since I'd stood on the street, hurling accusations at a man who had turned out not to be my husband. *How am I different now?* I wasn't. I would be an adulterer, too.

Sarah gave a little wave and secured a spot on one of the plush satin couches with Owen, curled around him like a kitten.

I paid the bill and took Will's hand. I led him to our room, where I hung the Do Not Disturb tag on the door, hoping Sarah would notice. We lay on my bed, and I kissed him fully, hard and insistent. Backing up, I slowly pulled my shirt up over my head, then shimmied my jeans down over my hips until I stood nude in front of him, shivering slightly from both the frosty hotel room air and the electrifying need to be touched.

I reached out and paused, tentative for a moment, at his belt buckle. He pulled his shirt over his head, and I leaned over to kiss his neck and bare shoulders. Teasingly, I ran my hand along the front of his zipper, feeling his response and hearing his guttural groan. His eyes rolled skyward, and a small grin formed on his lips. I smiled, my confidence restored. He ran his hands up my sides, grazing my breasts and burning my skin. I attempted to push him back onto the bed.

He smiled slyly, grasping my hips with his hands. "You can't be in charge all the time, Claire." He held my arms out, tracing his fingertips in excruciatingly slow circles down my torso and across my breasts. He bent his head close in an almost kiss. I could feel his breath on my skin, but he kept his palm low and warm on my belly, forcing me upright.

When his lips finally met my flesh just beneath my breast bone, I gasped. He tilted his head slightly, and I could see his smile of satisfaction. I ran my hands through his hair, my nails clawing gently at the back of his neck, as his mouth trailed hot and wet down my stomach and thighs. He paused, giving me a raised eyebrow.

I laughed self-consciously. The sound of my laughter echoing in the dim room had a clarifying effect. Time seemed to stop. I felt on the precipice of something profound; I felt alive, something I hadn't felt in six months. *Desired and desirable. How long had that been missing? Years, maybe?*

When our lips met, his mouth tasted of vodka and peppermint. His lips moved in cadenced rhythm with mine, and I pulled him closer, needing the connection. I felt his nakedness under my palm, his light feathery chest hair so different than Greg's, his smell, a woodsy, musky mixture that made my head spin. I kissed his neck, biting gently in the way Greg liked because I knew no other way to be with a man. He moaned softly, his breath coming in short bursts with a soft incantation, "Claire..." and for a second, I opened my eyes, startled. Greg had never said my name during sex, had barely said anything at all most of the time. And I couldn't stop comparing. The feel of Will's thick dark wavy hair in my fingers was a stark dichotomy to Greg's short, soft buzz. Will's leanness felt alien, his kisses foreign.

When I reached down to grip him and heard his sharp intake of breath, I once again felt in control, almost *powerful.* With careful precision, I moved into him, gently pushing him back on the bed, and straddled his hips. The familiar pressure as I sank onto him, dizzyingly pleasurable, brought me to the edge, and I moaned softly.

"Shh," Will whispered with a gentle smile.

We moved in a singular rhythm together, in tune, naturally synchronized. And as I watched Will's face, unfamiliar as a stranger's, it occurred to me that I could be my own person, anyone I wanted to be. I felt a liberating surge of power rise up, bringing with it a long buried heat of desire. Waves of pleasure thrummed from my core. Will's visceral cries interwove with mine as we climaxed.

Sated, I lay in the crook of his arm, our flesh moist and sticky where it met. Silently blissful. Oddly comfortable with this stranger. I half-expected him to come up with an excuse to leave, but he surprised me. Having never had a one-night stand, I didn't know what to expect. I anticipated more awkwardness. Maybe there would have been, if I'd not known the interlude for what it was, if I'd been thinking about a future with the man. *If I were single.*

I realized that I had technically cheated on my husband. Mulling it over, I discovered that I no longer cared. The sex had been at least as good as the best sex Greg and I had ever had.

"What are you going through?" Will asked. His fingers traced patterns on my palm.

"What?" I looked up at him. *Was I that transparent?*

"Last night, you said you're kind of going through something.

And then tonight, you show up, this... lioness on a hunt." He laughed. "So, I wondered."

I debated on what to tell him, if anything. "My husband left me."

He arched his eyebrows at me. "You're married?"

"Sort of. Well, technically, yes." I tried to stifle a giggle, which had to be from the martinis, but mortifyingly, I couldn't. I coughed to cover it up.

He propped himself up on his elbows. "Are you laughing? At me?" He looked mildly annoyed.

"Oh, God, Will, no! Listen, here's the whole crazy story. Six months ago, my husband went on a business trip and never came home. I have no idea what happened to him. He could have run away, or he could be dead. I found out later that he'd been having an affair, and he wasn't really the person I thought he was anyway." Oh, God. Information overload.

Will looked half-astonished, half-ready to run out the door, his mouth slack with disbelief.

I put my hand on his arm. "I was laughing because I feel bad for you. You didn't know you were going to end up with me and all my... baggage." I started laughing so hard, tears streamed out of my eyes.

Will smiled nervously, not quite getting the joke, but he had yet to make a break for it, so I took that as a good sign. I hiccupped and finally calmed.

"So, he what? Never came home?" he asked.

"Nope. Gone without a trace. New Jersey's finest can't even find him."

"That's crazy." He stared at me for a moment. "So what am I then? An angry screw? A way to get back at him?"

"No, not really. You would think so, I guess. And I *am* angry. But this... this doesn't *feel* angry. I don't feel like I'm using you to get back at anyone. And I've discovered things, you know? Things that he's kept a secret that a man shouldn't keep from his wife. It makes me think that maybe he never loved me the right way." I was rambling.

I didn't know Will well enough to explain how Greg may or may not have loved me.

Will resumed tracing patterns into my palm. "So, you didn't answer me. What was this to you? What *is* this to you?"

"An awakening," I replied, kissing him gently. "This is an awakening of the senses. A welcome back party."

His arms went around me as he hungrily returned my kiss. I pulled him on top of me, wrapping my legs around him.

"Well, it's a great party," he murmured.

When I woke up several hours later, sun streamed in through the windows. I sat up and looked around. I was alone in the room. I stretched languidly under the six-hundred-thread-count sheets, enjoying my first post-coital morning in a long time. I was startled by a soft knock on the door, followed by a quiet, "Hello?"

"Come in!" I called to Sarah. "I'm alone."

She came in carrying her black strappy sandals.

I giggled. "Oh, that must have been some walk of shame, girl. What are we, twenty-five?"

"Owen drove me here," she retorted. "I told him no way was I walking back at nine in the morning, holding my shoes and wearing the same clothes from the night before. I am past that point in my life."

"How was your night?" I asked, eyebrows wiggling suggestively.

"Uh-uh, you first. How was yours?"

"Oh, pretty wonderful. I can't believe you get to do this all the time!" I flopped back onto the pillows. "I've never had a one-night stand before!"

"When did he leave?"

"I have no clue."

She reached over and plucked something off the pillow next to my head. "Oh, my God. What an amateur. He left a note!"

Holding the sheet over me, I reached up for it. "Give me that! That might say something personal!" I grabbed it out of her hand.

Claire,

I had a wonderful time. Hope you get through your "something." Your husband has no idea what he left behind. Next time you're on the west coast, call me day or night. I still have your cell # and I'll call you next time I'm in New York. I'd love to meet up. And I really hope I see you again. I mean that. Love, Will.

"Well, that's about the sweetest Dear Jane letter I ever read," Sarah said.

"It's not a Dear Jane letter. That would imply that I'm being dumped, which implies that I wanted more than this one night. Which I don't."

Sarah stretched her arms wide, grinning and turning in a slow circle. "So how does it feel to be me?"

"It's a great party," I replied.

We spent our last day in San Diego doing a vineyard tour of southern California. Sarah deemed it "No Napa Valley. But pretty damn good." And that was okay by me. It was the happiest day I'd had in a long time. We were giggly, surely obnoxious to some. I thought of Greg barely at all, Will frequently, and Drew once when our vintner pompously instructed us to swirl and sniff the glass prior to tasting. I remembered Drew doing something similar, mockingly, and declaring the wine, "Woodsy. Or is it Woody?" and us breaking into laughter. *Where were we? A wine festival, years ago somewhere in New York state.* Greg was with us, but I had no memories of that trip that included him. I made a mental note to call Drew as soon as I got home and apologize for avoiding him the past few weeks.

That night, we ordered Chinese take-out and laid off the booze. I was too old to drink for two consecutive nights, and my digestive system was not thrilled with my recent tear. We rented girly movies about finding true love and happily ever after and talked about what a bunch of shit they were.

"Not all men are scum, Claire," Sarah amended.

"Not Owen?" I asked, realizing she had successfully evaded the "How was your night" question.

"Actually, no. To tell the truth, Owen is the first guy I've been genuinely interested in for a very long time."

"Really?" I was flabbergasted. Sarah, the queen of giving out a fake phone number *after* the one-night stand.

"Really. And I think he might feel the same way." She was quick to add, "But who knows? You can't tell with vacation flings."

I nodded, playing along. "Yeah, I mean they never go anywhere."

We fell asleep with the TV still on, knowing that we would part the next day and go back to reality. That was okay; I was ready for it.

CHAPTER 20

When I arrived home, I hugged the girls with ferocity. The trip had worked wonders for my state of mind, but I frequently felt incomplete, as if I'd lost an arm or a leg. Holding my girls, I realized that Leah and Hannah filled that void. While I had enjoyed the long, hot showers and the selfish indulgence of alcohol and rich food, I wouldn't trade lives with Sarah for anything. I breathed in the girls' strawberry hair. They always smelled like candy, even when they'd gone days without a bath, as if innocent sweetness wafted out of their pores. Mom said Leah had cried because she missed me, but had slept well all three nights. Amazing.

Hannah held my hand for the majority of the evening, as though the simple gesture could anchor me and keep me from leaving her again. After I put Leah to bed, Hannah and I sat on the couch. She informed me that Annie was no longer her best friend because Pop-pop was and that she liked spaghetti.

I expressed surprise at both admissions, and Hannah said gravely, "Mommy, things change when you're not here."

"I guess they do!" I tried not to smile. "I won't go away again for a long time, okay?"

"Did you go and try to find Daddy again?"

I had a stab of guilt. When I flew out there, that had been my intention. After my stranger chase through the streets of San Diego, the need to do the Greg Barnes tour had died. I decided to lie, thinking that alternate explanations would be too complicated. "I did look for Daddy. But I didn't find him."

Hannah absorbed that for a moment. "Do you think we'll ever find him?"

"I don't know."

She sagged against me briefly, and then in the way only a four-year-old can recover, she bolted upright. "Oh! I know what I forgot! I forgot to tell you that I want another puppy!"

"You do?"

"Yup, I just decided when you were away. Can we?"

The time had come for everyone to move on. I didn't have the heart to say no outright, but I was just starting to feel on my feet again. Dogs meant training and walks and things I wasn't sure I could keep up with. Yet. "What if we could get a cat instead? I think that would be nice, Hannah. We'll go to the ASPCA and adopt a cat that needs a home. What do you think?"

"Would he be a kitten? Like a baby?"

"Probably not. But that's okay. We'll give a cat a home when he doesn't have one. It's better than getting a kitten."

After a moment, she nodded. "Then he'll have a family. He'll have us, right?" Her big brown eyes, mirror images of Greg's, implored mine, seemingly desperate to get the right answer.

"Yes, he'll have us." I pulled her to me, and for what seemed like the hundredth time that day, kissed her head, smoothing her hair.

With my newfound resolve and my self-proclaimed "awakening," I viewed my house with a critical eye. When had things gone to pot? I realized we'd gone the entire winter with the screens in the doors, as Greg hadn't been there to replace them with storm windows. The back door where Cody had scratched his way out remained ripped. The gutters had clogged because Greg hadn't been around to clean them out in November after the trees shed their leaves. The winter hadn't been kind, and the blocked gutters had collected water, which had frozen, and because of the weight, the gutters sagged in places, straining their brackets. I wondered if I would stay in the house, with the big yard and all the work, if it remained just me. There were tough decisions in my future.

For the time being, I needed to get control over my home and learn how to do the things Greg had done. I watched a YouTube video on screen replacement, made a trip to Home Depot to pick up new mesh, and rescreened the patio door. That job took me half of a Saturday. Dad called twice to see if I needed any help, but I declined his offer. I borrowed a ladder from Pastor Joe because the one I found in the barn seemed rickety, and while Greg might have kept on using it, I wasn't about to break my leg or worse.

Monday, while Hannah was at school and Leah was napping, I started on the west-facing side of the house, pulling mounds of rotting organic material from the gutters. The April air was brisk, but the waterlogged leaves were held together by thawing ice, making removal easier. I did the same thing to the east side of the house the next day.

I noticed the grass getting long and searched my memory for when Greg usually did the first cut. Sometime in April or May? I'd have to tackle the riding mower at some point when I wasn't exhausted from gutter cleaning. I realized I hadn't given Greg the credit he deserved, as most of the husband duties around the house were turning out to be the more physical variety. My arms and back ached, and fleetingly, I thought about how fantastic a massage would feel. Only then did I realize that I had never offered one, in all the years being married, as Greg performed backbreaking labor in our home. *Maybe he found someone who would massage out every kink.*

Tuesday evening, I made a quick dinner of chicken nuggets and peas—about which Hannah complained—read appropriate bedtime stories, and tucked the girls into bed. I sat in the dimly lit living room, drinking a glass of white wine and staring blankly at the phone. Dreading the call I knew I had to make, I dialed the familiar number.

When Drew picked up, he sounded genuinely happy to hear from me.

"I'm sorry I haven't called," I blurted.

He chuckled softly. "I was starting to wonder."

"No, I'm..." I swirled the wine in my glass, thinking of how to explain. I drew a blank. "Just getting through, I guess. How are you?"

"I'm good. I'm working on another print series."

"Really? Tell me about it?"

"Are you sure? You might be offended."

"Of course."

"It's... um... businessmen. At lunchtime. In public parks... with women."

No wonder he had been hesitant. I was speechless. "Really? Isn't that... wrong or something?"

"No. I have permission to use the images from men and women in the picture. So it's not actually wrong, but it does look like clandestine affairs. But the weird part is most of the people I approached were husbands and wives meeting for lunch. So, innocent and harmless. But my photographs paint a slightly different picture."

"And they didn't mind?"

"Nope. In fact, most of them thought it was pretty cool. There were a few people who weren't married, and it ended up being... uh, a thing."

"A thing?" I laughed. "What kind of thing?"

"I got punched in the face once."

"You did not! Drew, that's terrible!"

"No, I've never been punched before. I felt kind of accomplished. Turns out the guy *was* cheating on his wife. I wouldn't delete the picture in front of him, so he demanded my camera. I said, 'No way.' So he punched me. Turns out, photography is a contact sport."

"I miss you!" I blurted.

After a long pause, he said, "I miss you, too, Claire."

"But...?" I could hear the silent 'but' as clear as day. I'd become so accustomed to it.

"But... nothing. Well, I'm seeing someone."

Of course. What did I want? What did I expect? Did it matter?

I hadn't called him for anything other than friendship. Then why did my chest ache? I didn't want to think about it. "Good!" I said enthusiastically. "Tell me about her."

"Maybe another time, okay?" His voice was gentle. I felt the impending dismissal before he said it.

"Well, I should go anyway," I said. "I think Leah is awake." Another lie. "Call me soon, okay? I want to hear about the new woman in your life when we both have more time." I forced a laugh.

"Are you all right? You sound kind of... maniacal, actually."

"I'm fine. But I've gotta go. Leah is crying. Love you. Call me later, okay? Bye." I hung up. *Why is everything so complicated?*

CHAPTER 21

T HE SATURDAY BEFORE LEAH'S FIRST *birthday party, Drew is coming for dinner and drinks and will spend the night in the guest room before the big party. Sarah is flying in tomorrow morning, and Drew will pick her up at the airport while Greg and I take care of last minute party things. The girls are at my parents to keep them out of the way. The weather has been warm for early September. Indian summer. I am weeding the garden; sweat is running down my forehead. I wipe my brow and feel a kiss between my shoulder blades. I turn to face Greg, who kisses me on the mouth. We're both covered in dirt and perspiration.*

"Hi!" I laugh. "What was that for?"

"You just looked beautiful." In the rise and fall of marital tides, we are at a high. He pulls me out of the garden and onto the grass. "I can't believe Leah is going to be a year old already."

"I know. It's crazy. It happened so fast. She's still a baby."

"Our last baby, unless..." His hands go to the top of my jeans, slowly unbuttoning. He kisses my stomach. "Unless you want to make another one..."

"Greg," I hiss. "The neighbors."

"What neighbors?" He pushes up my shirt.

He's right. The closest neighbors are a quarter-mile away and there are trees on all four sides of our property. We make love on the grass. Afterward, we lay half-clothed in our own yard. I giggle.

"I hope we don't get a FedEx delivery."

Greg laughs. "It could be the highlight of the driver's day."

"Do you actually want to have another baby?" I ask. Do we want three kids? Three plane tickets to Disney, three college tuitions, three seems so

much more than two. We always said we'd be done at two.

He shrugs. "I don't know. I guess lately I've been thinking about our life. I can't believe how lucky I am. I never thought I'd end up like this. I always expected to be alone. And poor. Struggling or something." He pulls me to him. "My life has exceeded my expectations in so many ways. Because of you." He kisses my forehead.

I love the way I feel in his arms, small, protected. We lie there for another half-hour before we get up, dress, and return to our chores that now seem so much less like chores. Briefly, I look around, wondering if anyone saw us. Doubtful. I say something to Greg, and he waves my concerns away.

A few hours later, we are showered and dressed with weeded gardens, cut grass, and a cleaner house. My parents drop off the girls, and I start dinner. Drew arrives amidst screaming excitement from Hannah and mimicked excitement from Leah.

Over dinner, all three of us make conversation. Sometimes Greg is reserved around Drew, but tonight, he is gregarious and jovial. He hands Drew a cigar, and I feel, for the first time, hopeful they will become friends. Parts of the evening, I feel like an outsider. I pout about that, as I'm not used to it. Greg is affectionate with me, more so than usual when we are around other people. He and Drew drink whiskey, a rarity for both men. Before bed, Drew reads the girls a bedtime story, and Hannah cannot believe her good fortune that Drew will be there when she wakes up in the morning.

We take our drinks outside, where Greg starts a fire in the fire pit. The men polish off half a bottle of Crown Royal. I stick to my white wine. I'm tipsy, but the men are drunk. Greg waves the white flag early, leaving Drew and me to put out the fire. Greg kisses me goodnight, a little longer than normal, and whispers in my ear that he loves me.

Drew and I stay up, drinking and talking. We debate about politics. Drew is staunchly liberal, active in his causes. Our debates are usually heated, but Drew is much more knowledgeable, as I have little time to give to others. This infuriates him, as he sees my selfish suburban bubble life as unappreciated good fortune. He says I am ignorant of struggle. I say he is ignorant of systemic abuse. He is angry in a way I've never seen him. He is *also drunker than I've ever seen him.*

"You are selfish and oblivious to the big world around you," he says, his arm swinging wildly. He knocks over a citronella candle on the patio table, and the wax snakes its way toward the edge.

"I don't think that's true," I say, stung by his accusation. "Yes, I'm absorbed in my life. I have two small children. I have to be. More people should be focused on their kids. Maybe there'd be less need for social do-gooders if more people raised their children properly."

"That's a completely oblivious thing to say. It discounts any extenuating factors. But that's how you are. Your life revolves around you. You don't account for how other people feel."

"Other people like who? Like homeless men on the streets of New York? No, I do not frequently account for homeless drunks on city streets when I make my daily life decisions."

"Other people like me, for instance." A beat. The air has shifted. Somehow we are no longer talking abstract politics. Things have gotten personal.

"What does that mean?"

"You have no idea how I feel, for example. You invite me to every holiday, every birthday party, to come here and sit and watch you and your husband either love or hate each other, depending on his moods. And I come. I laugh in all the right places and shake Greg's hand when I'd really love to sock him in the face. And I do that because you expect it. You have no clue what it costs me."

I grip the arm of the chair. I know deep down that what he is saying is true, but I've never acknowledged it, either to him or myself.

He stands up abruptly. "I'm sorry. I'm going to bed now. Before I say anything else I regret." He kisses my cheek and leaves me in the dark.

The embers of the fire crackle. I'm confused as to what just happened. With a sinking feeling, I turn to look at our bedroom window, which overlooks the patio and fire pit. I realize the windows are open to the September breeze. Mechanically, I clean up the patio, put the glasses in the dishwasher, and put away the whiskey. I pray that Greg didn't hear Drew's words. I'm only mildly concerned that Drew's and my friendship could change as a result of Drew's tirade because we've had encounters before and lived through them. Our relationship has always been an iceberg. The part the world sees is small and insignificant, where the largest, most complicated parts lie beneath the surface.

I go upstairs and undress quietly. When I climb into bed, Greg is awake. His arm goes around me, and we spoon. We don't speak. I have no idea if he heard Drew. I strain my ears, trying to imagine if I could hear a conversation taking place twenty feet below the window. I sleep fitfully, replaying the night's events with different endings in my dreams. When I wake in the morning, I am exhausted.

Sunday passes in a blur of activity. The house fills with family and friends. Drew picks up Sarah from the airport, and I am thrilled to see her. Throughout the day, I wonder if the night before was real. Everyone seems normal. Greg and Drew have resumed their banter, and I relax in the affable atmosphere. Leah cries when presented with her cake and everyone singing, but she loves her presents, ripping into the bright wrapping paper.

Sarah is staying for the week, taking Drew's place in the guest room. After the party, Drew packs up and gives the girls big hugs with promises to return as soon as he can.

"Come back and visit again soon, Drew," Greg says, shaking his hand. "Or we'll come to you one night. Leave the girls with Claire's parents and come have a wildly fun night in the city." He puts his arm around my waist. "That actually sounds like a lot of fun. Doesn't it, Claire?"

I nod. "Yeah."

"Sounds good," Drew says. "I'm sure I'll be back soon. Are you guys having your holiday party again this year?"

"I don't know," Greg replies. "I guess it depends on my mood."

The hint is subtle, but I get it immediately. I can't tell if Drew gets it, but he falters. Time stops for a beat, then resumes. Greg picks up Drew's bag and walks him out to the car; his hand is paternally clamped on Drew's shoulder. I stand alone in the hallway, while Sarah waves from the doorway. She picks up on nothing. We shut the door and go into the living room with Hannah and Leah. Life continues as usual. The effect is imperceptible.

Except to me.

CHAPTER 22

During the spring, I did all I could do to keep up with the grass, the gardens, and basic repairs. I lost a gutter anyway, despite my clearing attempts. For the replacement, I hired someone. I was done with Pastor Joe's ladder. The girls rode their new bikes in the driveway while I weeded, trimmed, and cleared fallen sticks from the yard. I mastered the riding mower after two or three mowings. I learned how to use the weed whacker. The lawn wasn't going to look great, as I didn't know Greg's whole regime of overseeding, aeration, and grub treatment, but I was proud of myself and felt confident the rest would come in time. I had nothing if not time.

I no longer considered I wouldn't need to learn those things. I no longer mentally added *if Greg's not home* to the end of thoughts or sentences. After eight months, I had finally accepted that he was not coming home. I was still angry sometimes, but not frequently. When I focused on it, which wasn't often, my anger was on behalf of the girls. If Greg had disappeared by choice, what he had done to them was unforgivable. I'd read that children were resilient, and I supposed that was true. I'd watched my kids adapt and move on in ways that amazed me—that part was Darwinian. What I didn't read, or talk about, was that adaptation came at a price. The girls were irreversibly changed, and that thought haunted me, sneaking up at unexpected moments and breaking my heart all over again.

They no longer asked for Greg every day. But Hannah was wary of everyone. Her small, pure heart had become guarded. When I left her at school or at my parents' house, she would ask me if I was definitely coming back. She had learned to see the world as unkind at too young an age. She smiled less frequently, and those smiles were hesitant, as though at any moment someone could snatch them away.

At Hannah's insistence, we did adopt a cat from the ASPCA. He wasn't a kitten, but he wasn't full-grown either. He was gray-striped with small, delicate white feet. The cat really took to Hannah, following her around the house and sleeping on her bed at night, curled in a tight gray coil of fur. Hannah named him Sunshine. When I asked why, she shrugged and said, "He looks like a storm cloud, but that's not a very happy name." The cat seemed to be helping, at least with Hannah.

Leah was different, too, but not as much. She had always been more headstrong than Hannah. She resisted me in almost every way, simply to assert her independence. I couldn't tell if her changes came from being parented from one perspective rather than two, or if she would have developed that way anyway. She was obstinate for the sake of being so, rather than for any real reason. Assertive to a fault, Leah fought discipline in a way that pliable Hannah never did. I roamed message boards at night, looking for disciplinary answers, when a year ago I would have bounced ideas off of Greg. Reward charts, time-outs, time-ins, and then more complicated, reverse reward charts, reverse time-outs, reverse time-ins, the suggestions made my head spin. When had raising a child gotten so complex? Or had it always been, but the complexity was divided in half, and therefore manageable?

One of those nights when I was scrolling through websites looking for help with potty training my stubborn Leah, my cell phone rang. Looking at the display, I noted a San Diego exchange, and for one crazy minute, I thought *Greg*. I immediately amended the thought. *Will.* I let it go to voicemail. My memories of our night together were precious to me. After I got back, I had considered calling him a few times, especially after a few glasses of wine in those quiet, lonely hours late at night. I didn't do it, in part because I didn't want to know the *real* Will. The Will in my mind was too perfect for any real flesh and blood human. I didn't want more heartbreak in my life. For that reason, I also avoided Drew. Although, I convinced myself that I wasn't actually avoiding Drew. *Our conversations take hours. And with everything I have to do, I don't have the time right now. I'll call tomorrow.*

I picked up my phone and dialed my voicemail. *Hi, Claire. It's Will Pierce. From San Diego. I hope you remember me. Anyway... uh... I was wondering how you were doing. I think of you. Call me sometime. Hope you're well. Bye now.*

I smiled. *Nice.* If nothing else, it was nice to have a man thinking of me.

I had a nine o'clock appointment the next day with Detective Reynolds. We had migrated to monthly meetings; he would come for coffee. Nothing ever changed. He assured me the case wasn't closed, and every once in a while, he'd call with a question about something he needed to follow up on from the file. But the investigation was all re-examination of old information. I looked forward to his visits, though, in part because they allowed me to hold a tether to my old life, but also because I genuinely enjoyed his company. He knew my situation and was endlessly sympathetic, unlike my former acquaintances from the neighborhood, church, or library.

People weren't deliberately cruel. They just didn't know what to say to me, so instead chose silence, avoidance of me entirely, or worse, pretending nothing had happened. Yes, I often thought Greg dying would have been easier.

My brain swam with too many thoughts. I took a shot of whiskey and went to bed. I woke up in the same position I fell asleep in.

Detective Reynolds sat at the breakfast table, drinking coffee. He always brought my favorite Boston Cream doughnuts. I didn't need the calories, since my grieving diet seemed to be ending. I filled out my clothes a little more and blamed the nightly bottles of wine. In my defense, some nights, I only drank half of a bottle.

"So, no more hunting trips planned?" he asked, half-smiling. He hadn't been surprised by my trek to San Diego, nor by the fact that I had failed to tell him about it until after I returned. He had, however, informed me that he had already checked out a Thai place across from Omni due to my last hunch, and they didn't find any record of Greg going there, and no one remembers seeing him. But the last time we knew of Greg being in San Diego was last May, almost a full year ago. So unless Greg did something particularly memorable, which I doubted, it seemed unlikely anyone *would* remember him.

"No." I spun the coffee mug in my hands. "I think I'm done for now. I need to be home. I need to stay focused on my kids. And..."

Detective Reynolds made no move to fill the silence. I loved that about him.

"And I'm not sure there's anything to find," I added. "Well, what's this month's theory?"

Every month, he seemed to ponder my question and answer it slightly differently. If nothing else, it gave me the illusion of progress.

"I'm starting to seriously consider the possibility he might be dead." He had always leaned more toward that theory than I did.

"If he died, then how would we not know it? Where is his body?"

"Oh, the possibilities are endless there. A victim of murder could be buried or thrown in the river, and we might never know."

It hit me how blasé the discussion was when we were talking about *my possibly dead husband.* I tried to force myself to feel *something,* but came up empty.

"The inheritance supports this," he continued. "It's a lot of money to leave behind."

"Unless he has a significant amount more, and that was a red herring," I suggested, playing devil's advocate. It all seemed farfetched for me, too, especially for the Greg I thought I knew. He was so *conventional.*

"Well, we looked into that. We subpoenaed his bank records from 2001 and 2002, as well as his mother's from when she was alive. The figure is about fifty thousand dollars short, but after her funeral—plus it looked like she donated some to charity—it came pretty close to the mark. There's a few thousand bucks we can't find. But that was eight years ago. Things get lost, you know?" He reached out and put his hand on mine. "We're still going to look for him, Claire. I know how badly you need closure."

I felt tears brim my eyelids. "Thanks, Matt. I hope you eventually figure it out." I wiped the tears away before Hannah or Leah could come bounding in from the living room and see them.

He leaned back again. "I want to. There are definitely some cases that get to you more than others. I want peace for you and your family. Unfortunately, a death in absentia ruling takes at least seven years."

"What does that mean?"

"If Greg is still missing six years from now, we can petition the courts to issue a death certificate without evidence of death."

"Six more years seems a lifetime from now. What will that do? A death certificate, I mean."

"For starters, you could file for life insurance." He stared at me intently. Gauging my reaction?

"I... I hadn't even thought about that. In fact," I said, feeling instantly stupid, "I have no idea how much Greg's life insurance policy is. Why don't I know that? Isn't that something a wife knows about her husband?"

He shrugged. "The strangest part to me is that we've had no reported sightings of Greg. We've had missing posters up around here and in Rochester for over six months now and nothing. Not one person has called to say they've seen him. It makes no sense. It's part of the reason I think he has to be dead. Men cannot change their appearance that easily."

Matt stood and put his cup in the sink. "I should head back to the station. I have another meeting in a bit. Are you going to be okay?"

"Thanks, Matt. Yes, I'll be fine. It's just something to think about. That's all." I walked him to the door, then went back to clean up and throw away the temptation of the two remaining doughnuts. The girls didn't need the sugar any more than I needed the extra calories.

I called Mom to fill her in on the monthly meeting. She offered to take the girls for a few hours so I could do some of the yardwork. The week before, we'd had a storm that brought down part of a tree. I needed to break up the tree limbs as much as I could, then Dad planned to take a chainsaw to the rest. In addition, the physical exercise would help me clear my head.

Mom came to pick up the kids, and I got dressed in an old T-shirt and jeans. I put on my iPod and was a quarter way through the mess when I caught a flash of movement. When I looked up, I nearly fainted. Bounding toward me, as if no time at all had passed, was Cody. His coat looked different, longer than we'd ever let it get, and he had a blue bandana around his neck.

"Oh, my God." I pulled off my headphones and knelt on the ground. Cody tackled me, licking my face. He smelled like dog shampoo and potpourri.

I grabbed him by the collar. "Seriously, you've been gone for eight months! Are you trying to kill me?" I wrapped my arms around his neck, something I had always done before. I rubbed his belly and began to think.

After a minute, I realized that I had grabbed him by the *collar*. We were terrible at keeping a collar on him. His head and neck were close enough in size to make a collar virtually impossible to keep on him. Instead of fighting it, I would typically leave his collar lying on the counter or on top of the fridge until we wanted to walk him, which was almost never because he had the run of the yard. I couldn't be sure, but I thought it likely the collar was still on top of the fridge. Then, what was this collar? I checked the tag. Cody's name was "Walter," and he apparently lived at an address about ten miles from our house. *What a completely terrible name for a dog,* was all

138

I could think. And then it occurred to me. Cody had a new home, a new family.

Cody had been ours first, and I had to fight the instinct to take him into the house and keep him. *But what if his new family had kids?*

I inspected him. His fur hung a bit long, but I grudgingly admitted that was more personal taste than hygiene. I pulled open his mouth. His teeth were white and clean. That was definitely above and beyond. I'd never had his teeth cleaned. His ears were clear, too.

I went to the barn, and Cody followed me. I dug out one of his old tennis balls and threw it as hard as I could—about halfway to the driveway. *Pathetic. I need to work out.* He picked it up, brought it back, and then did something he had rarely done when living with us. He dropped it. And sat. Like a real dog. Someone had taught him in less than a year what we'd been unable to in five years.

"Well, this is new!" I ruffled his ears. We played catch for about twenty minutes.

I checked my watch and saw that I had only an hour before the girls would be back. Sighing, I loaded Cody into the van. The house that matched the address on "Walter's" collar was a new construction home in a development about ten miles away. The houses were on acre lots with large fenced-in yards. I wondered how he had gotten out and managed to run ten miles home. *Not home anymore.* He was a canine Houdini when he wanted to be.

I kissed his head and knocked on the door.

A boy about eleven years old answered. "Walter!" He bent to hug Cody-Walter. "Mom! Some lady brought Walter back!"

A woman came rushing out on the porch. "Oh, my God, we were so worried! Thank you, thank you. We have no idea how he got out. We were visiting friends in Clinton, and one minute he was in their yard, and the next, *poof!* He was gone. Ben! Come look. Walter's back!"

A man and another young boy, around thirteen or fourteen, came out on the porch.

"Can we offer you anything?" the man asked. "I'm Ben Fields. And this is my wife, Amanda, and two boys, Jimmy and Leo. We were so worried about Walter. Amanda and Jimmy drove around all morning looking for him. We were about to call the ASPCA, but we were hoping someone would just find him and bring him back."

My eyes started to water. "No, thank you. I understand. Our dog ran away once. I'm glad I could help."

I gave a little wave and began to walk down the steps, off the porch. I knew I'd made the right decision. Our family had moved on. I couldn't see doing to Jimmy and Leo what had been done to Hannah and Leah.

I stopped and turned, wanting to know the answer to a question, but not sure how to ask. "How old is he?"

"We aren't sure," Ben said. "We found him about, oh, maybe a year ago now? We put up signs and called the ASPCA, but no one ever claimed him. He's such a great dog; we couldn't figure out why someone wouldn't want him back. He's an escape artist, though, as you can tell."

I almost laughed, wondering what they would say if I told them the truth. I felt a little sad that I never thought to call the ASPCA. *Would I have even seen the signs?* My memory of that time was of drowning. I had been reclusive, barely leaving the house, certainly not driving all around New Jersey. I doubted Dad had driven ten miles out to put up our posters.

I had chosen saving myself over saving Cody. Watching him with his new family, I realized Cody hadn't needed saving.

One of the boys—Jimmy or Leo, I wasn't sure—bounded off the steps with Walter behind him and ran toward the backyard. They shut the gate, and I could no longer see them.

Goodbye, Cody.

I climbed in the van and drove home.

CHAPTER 23

THE SUMMER ARRIVED WITH FEROCITY, setting more than one high-temperature record in the month of June alone. In July, we spent our days in the yard between a sprinkler and a baby pool. I achieved a nice summer tan, but the kids became restless. By midday, we had to seek refuge in the air-conditioned house, where we rambled around, irritated and snapping at each other.

I enrolled Hannah in day camp while preschool was out of session, and that helped break up the days. I still had not gone back to work, but the end of my sabbatical was looming. I had yet to make any firm decisions about my future. *At the end of summer,* I promised myself. In the meantime, we were bored.

"Why don't you take the girls to the Arnolds' summer home in Brigantine?" Mom suggested one day.

The Arnolds were my parents' closest friends and owned several homes all over the country. Mom and Dad rarely paid for a vacation, but the drawback was they always had to vacation with the Arnolds. Deb and Don were nice people, but Deb talked more than anyone I'd ever met, including my mother, which was a feat. Don hardly ever said a word, probably because he was so used to not being able to get one in edgewise.

"Would the Arnolds be there?" I asked pointedly.

"No, they're in... I'm not sure actually, possibly Africa, although in July? That seems odd. You'd think it would be too hot to safari in July, but then who knows? It's the other side of the world. Aren't their seasons different?"

"I have no idea. Listen, Ma, do you think they'd let us? That actually sounds like a great idea."

She shrugged. "I can give you Deb's cell phone number."

"Can you call them?" I suggested hopefully. I had no desire to talk to Deb. Who knew what she'd say? The call would surely be awkward. Most of my conversations with acquaintances were awkward.

Mom paused, clearly thinking along the same lines.

I put a hand to my forehead. "I've been through so much..."

Mom rolled her eyes. "There will be an expiration date on this, you know." She dug through her purse for her cell phone.

"Really? At some point, you'll stop having sympathy for me and my kids whose father ran away and possibly died? That seems kind of heartless."

Mom swatted me on the arm and dialed Deb's number, stepping inside to talk to her. Almost a full half-hour later she emerged, shaking her head. "That woman never stops. Yes, they're in Africa, and no, it's not hot. In fact, it's their winter! Isn't that neat?"

"Neat. What about the house?"

"Oh, Deb doesn't care. It's not baby-proofed. She was a little concerned over breakables. But they aren't renting it this year because they're going to be in Africa for three months. But I can go over to their house tomorrow—the one here in Clinton—and pick up the Brigantine key."

"Really? That would be fantastic!" I wondered why we had never done it before—Greg and I with the kids, as a family. I had actually never even thought about it. We'd always traveled for our vacations— North Carolina, Florida, and once, Maine.

I planned the trip for the following week, from Monday until we decided to come home. Probably a week or less, I figured. I packed and loaded the van with everything from bread and peanut butter to dishes, pots and pans, towels, bathing suits, and sunscreen. The doors to the van barely shut, and by the time we pulled out of the driveway, I was exhausted. We spent the first hour singing songs that all had the same lyrics, "We're going to the beach!" with different melodies as dictated by Hannah.

During the second half of the trip, which in total turned into three hours due to traffic—*Who goes to the beach on a Monday?*—I turned on the DVD player because I ran out of songs to turn into the "Going to the Beach" song. When we pulled into the driveway of the Arnolds' ranch a block from the ocean, I was so tired, all I wanted to do was nap. But since the kids had both slept during the third hour, they clamored for the beach *right now.*

I got everyone in bathing suits and lathered up with sunscreen, and we walked the block down to the public beach. Hot sand sank beneath our feet as we walked. Two other families were there, and I dropped our blankets, umbrella, and chairs between the two setups. I smiled and nodded a brief hello. Pulling the blanket tight, I anchored it with our bag and the cooler, then surveyed the area. The water lapped gently, and my cautious mothering side noted the lack of any real waves, only small swells advancing and receding.

The salt air was invigorating, and I inhaled deeply, feeling the heavy humidity in my lungs. The girls took their buckets and shovels to the water's edge, and I dragged my chair down after them. As I watched them dig in the sand, talking to each other in their own private language, I was surprised to realize I was crying. Tears fell freely down my cheeks. Free from anger and hate, I would periodically have moments where I simply *missed Greg.* I wasn't missing having a husband, or my kids having a father, but I missed the person he was, or at least the person I had known. I still believed I fundamentally knew him. I thought that when he buried Hannah in the sand last year and spent a half hour pretending she was lost and calling for her, even going as far as jumping in the ocean to look for her, causing her to giggle incessantly, that he wasn't pretending, that he was being himself. And I still loved that part of him. I knew that despite his sometimes serious and sullen moods, of the two of us, he was the sillier one. And our kids would have become better people if he was still in their lives.

The girls never looked up from their digging, and I reined in my emotions before they could turn and see their mother crying on the beach. I closed my eyes briefly, tipping my face to the sun feeling the warmth on my eyes, drying the tears. They had caught me crying a few times, and I thought it a good thing overall that they saw me grieving for their father, but it worried them. And Hannah always tried to make it better, her innate mothering bubbling to the surface, brows creased with concern beyond her years.

Back at the house, I made spaghetti and meatballs for dinner, which we ate while still wearing our bathing suits. The smell of sand and sunscreen had already permeated everything, and it was only the first day. I could feel the tension falling away, sliding off my shoulders like seaweed in the ocean. The knots in my back unfurled, and the anxiety I always seemed to carry with me, a twisted, sick feeling in my gut, melted away, leaving in its place only a small reminder of uneasiness, like a child's sand footprint.

Everyone got a bath, and we watched a movie on the small living room television. They insisted on sleeping in the same bed. *It's A-cation, Mommy. Do we have to have house rules on A-cation?* I relented, and they slept in a double bed in the room adjoined to my room. I watched them sleep, the rise and fall of the blankets in perfect unison, as though they had synched on purpose. Hannah sucked her thumb, and Leah's hands outstretched wildly, her temper evident even in dreams, with her Uglydoll lying next to her. They slept with their backs to each other, but touching. *Hiney to hiney,* Hannah would say. I fell asleep on the floor and woke in the morning with the sun.

⁂

The days blended together, as they tended to do on vacation. I planned no activities, save for going to the beach. I did want to try to find the boardwalk once, if there was one, but every night I told myself, *Tomorrow, we'll go.* I was simply enjoying the seclusion of our hideaway. I felt protected from the world, and all the evil in it. I tried every few days to get the girls back to the house for midday naps. As the sun and sand took their toll, the girls' energies drained, and their dispositions would deteriorate. During those naps, I would take a baby monitor and a book out to the pool in the backyard and read.

The Arnolds' aboveground pool was small, but it did the trick. I would float and, for an hour or so, get lost in another world. I read *Harry Potter and the Sorcerer's Stone* because the story seemed like something I would never accidentally relate to, and it was absorbing.

One day, when I checked my watch, I realized I had been floating and reading for over two hours. I dried off and ran inside to wake up the girls. If they slept any longer, they definitely wouldn't sleep at night. When I opened the door to their room, Hannah sat straight up in bed, blinking, startled from sleep. Leah's side was empty.

"Where's Leah?" I asked, alarmed.

Hannah shrugged, unconcerned, as her sister frequently went missing. Leah was usually found hiding somewhere nearby.

I pulled Hannah up by her hand. "Come on. Let's go find her." We went through the house calling "Le-AH!" in every room, looking under beds and in closets. I kept checking out the window of the back bedroom that overlooked the pool, relieved to keep seeing the calm, undisturbed water.

After ten minutes, I started to feel a tightening in my throat. "Leah! If you are hiding and you don't come out *right now*, I will put Uglydoll in time-out for a *whole day!*"

I ran back down the hall and checked the bed. I looked under the bed and in the closet. No Uglydoll. I went back to the kitchen and sat at the table to calm down and think. Panic scrambled my thoughts. Surely, she was hiding.

Hannah came out of the bathroom, shaking her head. "She's not in there." She sat in a chair next to me, watching my reaction. I stood up and grabbed her hand. There were so many places Leah could go.

And oh, God, the ocean—*only a block away.*

Pulling Hannah, and then eventually picking her up, I ran out the front door, down the block to the beach, yelling Leah's name the entire way. When we got to the sand, I put Hannah down and instructed her to wait by the gate.

"Do *not* move. Do you understand? Your feet are glued to the sand. *Glued*, got it? I need to find your sister."

Hannah nodded solemnly.

I ran toward the water, scanning the beach and screaming, "Leah!" as loud as I could. I ran parallel to the ocean to the jetty. Looking back, I saw Hannah parked where I'd left her. I scaled the rocks and looked over the other side. "Le-ah!"

No Leah.

I had no idea what to do. I ran as far as I could while still being able to see Hannah, up and down the shore. Leah was not on the beach. Backtracking to the house, we ran through the streets, calling Leah's name.

No Leah.

When we got back to the house, I thought to check the car. No luck. I instructed Hannah to go inside and look everywhere she could think of for Leah. I started at one end of the house; Hannah started at the other. The house was small. In fifteen minutes, we had both searched the entire house, closets and all.

No Leah.

I sat down on the porch and pulled out my cell phone. *A person should not have to file a missing persons report twice in the same year.* It was unreal that I had to go through it again.

I dialed 9-1-1. "I need to report a missing child."

⁘⁘⁘

As it happens, the response for a missing child is vastly different than for a grown man. Within ten minutes, four police cruisers had pulled up out front. Eight policemen descended on the living room like locusts, each with a distinct responsibility. I was reliving a nightmare.

"The last time I saw her was when I put her down for her nap."

"No, I don't have any pictures of her. We're on vacation." Then, I remembered I had digital pictures on my camera card, so I gave them those.

"I was in the pool during her nap." That explanation was received with not a few raised eyebrows and exchanged looks, which I ignored.

With a basic description of what she looked like and what she was wearing, they wasted no time in spreading out and combing the town. One of the officers instructed me to wait at the house in case she came back and call his cell phone if I found her.

I sat on the porch with Hannah, my head in my hands. After a few minutes, my cell phone rang. I answered immediately with hope flying.

"Hi, Claire," Drew said. "I'm glad you answered. I'm driving to your house. I need to talk to you about—"

"Drew, Leah is missing!"

"What?"

"I'm at the beach. They were taking a nap, and I went to wake them up, and Leah wasn't in her bed, and I looked all over for her, and the police said for me to—" A sob caught in my throat.

"I'm on my way. Where are you?"

"Brigantine. Please come." I gave him the address and hung up.

Hannah sat next to me, holding my hand in silent apprehension. A little adult. I sat on the porch for two hours, which felt more like six, until I saw Drew's car pull into the driveway.

He parked, and I ran out to his car. My knees gave out as I reached him, and he put his arms around me to hold me up. I sobbed into his collar.

Hannah came over, and Drew extended the hug to include her. "We'll find her, Claire. She hides, right? This isn't Greg. She isn't gone, okay?" He pulled me away, looking into my eyes. "We'll find her. She's hiding somewhere. That's all."

I believed him because I had no choice. With Drew there, I knew we'd find her, and everything would be fine.

He led me inside and poured me a glass of wine. "You need to relax. Here, drink a few of these, but not too many, and I'll be back." He left.

"Mommy, I'm hungry."

I checked the time—five o'clock. Leah would be hungry, too. I hoped that whatever she was doing, she would be reminded to come home to eat. *If she can find her way back. Stop thinking like that.* I made Hannah a peanut butter and jelly sandwich and turned on the TV. I set up a tray in front of *Dora the Explorer*. She raised an eyebrow at me.

"Yes, you can eat in front of the TV. Right now, you can do anything you want as long as you don't disappear on me."

I was too anxious to eat, but I gulped down a glass of wine and was halfway through the second when my cell phone rang. I snatched it up and answered with a breathless, "Hello?"

"This is Officer Jones. Has your daughter come home?"

"No," I said, heart sinking. I had hoped they would tell me they had her.

"In about an hour, if we still haven't found her, we're going to call the FBI."

I laughed—a crude, guttural sound. *They did so much to find my husband.* But surely a child would be different. I hung up, despondent, and stared at the kitchen table, waiting.

The front door flung open.

"Claire! I found Leah. I have her!" Drew walked in holding a very startled-looking Leah.

I grabbed her from Drew's arms and hugged her so tightly I thought I would break every small rib. I sobbed, crying in her hair, then sat on the floor with her simply because my legs would not support the weight of my relief. I kissed her cheeks, her hair, and ran

THOUGHT I KNEW YOU

my hands down her arms and legs.

"Oh, God, you're okay. You're okay. Where was she?"

I could tell by Drew's face that he didn't want to answer the question.

"Out on the jetty," he said softly.

"Oh, God." I couldn't stop crying. I couldn't catch my breath. I let Leah go and put my head between my knees.

Drew put his hand on my neck, his touch warm and soothing. "Take slow breaths, Claire. You're hyperventilating." He rubbed my back.

I raised my head. "Leah, if you *ever* do *anything* like that again, I will take your Uglydoll away forever. Do you understand me?"

She had tears in her eyes, and I knew she had no comprehension of what I had suffered. To Leah, nearly three years old, adventurous and unafraid of the world, she had merely been exploring. She nodded, understanding finally that she'd done something wrong.

Hannah cried and hugged Leah fiercely. "We thought you drowned in the ocean."

"I was on the rocks!" she protested. "I'm not a'posed to go in the ocean without Mommy."

I asked Drew to call the police and tell them she'd been found. "Drew, I don't get it. We looked on the jetty. I ran up and down the beach, calling for her. Leah, did you hear Mommy calling you?" I asked.

She shook her head, still wary of me.

I realized that she didn't have Uglydoll with her. "Leah, where's Uglydoll?"

"In the car," she said matter-of-factly.

The car? Why would Uglydoll be in the car? Unless. *Unless.* My heart sped up.

"Leah, were you in the car when Mommy was looking for you?"

"I was hiding! I was under the seat, and you couldn't see me."

She was there; she saw me search the car. I could have found her three hours ago. I had opened the car door and, in my panic, called her name, searched the seats with a cursory glance, and closed the door. To a child who loved to hide and had no idea how to read panic in a voice, she had probably been thrilled with her cleverness. I could envision her there, flattened under the seats with bated breath, waiting for me to come back and say, "Ah ha! I found you, Leah!" as I usually do when she hides. Then, she got bored and wandered down to the ocean. When? How? While we were in the house, before we called the police, was the only time that made sense. If I had looked out the window at any time while we were searching the house, I might have seen her.

My head pounded. Drew appeared out of nowhere, holding Uglydoll, retrieved from the car. Leah snatched her doll out of his hands and joined her sister on the couch for the rare treat of watching TV for an extra hour.

I poured another glass of wine and drank it down in two gulps.

"Can I do anything?" Drew asked, his hand on my back.

I looked at my watch—seven o'clock. "Yes. We need more wine. And pizza."

CHAPTER 24

D REW STAYED THE NIGHT BECAUSE we had split a bottle of wine, and he felt he shouldn't drive home. He disappeared into the guest room without a backward glance, and I wondered if my jitters were caused by the adrenaline of the day or something else. *My very own Johnny on the spot.*

The next day, as he packed to leave, I stood in the doorway of his room. "Sure you can't stay?" I was aiming for airy, but my words fell like lead weights to the floor between us. I self-consciously crossed my arms.

He half-smiled as he carefully folded yesterday's shirt into his duffel bag. "Dinner plans." He avoided eye contact, purposefully vague. My pride kept me from asking anything more.

Before he left, he awkwardly kissed my cheek, lingering a bit too long. His face felt stubbled and rough. I resisted the urge to wrap my arms around his neck, and for a moment, our breathing synced, and my heart picked up an uneven, staccato beat.

I stepped back, breaking the spell, and gave him a wide smile. "Call me, okay?"

He nodded and loped down the walk.

When I looked out the window five minutes later, the car was idling at the curb, but before I could open the front door, he pulled away.

*

Two days later, I packed up the car, loaded the girls in, and flipped on the DVD player to the Disney princess movie of their choice. An hour into the drive, I remembered the day Leah went missing, Drew had called to talk to me about something. I had been so caught up in Leah, I completely forgot to ask him about it. I picked up my cell phone and dialed his number.

"Hey!" I said when he picked up. "Remember a few days ago, when you called? You said you wanted to talk to me about something."

"Um, yeah, I remember." His voice was halting, evasive. In the background, I heard a voice. Female? I couldn't tell.

"Is this a bad time? I can call back later. I just remembered it..."

"Let me call you back in five minutes, okay?"

I said, "Sure," and we hung up. About fifteen minutes later, my phone rang again.

"Hi, sorry about that."

"No, it's fine. You didn't even have to call me back. Everything okay?"

"Yeah, it's fine. Remember how I had said I was seeing someone? She was here, but she had to leave."

"Oh." I didn't have any response prepared. I tried to come up with conversation. What would I have said if Sarah talked about a man she was seeing? "Tell me about her. What's her name?"

"Her name is Olivia. She's a food critic."

"Oh, that sounds fun!" I hoped I sounded enthusiastic. "How did you meet?"

"We met at a benefit. A mutual friend set us up. Like a blind date. It was so weird; I'd never been on a blind date before."

"Well... what's she like? You've been seeing her for a few months now, right?"

"Yeah, about three now. She's pretty great, very funny. I actually think you'd like her. It's what I was going to talk to you about. I want you to meet her."

I felt sucker punched. I could handle hearing about his girlfriends. Sort of. Meeting them would be another story. I briefly flashed back to all the years Drew had endured me being *married*. The shoe was on the other foot. I had pretended for years that he was unaffected by my love life, my dating, my *marriage*.

"Oh. It must be serious, then?" I tried to sound casual.

He coughed. "Yeah. I think it might be." He sighed. "Timing," he said softly.

"Yeah, it always sucks." But I knew that for Drew to want me to meet one of his girlfriends, he had to be at least halfway in love with her. *In love with her.* I banged the steering wheel with the heel of my hand. I thought of everything Drew had done for me in the last few months. And the years he'd remained my closest confidant when it must have killed him at times. He had always thought of me then. *The least I can do is think of him now.*

I put a fake smile on my face, even though he couldn't see it. I hoped the big smile at least made my next words feel believable. "I'd love to meet her, Drew. When?"

"Thanks for that. For pretending." He laughed quietly. "I don't know when. Soon. Can I bring her for dinner?"

"Yes, call me next week. We'll figure out a date." I made the excuse of not wanting to talk long while driving and ended the call.

I had my monthly meeting with Detective Reynolds the following Monday. He brought me the customary Boston Creams. After monitoring credit card history, bank accounts, and general social security activity—meaning Greg had not applied for another credit card, a name change, or opened any bank accounts—the police were noting Greg to be "most likely" deceased in his file. But since no direct evidence had been found, the file would remain open, but unsolved. After a year of Greg being missing—the anniversary was only two months away—our monthly meetings would be replaced by a brief appointment every six months, and then eventually, only if new information arose.

"I'm sorry, Claire. I really am. Do you have any questions?"

Do I have any questions? Sure. Does anyone have any answers? "What should I do now? How do we move on?" I picked at a piece of hardened jelly stuck to the table.

"I don't know. Maybe a memorial service wouldn't be a terrible idea." His eyes were compassionate. I always thought Matt Reynolds had the kindest smile I'd ever seen.

I mulled it over. No, it wouldn't be a terrible idea. I could tell the girls that Daddy was in Heaven. With Annie's Grandpa. I could start to close the door, exit Purgatory, stage right.

Would I have the gall to go through with it? Half of Clinton thought Greg had left me. Would I be a laughingstock if I had a memorial service for him? Seeds of doubt began to sprout in my mind. My anger over the last few months had been directed toward a man who had left me. What if he hadn't? What if something terrible had happened to him? While it wasn't the first time I wondered that, previous musings had always been through a thin veil of anger. Free of anger and resentment, I felt profoundly sad. I felt, for the first time, like a widow. Everything was upside down. Even if he hadn't left me, our marriage wasn't what I thought. I thought of the money, the probable affair, and all the ways in which I never knew Greg, how he had never let me know him. He had held himself hostage, a husband in law and practice only, emotionally checked out. His phony business trips. The Grand Del Mar, his apparent golf game. How could I memorialize someone I never knew?

Then, I thought of the girls. To keep my sanity, to not dissolve into bitter anger, I had to believe they knew Greg as a daddy, that to them, at least, he gave his entire self. Images of Greg the Dad flashed in my mind—Greg taking Hannah on a piggyback ride, rocking the newborn Leah in the middle of the night in the dimly lit nursery, teaching Hannah to play catch in the yard, letting them take turns on the riding mower while I watched nervously from the window. *The blades aren't running, Claire. I swear!* Yes, we could memorialize Greg, the father, and it would mean something.

It could very well mean everything.

⌒~∾૭ℭ∾~⌒

I arranged the memorial for the second Sunday in August, which also happened to be Greg's birthday. Pastor Joe agreed to give the service. I invited Mom, Dad, Drew, and Sarah. Some people from the community would show up, I knew—Melinda and Steve, some of Greg's old coworkers. The church congregation would be already there, as it was simply a service dedication. I asked my dad to speak, as I couldn't do it, and Greg had no close family. The Saturday prior to the service, I sat the girls down and told them that their daddy was in Heaven.

"Did the policeman find him?" Hannah asked.

"No, he didn't, sweetheart. But..." I faltered, unsure of how to continue. "It's the only thing that makes sense, Hannah. The police have all these alerts set up. So if Daddy used his credit card, or spent money, or really did anything, they would find him. And he hasn't. And you can't go this long without spending any money. He wouldn't be able to live anywhere or do anything. We've looked in hospitals all over, and we've had his picture up on the internet, on a special webpage for missing people."

"But what if he's not dead? What if he's hiding? Like Leah does, but bigger somehow?"

"That's okay, Hannah. Tomorrow, we're just going to talk about Daddy and how much we loved him. It's a special day to remember what a good daddy he was. And if he is hiding, and he comes home, we can tell him all about the day we had where we talked about how wonderful he was. Okay?"

She nodded uncertainly, and Leah mimicked the motion.

"The policeman is still going to look at those things I said earlier,

155

okay? His credit cards and spending money. We're not totally giving up, but it makes sense that Daddy is probably in Heaven." Their eyes were so heartbreaking, clouded with confusion, I couldn't look at them. Was I making things worse? There should be instructions for such an event. I had convinced myself that I couldn't screw up if I loved them enough, but what if I was wrong?

The day of the memorial service dawned unusually sunny and cool. Cloudless, the sky seemed too cheery, a day for flying kites or picnicking in the park, hiking through a forest or swimming in a lake, not for memorializing your *most likely* deceased husband.

As I lay in bed in the quiet of the morning, I had my own memorial for Greg. The girls needed the service, and to some extent, so did I. I needed the closure it could bring, the finality. I would get a label— *widow. Are you married? I'm a widow.* At least that sounded official, better than *sort of.*

As I lay in bed, I wondered how many of my memories were true? Memories were tricky that way. Time tinted perception, which altered the memory, bending it like light through a prism, until what a person remembered might only contain slivers of fact. The rest was just a colorful reflection of emotion—hope, denial, anger, fear. I knew our marriage hadn't been perfect, but like so many people with drifting marriages, I believed we had all the time in the world to figure it out. I believed we would be fine. When he said it was "work" or "stress," I bought it. Marriages ebbed and flowed. I never knew how little of Greg I had access to. I thought back to all the things we had never talked about.

That night with Drew, Greg had clearly heard us talking, heard Drew's anger. The words he repeated back the next day weren't a fluke. They were a hint. So why hadn't we talked about it? I had thought of Greg differently after that night. He always knew how Drew felt about me, aware of the undercurrent I'd inadvertently tried to suppress for years. Yet never once did he ask us to end our friendship. I wondered how long Greg had felt married to both Drew and me? I wondered how much of myself I had really given Greg. A part of my heart had always belonged to another man. Could I really be angry if Greg eventually gave part of himself to another woman?

Yet for ten years—two years of dating and seven of the eight years we were married— Greg had never seemed to falter in his dedication to me, our marriage, and our family. If we had talked, would things have been different? If he had asked me to temper back my friendship with Drew, how would I have reacted? I would have been angry, incredulous. *How could you? He's my best friend.* But would I have done it? To save my marriage? No. Without question. No. I wouldn't even have taken the suggestion seriously. Greg might have been my husband, but Drew was as necessary to my life as food or air.

In my mind, the truth dawned. So raw and bleeding, I couldn't accept it with my eyes open. Drew had *always* come first. He was there first. Simply, he was *loved* first. The failure of my marriage, if in fact it did fail, was *my* fault. Acknowledging that was the very least I could do for Greg on the morning of his memorial service. He may have stepped outside the marriage officially, and should that come to light, I could easily play the wounded party with believability. But in my core, deep down where it carried the most weight, I knew I never had both feet in our marriage from the beginning.

With a heavy heart, I got up and took a shower. It felt reminiscent of the days when Greg first disappeared, when I found it almost impossible to get out of bed. My feet were leaden, and my chest ached. Alone in the spray of water, in the quiet before the girls woke up, I sobbed for the last time that day.

When Pastor Joe had asked me if I wanted anything special at the memorial service, the only thing I specified was for my father to read some verses from Ecclesiastes. *Turn! Turn! Turn!* was Greg's favorite song. We been driving somewhere once, and the song came on the radio. He was singing the words, and I made a joke about how you'd think he grew up in the sixties.

I would have loved to live in the sixties!

Really? Why? So much insecurity. War, the civil rights movement, the Kennedy assassination, the Martin Luther King Jr. assassination. That's a lot of death for one decade. It would have been so sad.

Yeah, but a man on the moon, Kennedy elected, the war protests—people believed in what they did then. Instead of apathy or hopelessness, there was so much passion in the country. It was such a crazy time.

At the time, I thought it odd that Greg would ever use the word "passion" about anything. I dismissed him. I couldn't remember when that conversation took place. Years ago, I was sure. But the Bible quote the song was based on seemed apropos. *To everything there is a season, and a time to every purpose under the heaven: A time to be born, and a time to die...*

When Dad read, tears came to my eyes, but I couldn't cry. I thought of how Greg wouldn't see his girls grow up, go on a first date, go to the prom, graduate. He would never walk them down the aisle. I still couldn't cry. My self-realization that morning had shelled me, and I watched the service through invisible Plexiglas. The voices were muffled; the din of a crowded church was non-existent.

I had Leah on one side and Hannah on the other. Leah squirmed, and I did not scold. Hannah whispered to me, but I didn't answer her. As we filed out of the church, I was bombarded by people. Parishioners waiting to be able to *finally* offer their condolences, to officially acknowledge our newfound family of three, like an inverse marriage. Drew followed me and, as usual, understood without being told that I needed only his presence, not his words or his touch. I was gracious to the mourners. *Thank you for coming. It's so nice to see you. How's little Samantha doing?* After all, their relief was palpable. I had a label; I was Claire Barnes, a widow. *Her husband died mysteriously. Poor thing!* I had no reception after the service.

Mom, Dad, Sarah, and Drew came back to the house, and everyone went out of their way to be overtly happy, laughing and joking, playing with the kids. Sarah and Drew were happy to see each other again. They talked about city life, dating, and their lives, sharing war stories. I watched the scene unfold before me as though it took place in a Macy's window display at Christmas. *Death of a Husband.*

Later, Drew left to go back to the city, and Sarah went upstairs to take a nap. She thankfully planned to stay for the week. Under her tutelage, I hoped my drugged haze would go away. The memorial service had triggered a change in my mood, from anger and resolve to the true sadness of a mourning woman whose husband has tragically died, compounded by guilt that accompanied my morning insight into our marriage.

That evening, I went through the motions of the evening, dinner, bath, and bed. Sarah waited for me in the dimly lit living room. A glass of wine stood on the coffee table.

I sat next to her and put my head on her shoulder. "Thank you for coming today. Without you and Drew, I really don't know where I'd be. All I do is thank you two."

"That's because we're such great people." She smirked, swirling the wine in her glass. I smiled thinly. No, she wasn't going to let me wallow very long.

"Let's talk about Drew," she blurted.

"What about him?" I asked warily.

"What's going on there? With you two?"

"Sarah, really? Today was Greg's memorial service. Nothing about that question seems inappropriate to you?"

"Claire, come off it. You've been in mourning for a year now. You've run the whole gamut of emotions, some of which landed you in someone else's bed on the other side of the country. So let's not act like you just buried the man."

I sulked for a minute, then I caved. I knew Sarah. We could sit in silence all night; she always won.

"I don't know. I'm all over the map with Drew." I recounted the beach story. "I didn't want him to leave when he did. And then when I called him back and he sprang the Olivia thing on me, I was caught completely unaware."

"I think you're both afraid."

"Of what?"

"Of being anything more than friends. Your whole lives, you've had each other. If it doesn't work, you won't have anything anymore. You're both terrified."

"I think it's more complicated than that. Frankly, I'm scared of dating anyone right now. Drew would feel like the safest bet, I would think."

"What are you going to do when you have to meet his girlfriend?" she asked.

"The same thing he's been doing for the last ten years, I guess. Pretend." I didn't relish the thought. "I'm sure she's beautiful."

Sarah put her hand over her mouth and giggled. "Remember that one girlfriend in college? She was Austrian or something? What was her name?"

"Inga!" we said in unison. Yes, I remembered Inga, the Austrian model. Dumb as a Box of Rocks Inga. Yoga Instructor Inga. I hated her. Drew's guy friends made continuous infuriating comments about her bedroom prowess.

"What did you do to her again?" Sarah was looking upward, searching for the memory.

"I drew a mustache on her face at a party. She was half-passed out in the bathroom, and I used eyeliner."

Sarah dissolved into laughter. I could barely think about it. My face burned, not from guilt, but from humiliation. I never wanted to admit the effect Drew's love life had on me. He slowed down quite a bit in his old age, but his college years had been filled with women. Girls, really. Almost all of them were blondes, with a cumulative IQ significantly less than their nightly take at the Luscious Ladies gentleman's club. Yes, I was fairly sure that Olivia was beautiful. I hoped that I could manage to keep my eyeliner in my purse.

CHAPTER 25

SEPTEMBER BROUGHT TWO MAJOR MILESTONES. One should have been huge: Hannah's first day of kindergarten. But that event was usurped by the looming one-year anniversary at the end of the month. One full year without Greg.

When I put Hannah on the bus on the second of September and waved to her with one hand while blotting my eyes with a tissue with the other, I thought for the millionth time in the past year, *Her daddy should be here to see this.* I was quite used to the sentiment, sure that a milestone wouldn't pass when I wouldn't acknowledge Greg in some way.

I felt sentimental about the one-year mark. It was the anniversary of a horrific tragedy, but somehow, guiltily, I felt accomplished. I thought it was terrible, in a way, to feel any benefit from Greg's death, but I felt stronger, more sure of myself. I could clean a gutter! I could repair plumbing! I had learned a lot in the last year. *I am going to be okay.* Should Greg be there? Yes, without question. Did I wish things were different? Absolutely. But somehow, life went on. And I had come a long way from the sorrowful wreck of a woman who could barely get herself and her children dressed. I hadn't even sworn at a stranger in almost six months. So for that at least, I found a very small reason to celebrate.

I decided to acknowledge the anniversary on September twenty-eighth, the Tuesday that Greg left for his trip, the last day I had seen him. I didn't know the date he technically disappeared, or died, if we were going with the current theory.

The morning of September twenty-eighth dawned like every other morning. I got Hannah on the bus. I took Leah to the toddler gym and chatted with the other mothers while Miss Megan clapped her hands and directed all the children to circle time. But I was repeatedly jolted by memory. I found myself trying to remember what I had done last year at whatever exact time I had the thought. I couldn't. I could remember October first, that Friday when Greg didn't come home, but I had no memory of kissing my husband his last kiss goodbye. I was sure that I did kiss him goodbye; I always did. Later, I was struck by the fact that I couldn't remember our last words to each other. *I love you. Be safe.* That was what we always said. Try as I might, I could not specifically recall saying it.

I didn't remind Hannah and Leah about the anniversary. I went about the evening ritual, as if the day were like any other.

After I put them to bed, I sat in the living room with Greg's notebook and pen. I turned to the back of the book, where there were about twenty blank pages.

Dear Greg,

Today, I'm honoring you in my heart as you've been gone from our lives for one year. Not a day goes by that I don't think of you. Not a day goes by that I don't wonder what happened to you. I'm writing this to help with my never-ending quest for closure, and in the farfetched chance I ever see you again, may you read it and know how I felt.

First and foremost, I miss you. I miss your laugh. I miss our early mornings and our late nights and our private moments. Our marriage wasn't perfect, but I did believe that it was good. I have since learned that you kept things from me. Your inheritance. Apparently, you golf? You possibly had a girlfriend. You stayed at a lavish hotel together. I feel like a fool, naïve and trusting. For our marriage was so very dear to me and clearly not equally important to you. You held parts of yourself hostage, parts I never had access to. Because of that, I never really knew you. Which makes my whole life seem like a joke. For that, I am angry and may never forgive. I'll try.

The girls miss you. Even with all the things I am angry about, I cannot take away the fact that you were a wonderful father. Hannah has stopped asking for you daily. It was hard on Leah, but it's getting better. Our life is permanently altered now. And if it ever comes out that you chose this path, I will never forgive you.

I heal a little every day. I finally fixed the broken spindle in the banister. I replaced the doorknob in Hannah's room. I'm learning to do your household chores. It's tough work, being you and me at the same time, but I'm stronger than I ever imagined.

Love, Claire.

I opened one eye. Hannah stood at the foot of the bed, arms crossed in fury. I closed my eyes and prayed for it to be a dream. *Will I ever sleep past seven again?*

"Mommy, this is 'portant. Leah said that she wants to be Rapunzel, too. Today is trick or treat, and Leah's gonna ruin it. Wake up!"

"I'm awake, Han. I'm awake." I sat up and blinked. Geesh, the bedroom was a mess. "Well, Hannah, we have two Rapunzel dresses somewhere, I think, in the playroom. If Leah wants to be Rapunzel, too, I don't see why not."

"Because. The movie did *not* have *two* Rapunzels." She held up one finger an inch from my face. "It had *one* Rapunzel. And that's me. Because I have long blond hair, and Leah has curly brown hair. She can be Belle."

It was easily the fourth Halloween discussion that week.

"I am *not* Belle. I don't even *like* Belle. She wears ugly yellow. I want to be Rapunzel," Leah said from the doorway.

Hannah turned to her. "Leah, you are *the little sister*. You have to do what I tell you to do. And I say you have to be Belle."

I held up my hand. "Hannah, you know as well as I do that no one tells Leah what to do. Now listen. We have two trick or treat nights. One tonight here, and one tomorrow in Nanny and Pop-pop's neighborhood. You can be Rapunzel tonight, and Leah can be Rapunzel tomorrow."

"But—" two voices cried in unison.

"That's it. Take it or leave it," I commanded.

They filed out of the bedroom, angry at each other, but angrier at me. Newly joined in solidarity against a common enemy, they huddled in Hannah's room. I heard whispering. Swinging my legs over the side of the bed, I looked at the clock. Six thirty. *Good grief.*

That evening, I escorted two Rapunzels up and down the neighborhood streets. I made small talk with the neighbors and visited briefly with Robin and Rob Masters who, prior to Greg's memorial service, I hadn't seen in months.

"How are you holding up?" Robin asked, pouring me a cup of hot apple cider.

I shrugged. "Better every day," I said truthfully.

Robin and Rob had no children, but were about ten years older than I was. I never knew if they couldn't conceive or if they chose not to. They seemed to love children. I heard Hannah in the living room, explaining hers and Leah's costumes to Rob.

"I am Rapunzel, and this is Rapunzel's little sister," she said proudly.

"Oh, wow!" Rob exclaimed. "What is her name?"

"Rapunzel!" Leah replied, indignant.

I smiled at their ingenious solution.

"I can't imagine, Claire. I'm so sorry for this year. I know I've said it to you a few times, but if you ever need anything, we're always here."

I did know that, and I appreciated it. I briefly wondered why Greg and I hadn't become closer to the Masters than just sharing friendly neighborhood banter. We should have done dinners, picnics, or neighborly things. I made a mental note to try harder, to connect. *Small ripples.* So many things seemed like small ripples, minor effects of Greg's disappearance.

We drank our apple cider, traded small talk, and then waved goodbye as the girls and I continued on the very important business of Trick-or-Treating.

CHAPTER 26

SUCKED IT UP AND MADE plans to visit Drew the second weekend in November. I got the girls all hyped up to spend the night at Nanny and Pop-pop's and dropped them off Saturday afternoon.

I took the train from Annandale into Manhattan, where Drew would pick me up. I hadn't seen him since the memorial service and had only spoken to him once. Our friendship had changed over the past year. I didn't know if it was because I had needed him so much or because Greg was technically no longer in the picture. Our past few encounters had fallen into one of two categories: fraught with tension, or formal and distant.

I wondered what the evening would bring. I wondered what Olivia would be like. I hoped he was alone when he picked me up. My stomach lurched as I thought about seeing Drew with a woman. Maybe once, years ago, he had brought someone to dinner. I vaguely remembered her. How had Drew dealt for ten-plus years?

When I walked up the steps to the terminal at Penn Station, Drew stood right where he texted me he'd be—in front of the Au Bon Pain. I studied him in the few seconds before he saw me. He looked wonderful—tall and dark, open-faced, and friendly. He shifted his weight from one foot to the other, scanning the crowd. His eyes caught mine, and he broke into a wide grin and waved. When he hugged me, my heart thudded. *This is ridiculous*, I scolded. Drew was my best friend. He was seeing someone, seriously enough to want us to meet. He'd been watching me with Greg for years. I needed to calm down, but I didn't know how. He smelled like Drew, soap and shampoo, like home to me. What had I been thinking? *This is going to be impossible.*

"Hi," he said, ducking his head almost shyly. "You look great, Claire. I'm so glad you're here."

"Me too. I need a night out. I need you, actually." I put my head on his shoulder.

He gave me a quick squeeze. "Well, let's go. Wait till you see my apartment!" He led me through the crowd and to the street. We hailed a taxi.

"I can't believe you live in Harlem!" I also couldn't believe we were taking a taxi a hundred blocks. Drew must be rich.

"Stop, it's not like it used to be. The crime in southwest Harlem is incredibly low. When was the last time you went into the city? The eighties?"

I stared out the window, watching the city go by, like a silent movie running at the wrong speed. Traffic was surprisingly light. The opulence of the Upper West Side melded into rundown row homes of Morningside Heights. We turned on 119th Street, and the row homes faded into beautiful brownstones with sculpted steps and ornate front doors. The cab stopped, and Drew got out. The tree-lined street boasted historic and stately homes.

"These are gorgeous!" I exclaimed.

"See? And you doubted me." He grinned evilly.

His apartment was huge by New York standards, with hardwood floors and a large, elaborate fireplace. The kitchen was small, but he had two reasonably sized bedrooms—*two bedrooms. Unheard of!* The living room and dining room were one open room separated by a display of ten different-sized stained-glass windows hanging from chains, with smaller ones hanging from each to create a faux wall. Some had ornate, bursting lilies and roses in a kaleidoscope pattern, and others were simpler, alternating square patterns in basic colors, reminiscent of old New Jersey farmhouses. Light flooded around the frames, and the prism effect created hypnotic dancing spots of light throughout the room.

"Drew, did you do this? It's beautiful!"

He shrugged. "I needed a divider between the rooms, and walls are so last year, you know?"

I laughed. I had only been to one or two of Drew's previous apartments. His living area was clean, with a surprising sense of style. I briefly remembered what Greg's bachelor pad had looked like—all utility, simple furniture and faux wood. Drew's had flair—a small sculpture, a tray of sand and marbles on the coffee table, not a Yankee candle in sight. Very chic. Clearly, the handmade art was all one of kind, not chain store accessorized, like my own house.

When I said as much, he laughed. "Well, Claire, I *am* an artist. Which reminds me. Guess what we're doing tonight?"

"What?"

"We're going to a gallery opening." My jaw dropped. I had brought nothing to wear to an event like that.

"Don't panic. It's just a one-room gallery a few blocks over. They're showing my collection. Remember the one I told you about, with the lunchtime affairs?"

I nodded. How could I forget?

"It's called *Illicit*. Please don't say no. I want you to see it." His took my hand, his touch sent pulsing jolts up my arms, curling my toes.

"What do I wear?" I asked, slowly withdrawing my hand. My eyes held his for a beat.

"Anything you want. It's a small reception, probably less than twenty people. But it's the art world. Everyone dresses crazy. You'll be fine. Don't worry. And besides, you're going with me, and I'm the star of the evening." He performed a deep bow, tipping an imaginary hat.

I went to his guest room to unpack and figure out what to wear. I had packed the wrap dress Sarah had raved about in San Diego, but it looked so *Mom-ish*. I pulled out a pair of black leggings and a black boat-neck glitter sweater. The outfit was fashionable and not me at all. I had taken it off of a mannequin at a store where I had never shopped before because the shop was out-of-my-league trendy. I put the ensemble on in front of the mirror and could barely believe my reflection. I added a pair of pointy-toed flats and shyly opened the door.

Drew was relaxing on the couch, flipping through a magazine. He whistled when he saw me. "Claire, you have seriously changed your style!" He motioned for me to turn around. "I hardly recognize you. It's like you're one of my friends or something!"

I swatted at him, then dug through my purse for a mint. When I looked up, I met his gaze, his eyes reflecting desire and regret at once. For a moment, I wished I hadn't come.

He recovered so quickly, I wondered if I actually saw anything at all. "Come on. Let's go. I can't wait to show you off. I'm pretty sure all my friends think I've made you up." He put his arm around my shoulder, hugging me to him. We paused in the doorway, and he moved a piece of hair away from my face. I inhaled sharply, waiting. "I hope you like the photographs, Claire. I'm sorry if I offended you with the topic. But the truth is, somehow, I couldn't stop myself."

His gaze was so intense, I only half-listened. Things had shifted with me. Drew was no longer my closest friend when I was in need. Somehow, he had become an amazing, beautiful man. The longing was astounding. I've been denied by him so frequently in my life, I couldn't bring myself to initiate even a kiss. My insides twisted at the thought.

I stepped back and glanced at the wall across the room. "Listen, don't worry about it. It's fine." I smiled up at him with false bravado and kissed his cheek. "I can't wait to see them."

Then, I walked through the door and into the hall, deliberately breaking the spell. He followed, locking the door behind him. When he faced me again, we were back to Drew and Claire, the way things used to be, which was still sort of in-between.

The gallery looked like a regular brownstone, except the entire first floor had been converted to a one-room art showcase. As Drew had predicted, about twenty people were milling around, and when we walked in the door, Drew was greeted by a round of applause. He repeated his dramatic bow, then ran his hand through his hair, scratching at his neck nervously.

He grasped my hand. "Everyone, this is Claire Barnes. If you know me well enough, you've heard a lot about her. Be nice to her." He lowered his voice to a stage whisper. "She's from the *suburbs.*"

Titters of laughter followed his comment. *Nice. Thanks, Drew.* I was handed a bowl-like glass of merlot. Drew's friends seemed accommodating and kind, not what I'd expected from city artists. I had prepared myself for condescension, even scorn.

One of the most beautiful women I'd ever seen sidled up to Drew and kissed his cheek. She was tall, practically six feet, with olive skin and a dark tangle of formed curls highlighted red and blond. Chic beyond belief. Model thin, with the elegance to match, she gave me an inclusive, radiant smile. "Darling, you should hear what people said before you got here. I've heard people say 'buyers' already." Her voice was silky with an unidentifiable accent.

He raised his eyebrows at her and turned to me. "Claire, meet Olivia."

My heart sank. Her? She was *the* Olivia? I expected blond. I expected giggly and girlish, with unrealistic breast implants. I did not expect the most fantastic woman I'd ever laid eyes on. My leggings and sweater felt as sophisticated as Leah's footie pajamas.

"Claire, so nice to meet you. You can't imagine how much I've heard about you. It's like I know you already." She leaned in and, instead of shaking my hand, hugged me, enveloping me in Chanel No. 5. *Of course, what else? Was I even wearing perfume?*

All I could smell was the light baby fragrance of my hair. I'd run out of shampoo that morning and had to use Leah's. *Real sexy, Claire.* She linked her arm through mine and dragged me away from Drew. I looked back at him, and he shrugged as if to say, *I don't know. Have fun!*

"Have you seen his photos yet?" Olivia asked.

I shook my head. I had yet to speak. I *couldn't* speak.

"He's so worried about you. He thinks you're going to hate him when you do." She stopped and turned to me. "There are six photos behind you, arranged in a collection. I'll leave you to look at them and come back to get you." She disappeared into the small crowd. *This woman is very, very good,* I thought.

I turned and gazed at the display. My first impression: *These are beautiful.* Every picture captured complete vulnerability. Every photo portrayed the man's complete love and adoration for the woman beside him. The emotion was open and apparent in every shot. Some shots were in profile, while others were full facial, or wide-angle close-ups. The women were in various positions and with a variety of responses. One was on her blackberry, ignoring her lunch date. One was returning the passionate expression. One photo seemed to be of a kiss a fraction of a second before it happened—eyes closed, lips parted. The photos were completely raw and human. And yes, they did appear to be affairs. In one picture, the woman was furtively looking over her shoulder. The expressions so sensual, I found it hard to believe the couples were married. *Married couples don't look at each other like that. Do they?*

"What do you think?" Drew asked from behind me. "I've been watching you, but you haven't moved for five minutes. I couldn't wait any longer." I turned, and he looked nervous.

"Oh, Drew, they're breathtaking. They're amazing! I can't believe you took these."

"You're not mad?"

"No, not at all. This has nothing to do with me. These are beautiful. They're almost hard to look at because they're so... graphic. Not sexually, but raw human emotion boiled down to a single moment in time. And you captured that. These people were going about their day, meeting their spouses for lunch, and you snapped the shutter at the right moment to capture a whole life's emotion in one shot. It's crazy." I shook my head. "I'm explaining this terribly."

"No, you're saying it wonderfully. Thank you." He hugged me.

I rested my cheek on his chest, relaxing into the embrace, our bodies connecting down to our toes. His breathing quickened ever so slightly, but enough for me to detect it. For a split second, he pulled me closer, and I concentrated on the cadence of his heart. I imagined it speeding up, or maybe it wasn't my imagination. Matching my breathing to his, I watched his neck as he swallowed. *What if I kissed it? Right here?*

We broke apart, and he held my gaze for a second longer before we were interrupted by someone asking a question about the pictures. Drew's eyes found mine, saying... what? *I'm sorry?*

He introduced me to the person, then they made small talk. I looked around the room and spotted Olivia. She moved effortlessly from group to group, each clique opening to let her in immediately. She circulated and laughed, her hand on an arm, even a cheek—*Who does that?*—flirting with men and women alike, bestowing her light on everyone equally. She reminded me of Sarah, but even Sarah didn't shine that brilliantly.

She caught me looking, came over, and squeezed my hand. "What did you think?"

I realized that her eyes were different colors. The right one was a deep blue, almost purple, exotic in its own right, while the left one was green. The effect was mesmerizing.

"The pictures? They're amazing. Of course I'm not mad! I don't know why he would think I would be."

"That's what I told him. He is such a wonderful photographer." She gazed fondly across the room and gave Drew a little wave.

He waved back, his expression unreadable. For lack of things to do, I downed my merlot.

The rest of the evening passed quickly. I drank about three more large glasses of wine. Olivia doted on me like a mother hen. *Do you have*

enough to drink? Have you tried the appetizers? The canapés are amazing.
After the last of the gallery patrons had left, all that remained were
Drew, Olivia, me, and the owners, John and James, waiting to lock up
for the night.

"Drinks?" Olivia suggested.

Drew looked to me for an answer. It was almost midnight. I really
just wanted to sleep, but I gave a noncommittal shrug.

"Maybe one," Drew acquiesced.

We walked about five blocks to a pub, which surprised me. I would
have thought a martini bar or a trendy nightclub would be more their
speed. The place was dimly lit, a jukebox in the back played loud Janis
Joplin, and the bar spanned the entire right side. Booths and tables
peppered the back, heavy oak, nicked with years of use and abuse.

We sat in a booth, Drew and Olivia on one side, me on the other. I
felt out of place and awkward.

Olivia was bursting with excitement. She kissed Drew's cheek,
leaving a tiny remnant of sticky shine, like a small brand. "I'm so
thrilled. That was incredible!" Her arm linked through his, and he
looked equally excited.

"I know. I can't believe all the comments I received." He flushed
with pride. "Thank you so much for everything you did."

I almost replied, "You're welcome," but realized just in time
that he hadn't been talking to me. Of course not. What had I done?
Nothing. I showed up.

He gazed at Olivia with an expression I had seen on his face a
hundred times, a mixture of love, lust, and adoration.

I stood up unsteadily and excused myself to the bathroom. I stood
in front of the cracked mirror, took deep breaths. *Get a grip. Drew's
been watching me with Greg for years.* How many times had I kissed Greg
or told him I loved him in front of Drew? A million. I was instantly
sorry. *This is what Drew felt.*

I returned to the table, smiling as brilliantly as I could muster. *I
would have to fake this. Somehow.* Drew and Olivia were bent together,

heads touching, talking softly. I sat down, cleared my throat, and looked away.

Olivia stood up, leaned over, and kissed my cheek. "Claire, it was so wonderful to finally meet you. Can we all do lunch tomorrow before you go?"

"Sure, but are you leaving? Why?"

"I think you two need to catch up, and besides, I've been up since seven helping plan the opening. I'm exhausted."

"Well, it was nice to meet you. Great job on the reception, I think. I've never been to a gallery opening before."

She gave a small wave and was gone, out the door and swallowed into the New York streets.

I turned to Drew. "Was it something I said?"

"No, not at all. I think she just knew we needed some time together. She's... like that. She knows what you need without asking, it's so weird..." He gazed toward the door.

"You love her." I hadn't intended on saying it or even talking about Olivia. The words just came out.

He nodded. "I think I do." His eyes searched mine. "I was more sure before today."

"Why today?" It was a question with a known answer, unfair really.

He raked a hand through his hair. "You. Always you, Claire. My whole life..." He twirled the half-empty mug of his beer around in his hands, not making eye contact. "And now, here you are. Somewhat available. For the first time in our lives. But somehow, I'm not..."

I realized I was holding my breath. "What do you want, Drew?" I asked finally, watching my oldest friend wrestle with his emotions. I knew every line of his face, the curve of his jaw, every smile. I realized how unfair life had been to him, at least when it came to love. How unfair *I'd* been to him.

His eyes met mine, and his smile was wry. "I have no idea. For as long as I can remember, I've wanted only one thing. And now, I love two women. And even more unbelievably, two women seem to love me." He gave me a look then: *Am I reading this right?*

I studied the marred table surface and then nodded slowly, meeting his eyes. My heart hammered. He shook his head once and smiled wryly. *Figures.*

We sat for a while, silent and consumed with our own thoughts, surely similar, but both of us unable or unwilling to vent them. Finally, he motioned for the waitress and paid the tab.

We walked back to his apartment in oddly comfortable silence. I linked my arm through his and wondered how our friendship had bounced back and forth across the line, and *yet*, we still felt so easy. I decided the answer was because he was Drew, because I could say anything to him, and he would always be there. He had been there for me, regardless of what it cost him, all my life. Had I ever repaid him? No, not likely.

I was struck with a sudden strong urge to go home, to do something, for the first time, for my old friend. I could leave him alone and let him love another woman, a woman so fantastic that she'd left him alone with me, his unrequited love.

Surely, she knew about us. Even if he had never explicitly told her, she was too savvy not to see it, plain in front of her face. She was also too smart to want a man who wanted someone else. I realized then that her leaving us alone was a way to ferret out who he really loved, and I smiled. In another lifetime, I would have liked being friends with Olivia.

When we got back to Drew's apartment, I kissed him on the cheek and turned to go into the guest room. He grabbed my elbow and pulled me to him, his face inches from mine. His breath, hot on my neck, sent chills down my spine.

"Drew, think about it first, okay?" I pulled away. "Don't throw away what you have. Be sure of what you want." Gently, I disengaged his hand from my arm and walked into the guest room. I shut the door behind me and leaned against it. I heard him go into his room and close the door.

I got into bed and slept fitfully. I waited for the creaking door, the soft pad of footsteps. I wondered if he slept any better than I did. When the first light of the morning shone in my window, a quicksilver of pink and gold, I got up and packed. I found an envelope and a pen in the kitchen and wrote a quick note:

Figure out what will make you happy and do it. For once in your life, do something for you, not me.

I slipped out the front door, into the streets of New York. Oddly for a place known as "the city that never sleeps," the streets were deserted. I hailed a cab to Penn Station and hopped the first train to Annandale.

I cried the entire way home.

CHAPTER 27

THAT YEAR, I COOKED THANKSGIVING dinner in its entirety. Mom and Dad came over, and I invited Rob and Robin Masters. Surprisingly, they didn't have plans and happily accepted. I did not call Drew, and he did not call me. The evening felt festive, hopeful.

I thought of Greg a few times, recalling past Thanksgivings. Specifically, the year he had insisted on deep-frying a turkey. Mom was skeptical, but he swore it was the absolute juiciest turkey. He started at three in the afternoon, and at nine o'clock, we were *finally* sitting down to eat. He cut into the bird along the breast bone, and the inside shone white with a touch of pink. Mom looked as if she might cry. He ran to the closest grocery store and bought four leathery rotisserie chickens. He cut them up and presented them on the turkey platter, smothered in Mom's gravy. We almost didn't know the difference. Almost.

I recounted the story at the dinner table, and Hannah seemed to delight in the memory, although she couldn't have been more than a year old. *I have to bring him up more,* I thought. *Let her talk about him, let her remember him.*

With Thanksgiving over, I began preparations for Christmas, our second without Greg. I didn't count on Drew coming. I hadn't heard from him since the gallery opening. I was sad about that, but not overly so. I didn't doubt that we'd still be friends. We just needed time, and I had tons of that.

The first week in December, we went to the tree farm, something we used to do as a foursome. I let Leah pick the tree and told Hannah she could pick it the next year. I made Christmas lists and decorated the house. I even dug out all the Christmas CDs and sang with the girls.

Mom watched the kids while I trekked back to the mall. I was reminded of the previous year's trip, and for the millionth time, I was content with how far I'd come in the past year. There would be no overabundance of toys and no Drew to distract us. In some ways, Christmas could very well be harder.

I pushed the cart up and down the aisles of the toy store. Hannah wanted another Barbie. She'd also asked for a Wii. Greg had always been adamantly against video games. But I had researched age-appropriate games and decided I could set limits. The Wii, at least, had active games that involved jumping around and dancing. I purchased the game console, a combined gift for both girls, and a game for each. I added a few small things for their stockings and paid just under two hundred dollars, drastically different from last year's spending spree. We were back to normal, a new kind of normal. I drove home and stashed the gifts in my bedroom closet. I would wrap them on Christmas Eve, only a few short days away.

December's visit with Detective Reynolds came a week before Christmas, our last meeting before we started our semi-annual meetings. Hannah was at school in the morning, and I settled Leah in front of the *Mickey Mouse Clubhouse* while I made coffee.

Matt was fifteen minutes late, but I forgave him when he handed me a brown paper bag, the scent of sugar and cream drifting up as soon as I unfolded the top. He settled at the kitchen table and opened the file he usually brought with him to review latest developments with me. I had always thought it pathetically thin. It looked almost... thick.

True to form, he did not mince words. "Claire, there's been a development."

My heart thudded. I sat in a chair across from him and stared at the file.

"I don't beat around the bush, so I'm going to start the story and tell it to the end. You can interrupt if you have questions, but try to wait until I'm done, okay?"

I nodded. I glanced at Leah sitting on the floor in the living room, absorbed in the television.

"About a year ago, a car went into the Onondaga Lake. Do you know where that is?"

I shook my head.

"It's north of Syracuse, New York, about an hour and a half drive from Rochester. Two people were in the car, a woman and a man. A few months ago, I began researching unidentified deceased males in a concentric pattern around Rochester. I had a few leads, but none of them panned out. Eventually we identified them all, except for the passenger in this car. Their bodies were found about three months ago, in the car at the bottom of the lake. The police were trolling the lake for a teenage girl missing from the Syracuse area, believed to have drowned. They found the car at the bottom. The lake is sixty-five feet at its deepest. It was a rental car, leased to a woman named..." He consulted his file. "Melissa Richards. Does that name sound familiar to you?"

"No, I've never heard it before."

"Basically, they located two pelvic bones held in place by seatbelts and the crushed car. There was a femur and a tibia found in the car, but no other bones. They believe the driver was a woman and the passenger was a man, based on the width of the pelvic bones. Do you have any questions so far?"

"What happened to the rest of the bones?" I asked, curious as to how two whole skeletons could just disappear.

He coughed and looked down at the file. "When the car went into the lake, the passenger broke the window, trying to get out, which had to have happened prior to the car sinking, otherwise, the pressure would be too great. Apparently, neither could get out of their seatbelts, so they drowned." He averted his eyes as he said the last words. "And the Onondaga Lake is unique in that it is the fastest flushing natural lake in the United States, about four or five times in a heavy rainfall year. The lake discharges into the Seneca River and the water eventually ends up in Lake Ontario. So with that depth, and that level of water exchange, we wouldn't expect to find intact skeletons nine months after they were submerged." He spoke in a clinical voice, devoid of emotion.

I pushed images of Greg in a sinking car out of my mind. I thought back to the hairbrush and other personal items of Greg's that the police had taken from the house. "What about DNA?" I read the news, and knew they could do amazing things with bones.

"Normally, yes, we could work on that, but contrary to what you see in the movies, it's nearly impossible to extract a viable DNA sample from bones that have been underwater for almost a year. So we went back to Melissa Richards. Richards had been reported as missing around the same time as your husband, and her case was closed a month ago when it was concluded that she was in the car. She was from Syracuse. Did Greg have any connection to Syracuse at all that you can think of?"

I shook my head. "Nothing other than the obvious connection to Rochester."

"I've been working with the Syracuse police, and they've dissected every avenue of Richards's life. We looked into boyfriends, family members, and friends. There is no other person in her life that would be an obvious candidate for the passenger. She was last seen alone."

"Matt," I began finally, not exactly sure what I was going to ask with the questions tumbling fast and furious over each other in my mind. "Do you really believe Greg was in the car with her?"

"It's worth considering," he replied heavily. "But I don't know that we'll ever know for sure."

After Detective Reynolds left, I called Mom and relayed the whole conversation.

"How are you? Are you okay?" she asked.

"Yeah, I'm okay. I'm just so tired of it. I had the memorial. I need him to be dead in my mind. Isn't that terrible? That's awful. I can't think about it anymore. I am so sick of wondering where he is, and this isn't any better. It's not any closer really to having a definitive answer. As far as I can tell, they aren't going to be able to prove it's him. So I'm not actually any better off."

"What does Detective Reynolds think?"

"He never says what he thinks. He just says what he can or can't prove. I'm so frustrated. I need this year to be over."

"Do you want me to come over?" Mom asked.

"No. I need to go meet the bus in an hour or so anyway. Thanks for listening."

We hung up, and I checked on Leah before going upstairs to Greg's study. I braced myself for the smell as I opened the door, but it seemed to have dissipated and didn't hit me as hard. I grabbed his brown leather journal and went back downstairs to sit at the island in the kitchen so I could keep an eye on Leah.

Slowly turning every page, I looked for any reference to a Melissa or MR or Syracuse. Nothing. I studied the note *Call Karen at Omni S.D.* When had it been written? I tried to figure it out based on the location in the book, but it was jotted sideways, so if he couldn't be bothered to turn the book upright, then would he have made sure to turn to the next available page? No, probably not. On the next page of the book, "2009 Resolutions" had been written and underlined twice. If the chronology was to be believed, *Call Karen* was written sometime in late 2008 or early 2009. I didn't think that was likely if Karen was the mystery woman. Our marriage was great in early 2009. No, I believed the note had been jotted on the backside of a randomly opened page, sideways, in a hurry.

I reread all the pages. Some comments were still endearing. Others were more puzzling. *I carry your heart with me. I carry it in my heart.* A line from a poem, maybe? And jotted next to it was "C!" which may have been intended for me. But Greg hadn't liked poetry much. *Or at least the Greg I knew didn't.* I felt a pang of tenderness. I wish I had known the real Greg. He had held everything close to the vest, protected. *What were you protecting yourself from, Greg?* I closed the book and got Leah ready to go pick up Hannah from the bus stop.

CHAPTER 28

WE AWOKE ON CHRISTMAS EVE morning to discover an unexpected snowstorm had hit Clinton. Almost ten inches of snow had fallen, and the grass and trees were covered in a marshmallow blanket that evoked Christmas spirit. Among the clamoring of high voices, I dug out snow suits and boots from the previous year—too tight all around, but good enough for one day.

After building a lopsided snowman and having a snowball fight that ended in tears—because with a three-year-old, most activities involved some tears—we retired in the comfort of the living room with mugs of hot cocoa. We hunkered down for the evening and played Memory and Candy Land.

When darkness fell, we all dozed in the living room, watching *A Charlie Brown Christmas*. I carried both girls up to bed. I watched them as they smiled in their sleep, dreaming of Christmastime magic, Santa, reindeer, and candy canes. *As perfect a day as I could ask for.* With Christmas music softly playing in the background, I lugged all the presents downstairs and wrapped them—brightly colored packages under a lit Christmas tree.

For the first time, I was alone on a Christmas Eve. I curled up on the couch, with the music and the lit tree, and sipped a glass of wine while I reflected on the year. Just as I was about to call it a night and head to bed, I heard a soft knock. Thinking I was imagining things, I waited. I heard it again. Someone was definitely knocking on the door.

I tiptoed down the hall and peered through the peephole. Drew stood on the porch, his hands in his pockets, staring at his shoes.

I opened the door. "Drew! What are you doing here?"

He stepped over the threshold and gently, unexpectedly, his hands curved around my jaw, and his lips crushed to mine. My mouth opened automatically. He pulled me to him, running his hands down my arms, then around my back. He shifted his weight and pushed me back against the door jamb. The desire swelled up in me so fast I couldn't contain it and let out a sharp gasp. He pushed my sweater up, cupped my breasts, then trailed his fingers down my stomach. I couldn't keep track of his hands. He kissed my neck, then sank to his knees and kissed my stomach. He stopped and rested his head against the top of my jeans. We were both breathing heavily, and my hands were immersed in his thick hair. I caught my breath and knelt on the floor in front of him.

"There is only one woman in my life, Claire." His face was hopeful, filled with love, anticipation.

I kissed him, my ears thundering. I felt a release I had never felt, even with Greg. Everything about him felt different from Greg, as if I'd come home. He tipped my head and kissed my lips gently.

I stood up and led him into the living room, where I poured him a glass of wine with shaky hands. We sat on the couch on opposite ends of the couch, facing each other.

"What—"

"How—"

We spoke at the same time and laughed self-consciously. He nodded for me to go first.

"Why did you come back? What happened? What does this mean?"

The lights from the Christmas tree twinkled in his eyes as he smiled shyly. "I tried, Claire. I did. After you left, I talked myself into believing it was for the best. I needed to be with someone, to be focused on someone other than you. For once in my life. And Olivia... she was great. We were great... but she knew. She knew before I did. She broke it off last week."

"Are you here because she broke it off?" I asked, offended.

"No... no." He sighed. "I'm here because she was smart enough to do what was best for me when I couldn't."

"What do you want?" I was thinking of his life in the city and my life in the suburbs. *It can't actually work. Can it?* Was love enough? I envisioned Olivia in Drew's world. She knew the people, the politics. I was an outsider, figuratively and geographically. My life was about *Sesame Street* and preschool. I knew nothing of art shows and gallery openings.

He bridged the gap between us on the couch and touched my hand. "I want you. In my life. Every day. I have wanted that for as long as I can remember."

We laced our fingers together, and I studied our hands. I knew Drew's hands as well as my own—long, thin fingers with large knuckles, hands that fixed things, hands that kept me from falling during every rough spot in my life. He pulled me toward him.

I leaned against him. We were going down a path both of us had only dreamed about. I unbuttoned his shirt and slowly explored his chest and stomach with my hands. I leaned forward to kiss him. I heard his sharp intake of breath as I worked the button on his jeans. I stood and pulled my sweater up over my head, then worked my jeans down over my hips. I straddled him, taking him inside me in one smooth motion.

We moved together, languidly and unhurried, relishing the moment for which we had both waited so long. I gazed in his eyes as we climaxed.

He whispered, "I love you."

I love you, too, my heart responded.

I woke up on Christmas morning, wrapped in Drew's arms on the living room couch, covered with a fleece, holiday-themed throw. I prodded Drew awake, then kissed him, thinking for the first time how fantastic it felt to be able to do that. *Like something I never knew that I always wanted to do.*

"Get up," I whispered, giggling.

"What? Why?" He struggled to sit up, rubbing the sleep from his eyes.

"Because if we don't put clothes on soon, the girls are going to really have a memorable Christmas."

He grinned. "I think we can safely call this a memorable Christmas." He leaned forward to kiss my neck.

I reluctantly pushed him away. "Go. Clothes. *Now.* We've got maybe five minutes." Pulling the blanket up over me, I ran on tiptoe as quietly as I could up the stairs and into my bedroom.

I changed into pajamas and was back downstairs mere minutes before the clattering of little feet thundered down the stairs. The girls stopped abruptly when they saw Drew.

"Santa brought us Drew," I told them.

They squealed with delight, jumping on his lap simultaneously. Drew mimicked their exuberance until the cacophony in the living room became so great that I held two fingers to my mouth and whistled. Everyone stopped and looked at me.

"She really ruins everything, right?" Drew whispered to Hannah.

She nodded seriously. *No fun at all,* she mouthed back.

"Okay, it's Christmas. Santa brought Drew, but he also brought some presents. And I need coffee. And breakfast. What do you want to do first?" I asked with mock seriousness.

"Presents!" they shouted.

"Presents *after* coffee," I corrected.

They wiggled with anticipation as they sat in front of the tree, waiting for me to bring in the coffee. I sat on the opposite end of the couch from Drew. He touched my hand lightly as I passed him his coffee. *Distracting electricity.* I couldn't reconcile our previous night's activities with my life that included the girls. While everyone opened their presents, I found my mind wandering to the night before—his tentative, but soft touch, his almost shy expression, as though the moment could vanish in a puff of smoke. And I blushed, realizing Drew was watching me. He gave me a sly smile. I'd forgotten how easily he could read my face, my mind. I had no secrets from Drew. My emotions were an open book to him, written in a language that only he knew. *Yes, this is going to be different.*

The girls were thrilled at the Wii and begging Drew to hook it up for them immediately. They played in their pajamas until my parents came over at one o'clock.

"Drew!" Mom exclaimed. "What are you doing here?"

"Oh, I thought I'd come by for some Christmas ham."

We were apparently on the same page. I wasn't sure how or when to tell my parents that I may or may not have a... a boyfriend. The word sounded so juvenile. How does a grown woman, an apparent widow, acquire a *boyfriend*? Was there some other more socially acceptable word? Lover was too ridiculous. Partner was too... politically correct.

Mom looked thrilled to see him and patted his cheek affectionately. He winked at me.

She carried the ham in a roasting pan covered in cellophane. "I'm going to pop this in," she said.

Dad joined the girls in the living room, where Hannah was anxious to show him her new toys. Throughout the evening, I kept catching Drew's eye, and he would wink or smile. I found myself wondering if he was really content playing house with someone else's kids, in the suburbs. He looked at me with such apparent love that I quickly quelled the thought. When we passed in the kitchen, he touched my hand. Or my shoulder. Or once, he discreetly patted my butt, causing my knees to turn to jelly.

After dinner, Mom and I sent the kids and the men to living room while we cleaned up the dinner dishes.

"How long has this been going on?" she asked.

Or maybe not so discreetly. "What?" I asked, trying to sound innocent.

"You *know* what. Careful here, Claire. I want you to be happy;

you've been through so much. But you're not alone in this, and those kids are fragile. They've had a rough year." She was drying a dish, avoiding eye contact. Her words were true and tough, but her voice was gentle. I remained silent, choosing to neither confirm nor deny. "And I also believe that man has been in love with you all his life. Make sure you know what you're doing, or there will be four broken hearts in this house."

I nodded. *Message understood.* She kissed my cheek and joined my family in the living room amidst shouts and squeals of laughter as Hannah and Drew competed in Wii bowling.

I couldn't remember a happier Christmas.

CHAPTER 29

"HANNAH! LEAH! LET'S GO!"

"Seriously, leaving the house in a reasonable amount of time isn't a thing that happens," I muttered. Macaroni salad, juice boxes, a half-eaten bag of hot dogs—just in case—and goldfish crackers all went into the soft-sided cooler. *Where did I put my camera?* I opened the cabinet I usually kept it in and groaned in frustration.

"Relax." Drew put his arm around my waist. He lifted my hair and kissed the back of my neck. "You are way too stressed about this."

"It's our first outing together. As a couple. With all of my old friends. I'm so nervous."

"I should be nervous, not you. Do I look nervous?"

I shook my head. No. Drew was never nervous.

"Do you know where I put the birthday present?" I asked.

"It's in the car. Please. Stop." He pulled me to him and kissed my lips.

My mouth opened, and he gently pushed me against the counter. My knees weakened. *This is unnatural. How easily he can do this to me. How it hasn't faded, even a little.*

He pulled away. "See? I relaxed you!" He smirked.

"You did something to me, all right. Now, please be helpful. Can you go get Hannah and Leah and drag them down here? It's Hannah's best friend's birthday. You'd think we wouldn't be the last ones there."

He laughed as he walked down the hall. His long legs covered the distance in less than five steps, and he was up the stairs in a matter of seconds.

"We're having a race!" His loud booming voice echoed off the foyer walls. "The first person, myself included, to get in the car, strapped in, and ready to go to the party will be allowed to go on the swings first at Annie's house. On your mark, get set, *go!*"

Three sets of footsteps, two light, one heavy, thundered down the steps. Within a minute, everyone was in the van, frantically buckling seatbelts.

After tossing the cooler in the trunk, I jumped into the driver's seat and turned the key.

"You like?" he asked, grinning.

"Yes, I like. Although a race down the steps? Probably not the best idea..."

He shrugged. "You never like my methods, yet you don't mind the success rate. Besides, I totally won that race."

"Uncle Drew didn't win. I did." Hannah pouted.

"Just call him Drew, Hannah." I had been trying to get the girls to drop the "Uncle" for a while. I took a deep breath, calming my frayed nerves.

Steve and Melinda had never met Drew, although when I had seen Melinda in the grocery store a few weeks ago, she mentioned she had heard that I was seeing someone. I wondered how she'd heard. Was it from a well-wisher passing along happy news or something whispered furtively behind a hand, with a knowing smile? *Her husband might not even be dead, you know.*

It had been six months, and Drew insisted that I needed to stop caring about other people's perceptions. For the first two months of our courtship, I refused to go to any restaurant where I might see someone from the neighborhood or church. That generally meant we had to drive twenty minutes in any direction to have a meal. I didn't rehire Charlotte as my date-night babysitter; I found a girl from the community college bulletin board. Drew grew tired of secret dating, but was patient with me. Annie's birthday party marked the first time

I had brought Drew to any neighborhood function. *Greg's replacement.* I tried not to think like that, but I knew others would.

"Okay, so whose house are we going to?" Drew asked again. Fact I never knew: Drew had a terrible time remembering names.

"Melinda and Steve. They have one daughter, Annie, who is Hannah's best friend. You've met her. Rob and Robin will be there, and you've met them." A few weeks ago, we had taken the girls to dinner at the Masters's house. I'd had the same fears that night as I had today, but I knew Robin and Rob wanted nothing but the best for me. Drew had brought an expensive bottle of wine and a bottle of whiskey. By the end of the night, everyone was talking like old friends.

Robin had pulled me aside as we were leaving. "Claire, Drew is wonderful. I'm so glad to see you happy."

We embraced, and I felt thankful to have an ally in the neighborhood. When I said that to Drew, he'd sighed. "An ally implies some kind of war, Claire. How do you even know anyone will care?"

As we pulled into the driveway, Melinda met us at the van. "Hi, I'm so glad you came!" she squealed, hugging me, then opening the back door to let the girls out of the car.

Hannah bounded right for the swing set and Annie, leaving Leah in her wake.

Taking the cooler from my arm, Melinda extended her hand to Drew. "I'm Melinda," she cooed.

I watched her, oddly unaffected by her flirting. She walked uncomfortably close to Drew, and I gauged his reaction. He turned around, caught my eye, and winked. I had told him about Melinda's reputation as the neighborhood floozy. *I have no idea how she'll be to you.* Drew, with his obvious striking looks, commanded her full attention. He was attentive, even ironically flirtatious, in return. She clucked around him, handing him a beer from the fridge and peppering him with questions. Where did he live? What did he do? Every answer was met with a "Really?" or a "Wow, that's so interesting!" as though he were a CIA operative, instead of a photographer.

As I unpacked the macaroni salad, I pretended to ignore them. I was curious to see how Drew would fit in with the shark pit of suburbia. He wasn't as obtuse as Greg, who had been oblivious to the gossip and malice. He was an artist, a student of human nature. *I can only imagine what his next photography collection will be.* I caught myself smiling.

"How are you holding up?" Melinda asked me.

I looked at her, startled. Her head was tilted, her eyebrows knitted—her insincere concerned face. I secretly called it the "fish face" because the expression was always accompanied by a badly disguised effort to ferret out some morsel of information to pass along to the masses. *I saw Claire Barnes in Stop & Shop today, and you'll never believe what she told me...* as though delivering their fresh catch of the day.

"Oh, I'm doing well," I replied, treading carefully. "You know, it will never be easy, but I have a strong support system. So that's been great." Drew rested his hand on my shoulder.

"Well, that's important," she replied with a knowing smile. "And Drew here, I'm sure he helps, too."

"Oh, well, Drew has been a friend since we were kids. He's been fantastically supportive," I said.

"Oh! So... you're just friends, then?" She pointed at us, waving her finger back and forth, curiosity disguised as concern.

"We were very close friends growing up," I said. "And not that it's anyone else's business, but yes, we have become an item."

"Oh, well, are you—" Melinda began, her concerned façade all but dropped in the excitement of such a juicy confirmation.

I cut her off, holding up my hand. "Melinda, thank you so much for asking about me. But at this point, I think I've said all I care to say. I'd also prefer it not become gossip fodder, if you can help yourself."

She took a step back. "Claire, I completely understand." She put her hand on my arm. "If you guys need *anything* at all, let me know." She hastily went inside to greet other, but surely less interesting, guests.

Drew turned to look at me in amazement. "Seriously? I think I was wrong. Maybe we do need allies."

"Welcome to the suburbs." I laughed. "You thought the city was tough? You have no idea. To be fair, she's the worst one. Everyone else will be more subtle. And probably genuinely care less."

"She makes me so sad," he commented.

I looked up in questioning surprise. Melinda made me a lot of things, but never, ever sad.

"Think about it," he said. "To care that much about someone else's life, your own life has to be pretty unfulfilling."

My mind flashed to Melinda's half-drunken attempts to seduce Greg two years ago. *What must her marriage be like?* Steve always seemed so... dull. Drew, an outsider, had shone new light on the whole party with one simple observation. I reached up, not caring who saw, and kissed him. "I love you, Drew Elliot."

The night before, I had lectured him. "Please, no PDA, okay?"

He replied with his usual sarcasm. "Someday, though, right? Someday, we can make out in the middle of a church barbeque? I've always wanted to. Please?"

I smacked him with my magazine. "You are never serious."

"You're serious enough for both of us," he had replied.

He kissed me back, eyes widened in surprise. "You said no PDA," he whispered.

"That was before. For some reason, I don't really care that much anymore."

CHAPTER 30

A FEW WEEKS LATER, WE HAD our first real fight. *The house.* The house was the thorn in our sides, the pea under the mattress. Drew protested very little in life, his easygoing side a nice complement to my detail-oriented type-A. I found, through time, that when he did stake a claim, I should take it seriously. I tried to abide by my own self-imposed rule; however, we struggled with the house. We painted the bedroom, bought a new bed, and rearranged the furniture. Nothing in the bedroom resembled the room I had shared with Greg. But Drew couldn't get past it. He wanted me to sell the house. He wanted us to move and find a new house to make our own. He felt like Greg's replacement, the new daddy, in the same house, filling the same role.

"Lots of people get *married* twice. And then, the second husband is always second. It's in the name!" I protested. "I can't help that. We're not even married yet..." I skirted another issue. "... but I feel like I already have to defend having a first husband to you."

"I've never asked you to defend having a first husband. That's ridiculous. But I feel like I'm renting space in Greg's life. Can't you see that? I don't question your love for me. Asking you to move is not like asking you who you loved more. I need us to start fresh, so I can feel like this is my place in life."

"It's just a house. You're making too much of this," I insisted. "This is your place in life. If you want it to be."

He threw up his hands and stomped outside.

Having quasi-lived together for seven months, I knew we were both coming to a head with our purgatory life. He still maintained his brownstone in Harlem, but he stayed with us most of the time, commuting in when necessary. The arrangement worked, albeit for the short term. Admittedly, I saw his point. My hesitation stemmed from my love for my house—the big yard, the barn, the privacy, the house's age. I knew we could find something that I would love again, particularly with Drew's income, but my house was my *home*. Stubbornly, unfairly, I held onto it.

Drew, almost never stubborn and rarely unfair, returned fifteen minutes later. He drew me in and held me. We made no concession, reached no agreement. But the argument had ended.

"I hate fighting with you." He looked so forlorn, I almost laughed out loud. Having been married, I knew that fighting came with the territory.

I hugged him back and reassured him that a fight was just a fight and I wasn't even mad. I simply didn't want to move. He kissed me gently, thumbing my jaw and bringing goose bumps to my arms. The kiss deepened, our mouths parting. So easily ready, willing, and panting for him, I could feel him respond in kind.

Gently, he pulled away. "The kids are upstairs."

My hand danced along his belly, teasingly. "Later."

He groaned, looking upward. "You know, I could find a woman without kids," he muttered.

"I think you tried that for ten years," I replied, raising my eyebrows. He laughed. "Touché."

In the end, we decided that if Drew still felt strongly about it at the end of the year, we'd put the house on the market. We'd find a house that would have all the things I loved about my house and one close to my parents. I secretly hoped that by the end of the year, the ghost of Greg would be eradicated, and the house would feel more like home to Drew. To that end, I insisted, he had to stop renting the brownstone, or at least sublet it.

We spent a Saturday cleaning out Greg's study. I boxed up all of his files, his computer, and his paperwork. I hesitated with his brown leather journal, thumbing through the worn pages. They were dog-eared from nights of close examination when he had first left, as I looked for clues hidden in the shorthand scribbling. I stopped at the page with the poem.

I carry your heart with me.
I carry it in my heart.
C!

I felt a hand on my shoulder. I looked up into Drew's bright blue eyes and saw no fear, no jealousy, just compassion.

"What do *you* think happened to Greg?" I asked. I must have asked him that question a hundred times, but he always answered differently, a variation on the theme of *Who the hell knows?*

"I don't know. I really don't. But since Detective Reynolds came up with that car, all I can think is that was him at the bottom of Lake Onondaga. With Melissa Richards. It's the only thing that makes any sense, you know?"

I nodded. I had thought the same thing, but never said it aloud. "Do you think he was dating Melissa Richards? And if so, then who was Karen?"

He joined me on the floor of the study, sitting cross-legged next to me. "Could he have had two mistresses?"

"I have no idea. I didn't know he had one." I paged carefully through the leather journal. "How would you feel if I kept this? If I didn't put it into storage?"

He thought for a moment and finally shrugged. "It's part of you. I don't believe you'll ever close the door on that life. I wouldn't want you to; it made you who you are. It eventually brought us together. I think you'll always wonder and question. And I'm okay with that."

I loved that most about Drew. We had no secrets. Talking was the cornerstone of our relationship. I knew all of his clients, all of his buyers, and all the galleries he frequented. Since I'd resigned from my job, he knew my days in excruciating detail. And they all involved activities with the kids. He asked my advice on things and valued my opinions. Our evenings were filled with music and chatter, and after the kids were put to bed, the television rarely went on. I loved the candidness of our relationship, so different from the eggshell environment I had my last year with Greg, where every question turned into an inquisition, every answer testy. I tried not to compare, but it was impossible. Even in our best days, Greg and I had rarely talked as frequently and with the same intensity as Drew and I did. It was a depth to life I never knew existed.

"I still wonder every day," I said, running my hand over the soft leather cover.

"I know. I know you do. Me, too, you know? Not for the same reasons, of course."

"What are your reasons?" I asked.

"Well, first, it's plain bizarre. A *Twilight Zone* episode. So yeah, of course I'd love to know the truth. But secondly, I worry every day that this will end, the way everyone does when they're in love. But I have the added worry of not knowing if your ex-but-not-ex-husband could come waltzing back into your life at any time. It's hard to be a hundred percent comfortable when there may never be finality, you know?"

I nodded. I did know. It had crossed my mind before: what if Greg had run away and decided to come back? What would I do? I shook my head. Greg and Claire were over, regardless of his being alive or dead. It was hard to admit, and I had yet to say it out loud, but I had something with Drew that I had never had with Greg. I could never give that up. It was as though I had lived my whole life missing a sense, and Drew had given it back to me. My life seemed richer. Food tasted better; colors seemed brighter. I saw humor in situations that would have plain irritated me previously. It wasn't that I'd had a bad life with Greg. I just never knew it could be so good. Instead of saying all of that, as I wasn't ready to admit to the relative emptiness of my life before, I touched his hand and said, "There's finality. That's not something you need to worry about."

Drew moved the desk and the filing cabinets out to the barn to be put up later on eBay. Standing in the almost empty study, I inhaled deeply. The room still had the same smell, like leather and man. Drew was going to use it as his office, a place to consolidate paperwork from his sales and possibly meet buyers.

"Mommy, where's all Daddy's stuff?" Hannah stood uncertainly in the doorway. Somehow, she'd become a small adult.

"Hannah, sit down." I sat back down on the floor, tucking Greg's journal under my leg. She plopped down next to me. I took a deep breath. "Hannah, Drew is going to live here now."

"He already lives here," she replied matter-of-factly.

"Yes, but he's going to *officially* live here. He's going to use Daddy's old study for his office." I gauged her reaction. There wasn't one—textbook Hannah. "Does that bother you at all?"

She shook her head and looked around at the bare walls. In the world of a six-year-old, a year and a half was a lifetime. The memories of her father were fading. My serious daughter was so much like her father it occasionally made me cry. She even looked like him. She was sullen and withdrawn sometimes, other times thoughtful beyond belief. But she was always kind and incredibly clever with a whip-smart memory. So much like Greg.

"Hannah, what do you remember about Daddy?" I wanted her to remember Greg.

She looked thoughtful, picking at her fingernail, a brooding prophecy of her teenage self. "I remember... our camping trip."

I searched my memory. Hannah had been three. We had gone camping in Massachusetts, near Boston. It rained all four days, ruining our plans to see a Red Sox game. We ended up seeing two movies in the closest town. I didn't remember it being particularly fun. I vaguely recalled begging for a hotel room, and Greg being adamant about staying at the campsite. Why? I couldn't remember.

"What do you remember most about it?" I asked.

"We played Memory every night and Candy Land. But you tried to make me play by the rules, and then Daddy said I didn't have to."

Ah, yes. We'd huddled in our large tent, sitting between two air mattresses and playing board games on the floor. I remembered being cold and frustrated at Leah, who kept tipping the board or picking up the memory cards with the curiosity of a one-year-old. Greg was jovial, as if we were having a great time. We took home mounds of mildewed laundry. I remembered laying down the gauntlet: we weren't camping again until the kids were old enough to have their own tent.

Not everything has to be so tragic, Claire.

I have no idea what you're talking about. Nothing here is tragic, it's just irritating. Particularly because the whole trip was a disaster.

You can't control the weather; it's not worth getting mad over. Besides, I actually had a good time.

No, you didn't. That's not possible. We did absolutely nothing that was any fun at all. You're just saying that to get under my skin, and it's childish.

Suit yourself, but the only one acting like a child around here is you.

I had stomped around for days, seeming unable to get warm. All our clothes smelled musty even after several runs through the washer.

I couldn't fathom why that memory stuck out in Hannah's mind. "What did you like most about the camping trip?"

She shrugged. "Daddy was so happy," she said with childlike simplicity. "That made it fun."

CHAPTER 31

WE EXPANDED THE GARDENS, BECAUSE as it turned out, Drew had an unexpected gift for growing things. In the spring and summer, he grew peppers, tomatoes, and strawberries, and in the back, along the barn, thick, unruly black raspberry bushes. He showed Hannah and Leah how to pick them and waved off my protests of making sure they were washed before the girls ate them.

"They don't taste as good unless you eat them right off the bush," Leah parroted.

Drew popped one in my mouth before I could argue, and all I could do was agree. He kissed me, leaving the tart remnants of raspberry on my lips.

In mid-July, Sarah visited for a week.

"Good god," she complained. "I forgot about the humidity!"

The five of us rattled around in the house, bumping into each other, hot and bored, until I loaded everyone into the van and drove the two hours out to Brigantine. Borrowing the Arnolds' beach house while they were in Mexico, we lazily spent our days at the beach or the pool, and the evenings on the patio, drinking and talking. The girls stayed up later than I would have liked, watching fireworks or running up and down in the surf. We cooked dinners of seafood and salads, rich, buttery lobster we ate with our hands outside while wearing bathing suits. The time was idyllic.

Drew tried his hand at cooking, and while the first two meals were only so-so, his patience and good humor won out. On the third night, he made a shrimp and crab ravioli with sherry cream sauce.

We ate until our clothes were stretched tight across our bellies, and I worried that the girls would get sick. At twilight, we trekked lawn chairs and blankets down the block to the beach and lay like beached whales, watching fireworks until late in the evening.

I asked Sarah to keep an eye on the kids while Drew and I walked hand in hand in the surf. I leaned my head on his shoulder, sighing happily.

"I want this forever," Drew said, pulling me to him, our hips bumping as we walked. "The girls, you, vacations, us being a family."

I nodded sleepily, a tad drunk on the bottle of wine we polished off back at the blanket. He stopped and turned me to face him. His face was so serious, an expression I'd rarely seen.

"I mean it, Claire. I want..." He looked toward the black void of the water. "I want to marry you. Someday."

I hesitated. I didn't know what to say, except the truth. "I want that, too, Drew. But how? Greg won't be declared deceased for another five years. The only way I could get married again would be to divorce him." I took his hand and kissed his palm. "Can I divorce Greg if I don't know where he is? I have no idea how that works. And to be honest, I'm not sure I could do it. I have to think about it."

He pulled me into a hug and kissed the top of my head. "I'll be patient, Claire. I will. Think about it, okay?"

I nodded and promised that I would. We stayed like that for a while, breathing together. We walked back toward the blanket in comfortable silence, lost in our own, surely similar, thoughts.

As we approached, Sarah waved. "I thought you guys sailed away," she whispered.

The girls were each sleeping soundly. Drew carried Hannah, I carried Leah, and we made our way back to the house. After we tucked them in, Drew retired to bed, while Sarah and I sat out on the patio, talking and catching up.

"I've never seen you so relaxed. So happy," Sarah observed.

"Oh, love, you should try it sometime. It really is the best drug."

I laughed.

"I guess so! You're not the Claire I know, worried or anxious. You're fun now," she joked.

"Hey, I'm fun. Remember San Diego?" I pouted.

"I do. I still talk to Owen sometimes. And Will asks about you all the time."

"Really? He was gawgeous!" I giggled. Will held a special place in my heart, my first and only foray into living single.

She nodded. "Yes, but you should see yourself now. You come alive when Drew's around." She swirled her wine glass. "I'm jealous."

I looked up in surprise. Sarah, the self-proclaimed perpetual bachelorette, was jealous of me?

"Yes, that's right," she said. "Make fun of me. Go ahead. But you make me think about my life. I'm not getting younger. I won't always have a date on Friday and Saturday nights. Right now, I make no more than three phone calls, and I've got a man to hang out with, and later, to keep me warm. I don't want to go through life alone. So what happens when all my 'Guy Fridays' find wives?"

"So you want this? Marriage, kids, the works?"

She shrugged. "You make it look so easy."

"With the right person, it's a lot easier," I agreed. I didn't say the whole truth—that making a life together with the wrong person was like pushing a boulder up a hill. While making a life with the right person was like having a wheelbarrow instead of a boulder, taking turns pushing each other on the inclines. That was the thing I could not say out loud. Had life with Greg been akin to pushing a boulder? Was it possible to marry the wrong person when that marriage had produced two of the most beautiful children ever? Or what if there was no right and wrong person, just different people? If I could go back, would I have made a different choice? No, of course not. I would trade my happiness for Leah and Hannah. If I could reverse the events of the last two years, would I, and thus take away Drew? But then, Leah and Hannah would have their daddy. I couldn't think about it;

it made my head and my heart hurt. No clean answer existed. Instead of saying all that, I replied, "Nothing is ever easy, Sarah. If you wait for easy, you'll die alone."

When we finally trudged, half-drunk and very tired, to our respective rooms, I crept into bed, careful not to wake Drew. He stirred beside me, and his arm encircled my waist. I kissed his forehead. Silently, effortlessly, he slid my body under his, his hands in my hair, his mouth on my neck. I was instantly ready and clung to him, desperate from the alcohol and heavy conversation. Quickly, wordlessly, we made love. He tasted of sand and sweat, wine and butter. We pulled, scratched, rough and coarse, a confirmation of reality, erasing my inner hypothetical questions.

Afterward, I lightly stroked his back. We fell asleep, his arm curled around me, pulling me into the curve of his body, without ever saying a word.

When we packed the van four days later, we were all five pounds heavier, tanned, and permanently slick with sunscreen. I was swearing off wine for at least a week, a bit embarrassed by the recycling bin at the curb as we pulled away. Sarah left the day after we got home, and after the unpacking, laundry, food shopping, and all the other miscellaneous chores that come from a restful week away, life returned to its normal rhythm.

Hannah and Leah had a month of day camp before returning to school. Leah was starting preschool; I could hardly believe it. Hannah would be in first grade.

Drew went into the city for a day to meet with a gallery owner and plan an opening. He had been uninspired lately and was going to stay overnight, stalking the parks and looking for unwitting subjects, or at least motivation. He claimed that living with me made him happy, and happiness made him lazy. He said he was too content to seek out the misery and sadness in society, and pictures of happy people didn't sell as well, not to mention the great reduction in subjects.

I had the house to myself, which was a rare treat. I recalled the conversation with Drew on the beach. Sitting down at the computer, I did a quick Google search. After a few minutes of reading, I mulled over my findings. I could file for a divorce. Did I want to? I wasn't sure. If something had happened to Greg, if he'd died, then clearly divorcing him would hurt no one. What about Hannah? Would she have to know? Would she even understand? Leah was too little. If Greg was missing by his own choice, then I should have no reservations about divorcing him. I couldn't reconcile all my questions.

Dad always said that when life gets too complicated, start by asking yourself what you *want*. Define it in one sentence and work backward. I pulled out a piece of paper and asked myself, *What do I want?* Without hesitation, the answer came. I wanted Drew. Working backward, Drew wanted marriage. Would he stay without marriage? It was hard to say. Marriage acted like a glue when the rest of a carefully constructed life fell apart. It kept a couple together through hardships until they could rebuild. I didn't believe in long-term relationships without marriage. Things wouldn't stay blissful forever; life—messy, complicated, hectic, frustrating, and sometimes downright disastrous—would get in the way. That, I knew better than most. I picked up the phone and dialed my lawyer.

Divorcing a missing person was relatively simple and took less than a month. Half of our assets had to be placed in escrow until Greg was found or declared deceased. Everything else was mine. If I were to sell the house, I had to reserve half of the estate in the escrow account. I signed an affidavit that stated that I had attempted to look for the missing person by phone, street address, internet searching, and even social networking websites. Matt Reynolds signed a similar affidavit and appeared at a court hearing as a witness to our search. He provided a judge with an inch-thick case file, including his investigation leading to Lake Onodaga. The judge made his determination on the spot, and I went from a widow to a divorcee. I attended the hearing without Drew, by my choice, but when I got home, he held me gently, knowing that the ruling was bittersweet.

The divorce had to be publicly announced in three newspapers as part of due diligence. In the event that Greg was hiding in the next county over, the court had to be able to say he had been publicly served. I dreaded that, knowing it was always possible that my incredible story would be picked up and splashed across headlines, which would give everyone entitlement to an opinion. I had enough guilt and didn't need more from public opinion, from people who didn't know the facts. I waited, but there was no blowback.

Overall, the divorce had little impact on my day-to-day life. I felt slightly freer to plan my future with Drew, but since I had believed Greg to be dead for some time, that wasn't an emotional freedom, but a legal one. We started to speak of marriage abstractly, the way people did when they first start thinking it was a real possibility, as in *Someday when we're married...* I wasn't sure when that day would be, but if there was one thing I'd learned, it was that life could sometimes change drastically from year to year. There was a certain wisdom in patiently waiting for life to happen. I planned on being a divorcee for a while before I became a wife again.

One Thursday, I sat at the kitchen island, lazily doing a crossword puzzle. In the back of my mind, I thought about being married again, about officially sharing my home, my finances, and my life with another person, as opposed to the separate-yet-equal life I was currently leading. The doorbell rang, interrupting my reverie. Drying my hands on a dishtowel as I walked down the hall, I tried to remember if it was time for Girl Scout cookie sales. I opened the door.

"Hi, Matt. Did we have a meeting today? I must have completely forgotten." I turned to walk back down the hall, then I realized we couldn't have a meeting. Our last meeting had been three and a half months ago, in May. We wouldn't meet again until—I did the math—November.

When I turned back, he still stood in the doorway. "Claire, can we come in?" he asked, his face unreadable.

We? I noticed a tall, gangly man behind him. He wore a navy blue suit and had a mustache and wire-rimmed glasses. I tried to place him and failed.

"Sure, come on in." My breath caught. Had there been a development? For one split, awful second, I fervently hoped they had come to tell me Greg was dead. The room began to spin. I studied Matt's face, and suddenly, I knew. "Matt, what's going on?"

He motioned me into the living room. "Claire, please, sit down, okay?" His hand felt heavy and warm on my back. He was being too nice, too gentle, the way a person acted when he was about to shatter someone's world.

I sat. *Please, just say it.*

"Claire, we found Greg."

The room tilted. The last thing I heard before my world went black was, "He's alive."

CHAPTER 32

WHEN I CAME TO, MATT stood over me, concern creasing his brow.

He helped me up, then brought me a glass of water. He gestured at the tall thin man behind him. "Claire, this is Detective Ron Ferras. He's from the Toronto police department. Greg is in Toronto, in Canada." He waited for me to nod. "He's in a federal care facility. Two years ago, Greg was mugged in downtown Toronto. Whoever mugged him then also pushed him off the curb in front of an oncoming car. The driver of the car called 911. He was taken to St. Michael's Hospital, where he received treatment for nine months."

The questions formed faster than I could ask them, as if I had lost the ability to speak. Why was he in Canada? Nothing made sense.

He continued, "When he remained in a persistent vegetative state, he was transferred out of the hospital and into a rehabilitation facility. That's where he has been until six months ago."

I had been staring at my hands, numbly. But at that, my head snapped up, and I met Matt's eyes. I saw sympathy, apology, and something else. Pity?

"What happened six months ago?" I asked.

"He woke up."

On Saturday, two days later, I sat in the front seat of Matt Reynold's Suburban. Drew stayed home with the girls; we hadn't told them anything. Until I knew what we were up against, I wanted to keep them innocent for as long as possible. The last two days had been awful. Drew and I did not speak much, my silence from shock, his from terror. I had nothing in me to reassure him, as I put on a performance every minute of every day for Hannah and Leah.

Three times, I had to ask Matt to pull over while I retched on the side of the interstate. The trip was eight hours long, and I was prone to motion sickness, which seemed to be exacerbated by fear. I called Mom twice to check on Hannah and Leah. She asked very few questions, just if I was all right. *I'll never be all right again. Why was Greg in Canada?*

I had a sudden thought. "You said there was an alert on Greg's passport. Why didn't it work?"

Matt tapped his fingers on the steering wheel. "He may have gone into Canada before we activated the alert. We did pull border control records at the time, but customs doesn't scan everyone's passport. Canada is a bit more... lackadaisical in their border control."

"I just thought... since 9/11... governments were tracking who was going in and out. Seems paranoid, I guess."

"No, I think it's a common misconception."

When we crossed the border into Canada, we were waved through without so much as a glance. Matt raised his eyebrows at me, as if to say, *See?* I called Drew to tell him we had crossed the border.

As we exited the highway, going into Toronto, Matt explained, "We're going to a rehab facility. It's like a nursing home. We'll speak to Greg's doctors and his therapists first. He has several of each. Greg spends six to eight hours a day in this facility, but he lives in a community home. It's a transitional place, like a halfway house for the brain injured."

"What does 'brain injured' mean?" I asked, feeling stupid.

"That's Greg's current diagnosis. I'm sure it's more complicated, but basically, when he was hit by the car, his head was struck with such force that his brain was severely damaged. In many cases of traumatic brain injury, a vegetative state aids with healing. It's the body's way of shutting down to the most basic levels, like hibernation. Healing of the brain is the hardest, most arduous and slowest process the body can do."

"How do you know all this?" I asked.

"After Detective Ferras came to tell me that Greg was awake, I researched it."

My mind came alive. Which was when? Where had Greg been for six months? Why did they wait so long to find us? I wished for a pen and paper so I could write down all my questions. "So if Greg woke up six months ago, why are we only hearing about this now?"

"Two weeks ago, Greg started remembering who he is."

"So he woke up six months ago with no memory of who he is?" I asked, incredulous. That was a movie plot, not someone's real life. *My real life.*

Matt shook his head. "We'll find out the details from Greg's doctors. But from what I understand, he didn't know his name for the first five and a half months."

"This is all too much. It's like a soap opera." I rubbed my forehead, massaging the information into my brain.

I gazed out the window, trying to organize my questions, my thoughts. I had no feelings; I was numb. If Greg was alive, what did I know to be true with certainty? The answer: nothing.

I felt a piercing guilt. I have been living with, loving, and making love to another man while my husband lay in a hospital in another country. Then, I callously divorced him. I motioned for Matt to pull over again, so I could heave my guilt onto the pavement. Once finished, I sat in the gravel and sobbed. Matt rubbed my back gently.

Take me back to New Jersey, I wanted to beg. But I could never go back, not in the same way. Nothing would ever be the same again.

The rehabilitation facility was a gray brick building in a hospital complex. It looked like every other hospital complex I'd ever seen. Matt led the way across the lobby to an information desk. I hung back, staring at my hands, my feet, or the floor. He spoke softly to the receptionist and then motioned for me to follow. I felt seized by panic. Were we going to see Greg? I bent over at the waist, unable to breathe. Matt started toward me, and I felt a pang of pity for the wonderful, quiet man with the sad eyes who seemed to do nothing but comfort me in times of crisis. I held up my hand and motioned for him to give me a moment. He stopped and waited patiently. After a few minutes, we continued down the hall.

"We're going to a conference room to meet with Greg's doctors and therapists," he whispered.

The conference room held a long table and could have been a corporate room at Advent. A projector stood in the corner, and three people sat around the table in oversized plush rolling chairs. The two men and a woman appeared diminutive, like children. They offered kind words, but behind the kindness lay a quiet curiosity; I was a human-interest story. The men introduced themselves as Greg's neurologist, Dr. Benedict, and his primary physician, Dr. Ludlow.

The woman opened a file. "My name is Dr. Goodman. I am Greg's cognitive therapist. Greg has four therapists right now. That number will go down later, but I am the best person to speak to Greg's current state of mind and his abilities, mental, physical, and emotional. I'm sure you understand. This is a terribly emotional event for him." She spoke in a clinical tone, her voice devoid of any warmth and humanity.

I disliked her instantly. *Yes, I'm pretty sure I get that. Terrible, check. Emotional, check.* "Can we start at the beginning, please, Dr. Goodman?" I asked, quietly but forcefully.

Dr. Goodman nodded briskly. "Almost two years ago, Greg was robbed at gunpoint on a street in downtown Toronto at ten o'clock at night. Greg fought back, but the man who robbed him pushed him into the street and ran away. He was struck by an oncoming car, and the driver called 911. The driver had seen the altercation before he hit Greg, and he gave a statement to the police. But that's all we knew of Greg since, with his wallet gone, there was no identification, credit cards, cell phone, or even receipts in his pockets, nothing. He was taken to St. Michael's Hospital, where he remained in a vegetative state for about nine months. After nine months with virtually no change, he was classified as a permanent vegetative state and transferred here. This is a rehabilitation facility that also acts as a long-term care facility. Eight months ago, Greg started experiencing spontaneous consciousness, sometimes for only minutes or hours, and once for a day. Then about six months ago, he woke fully. At that time, he remembered nothing about himself. Greg's memory loss was unique in that he retained a semantic memory, which is the ability to perform learned tasks, like reading. However, his episodic memory was gone. That is the portion of memory devoted to life experiences. He remembered nothing—no childhood, no family. He had no idea who the Prime Minister of Canada was or the President of the United States; we asked both, not sure if he was Canadian or American. He can, however, tie his own shoes. This is extraordinary. Most people in PVS for six months or longer must relearn everything. Greg had an astonishing baseline. But he still had no concept of himself. That was our biggest obstacle to progress, as it was very frustrating to him. Frustration hinders progress. Unfortunately, patients with TBI are—"

"I'm sorry," I interrupted. "What are TBI and PVS?"

"TBI stands for 'Traumatic Brain Injury.' That is what caused Greg's PVS, which is 'Persistent Vegetative State.' You might call it a coma. They are essentially the same thing with some minor technical differences." She shrugged nonchalantly.

Her blasé demeanor unnerved me. So casual, so laid-back. I wanted to grab her shoulders and shake her. "So where is he now? Can I see him?" I clutched the arms of the chair, my nails digging into the fabric. Impatient with their explanations and stories, I needed simply to *see* him, to verify with my own eyes that the man they were talking about was, in fact, my husband.

They exchanged glances, secretly communicating with their eyes. I felt like a pariah.

One of the men cleared his throat. "Claire..." I was surprised at his use of my first name, as if we were friends. "We think you should listen to the entire story before you see him. So you understand what to expect at this point."

"Okay, fine. What should I expect?" I realized that my leg was shaking, bouncing, really, with nervous energy I couldn't contain. Taking a deep breath, I forced my leg still with my hand and sat back in the chair, willing my body to appear relaxed.

Dr. Goodman turned to a new page in the file. "Greg has been in physical, occupational, and cognitive therapy for six months. A month ago, he moved to a group home, which is a government-funded housing specifically for patients with TBI in various stages of recovery. It's the first step toward independence and reintroduction back into society. It teaches things like cooperative living, basic sharing skills, and relating and interactive skills. Now, fortunately in Greg's case, he did pretty well with that. Like I said, his semantic memory is astonishing. It is probably the reason for his quick recovery."

"Greg had a nearly photographic memory," I replied, tracing a scratch on the table. "He was a corporate trainer, and he never needed notes, never forgot names or faces."

Dr. Goodman made an *ah* sound and nodded, as if my comment had made everything magically make sense. "Claire..." She cleared her throat, transitioning her clinical lecture to a more personal tone. "Two weeks ago, Greg was walking down the street, and he was drawn to a real estate office by the name on the shingle. He went into the office and was given a business card."

She pushed a business card across the table. The thick paper was worn and creased, dog-eared and soft around the edges. A bit of dirt was smudged across the front, as though someone had repeatedly run a soiled finger over the lettering. *Claire Barnes, Toronto Realty.*

Guiding you home! Call us now for a free evaluation!

Dr. Goodman continued, "He became so agitated in the realtor's office that they had to call the therapist at the group home to come and get him. He didn't sleep for forty-eight hours, so we had to give him a mild sedative. When he woke up almost a full day later, he remembered his name and you. The nurse on duty found you on the internet and called the police, who called Detective Reynolds. That was three days ago."

"So where is he now?" I asked again.

"He's down the hall," Dr. Goodman said. I must have appeared to jump out of my chair because she up held her hand. "There are a few more things you should know. First, he is not the man you married, most assuredly. We did not know him before, but we have yet to meet a TBI patient who is the same person before and after an accident. Parts of his brain no longer function well, in the same way, or at all. You *must* understand that. Secondly, he will not look the same. He has essentially been lying down for two years. His muscles atrophied. In addition, patients in PVS can actually become significantly shorter. This is because when you don't use your back muscles, your bones will weaken, and your spine will irreversibly contract. I know from his medical records here that he was a significantly taller man prior to the accident."

Greg used to be a large man, tall and broad, seeming to absorb all the empty space in a room. Whenever I thought of Greg, I thought of the breadth of his chest, the solidarity of his body and his voice, which boomed with self-assurance.

"Third, you may hear people call him Glen. When he woke up, he didn't have a name, and he had no family here to tell him his name. A name is a large part of an identity. Someone, a nurse I think, gave him a baby naming book and asked him to go through it. I suggested he look for a name that jumped out at him. He picked Glen. Knowing his name is actually Greg, that makes a great deal of sense. They're so similar. I suspect that he will revert to Greg because he identifies with his old life. He remembers you, his mother, his daughter Hannah, and your parents." She looked questioningly at me to confirm that these people did, in fact, exist.

"Greg's mother has been dead for almost ten years. And we have another daughter, Leah. She's younger than Hannah, so she was only two when Greg... disappeared."

"He knows his mother is not living, but he never mentioned Leah." I felt my jaw drop in a silent *oh,* and she continued quickly. "The earliest and latest memories are the last to recover, if they ever do. So the baby memories we have, those quick snatches of time that are snapshots in our mind? For him, those might be long gone. The last year or two of his life before the accident might come back eventually, but it's not guaranteed. He never mentioned Leah, so I'm guessing he doesn't remember her." She sat next to me, with her soft cool hand covering mine, seeming human for the first time, and explained, in detail, all the ways in which I would no longer know my husband, or more accurately, all the ways in which he would no longer know me. The medical jargon flew over my head, but certain phrases sliced through me, sharp and cold, a surgical knife carefully bisecting my life. *Learned behavior... impulsive... skewed moral compass... increased anger and irritability...*

Finally, to my relief, she seemed to run out of facts. "Claire, are you ready to see Greg?"

I felt lightheaded, but I nodded. She stood and motioned for me to follow. We left the conference room and walked down the hall, where I would see my husband for the first time in over two years.

CHAPTER 33

I HESITATED AT THE DOOR.

"When you're ready," Dr. Goodman said.

When I gathered my nerve and pushed open the door, he stood at the window on the opposite side of the room, his back to me. He was unrecognizably short and very thin, and for a moment, I felt a wilting relief. *It's not him. Thank God.* My vision wavered and I grabbed the doorframe for support.

He turned, and his face was thinner than I remembered, but unmistakable. I knew it as well as my own. *Greg.* I recognized his deep brown eyes and his easy smile, which he gave me almost immediately. "Claire, I'm so glad you came. I wasn't sure you would."

He looked like a runner, although judging by what I'd been told, he couldn't have run down the hall if he wanted to. The relief ebbed away, leaving a tumultuous sick feeling in its wake. The desire to turn and run was overwhelming.

Awkwardly, we approached each other. When he hugged me, his arms felt foreign. He didn't even smell the same. It was like hugging a stranger. I didn't realize I was crying until he wiped my cheek.

"This is so weird," I said.

He shrugged. "In my mind, I could have seen you yesterday."

"What is your last memory of me?" I had no idea where the timeline in his mind had stopped. I needed a reference.

He looked upward, as if searching his fleeting memory for permanent pictures. "I'm not sure. I remember you finding out you were pregnant. Are you pregnant?" He looked confused.

I shook my head. "We had Leah four years ago." I started to cry again; I really couldn't believe he had no memory of Leah. When the girls saw him, he would have to pretend. *Oh God, when would that be?* "Why are you in Toronto?" I asked. He shook his head.

"I don't know. Did we move here?"

I realized his answers would not be helpful. I was getting no closure from the meeting. It would only bring more questions. But I had to know, had to ask, "Who is Karen?"

He shook his head again. "I have no idea. Who is Karen?" He looked from me to Dr. Goodman.

I put my head in my hands, closed my eyes, and willed myself not to cry.

"Are you happy?" Greg asked. "Did Hannah miss me?" His questions were childlike.

Dr. Goodman had spoken about that, too. The sophistication a person gained with age was gone. The learned deception of hiding emotions, finely honed in most adults, had been stripped away by the injury. He wore them on his sleeve.

"I'm happy you're alive, Greg." That, at least, was the truth. My children had a father again. The confusion of that would eventually pass. To have their father back was permanent.

I searched the large room, awkwardly looking for a place for us to sit and talk. In one corner stood a round table with two chairs and in the other, a long corporate-looking couch. In the middle of the room was a hospital bed, and at the foot of the bed was an entertainment console and a television. The bed was stripped bare and uninviting.

I motioned to the couch, and as we sat, I reached over and, out of sheer habit, lightly touched his knee. The gesture was so natural and easy, and I marveled at how it hadn't faded with years of disuse. He put his arm around me, and we stayed that way for a moment, faintly rocking like the gentle sway of a boat. He seemed unable to sit still, physically moved by some unknown source of energy, like a toddler.

"Are you going to take me home today?" he asked.

Dr. Goodman answered, "Greg, you still need therapy six to eight hours a day. You can't go home yet. I'm sorry."

"Greg, tell me how you remembered," I said. Dr. Goodman had said that talking about remembering would help him remember more. He'd had no one to spoon-feed him memories, which were just foundations for more memories, so in his situation, it was a wonder he ever remembered anything at all.

"I had a card that had your name on it."

I nodded, encouraging him.

"I stared at it, trying to figure out why that card meant so much to me. And then I remembered you. What you looked like. You were playing in the leaves with a little girl who had blond hair in a ponytail and wore a blue coat."

"Hannah had a blue coat, light blue. It's Leah's now."

"Who's Leah?" he asked. He looked at Dr. Goodman, who jumped in again to explain that Leah was his daughter, the child I was pregnant with in his memory.

I tried not to scream. Instead, I said, "Tell me more."

"And then I just knew. I knew you were Claire, and I was Greg. It took me a few hours, but then I remembered the little girl was Hannah. And Cody, our dog! How's Cody?"

"Cody ran away. Actually the same day you... disappeared. Do you remember your accident?" I asked cautiously.

"No. I don't remember anything. The last thing I remember is you being pregnant, I think, because I don't remember the baby."

"Leah," I said, forcefully.

"Right. Leah." He smiled innocently. "I'm glad you came, Claire."

"I'm glad I came, too, Greg," I lied.

That night, I paced my hotel room. I couldn't relax. I was so incredibly tired, but I could not stop thinking. I called Drew, both dreading and desperately needing the call.

"Are you okay?" he asked immediately.

"Yes and... no." I didn't know how to answer the question, how to convey my emotions. I needed to hear his voice. I wished he was next to me. Then, I felt guilty. *Drew is not your husband. How and when should I tell Greg that he's not my husband any longer either?* I sobbed then, the tears coming for the first time in torrents, soaking the sleeve of my hand holding the phone. My nose ran, and I let out a loud, blubbery cry like one of Leah's. *Oh, Leah, how will you deal with this when I can't?* After a few minutes, my crying subsided.

"Do you want me to come there?" Drew asked hesitantly.

I shook my head, but then realized he couldn't see me. "No, please don't come here. I don't know what to do, how this is going to work." I meant Greg, but I realized Drew would think I meant him. I was too tired to explain. All I could do was tell Drew the truth. "I love you. Don't worry about that, okay?" Guilt sneaked back in, but I quelled it. Loving Drew was the one thing I was sure of, guilt or no.

"I love you, too, Claire. Of course I worry, especially right now, but I don't want you to think about that, okay?"

We fell silent then, so much to say, to ask, the weight of words between us.

"Did you see Greg?" he finally asked.

I pictured Greg, small and childlike looking out the window, his back toward the door. Then I remembered the expression on his face when he turned. "Yes, I saw him. It's definitely Greg. I... I don't know what I thought. I guess I thought I'd come here, and it would be a mistake, that it wouldn't be him." I thought of Greg's first words to me: *I'm glad you came. I wasn't sure you would.* "Drew..." I had to get off the phone, but I owed Drew some kind of explanation. One I didn't have. "I don't want you to worry. I love you. That's the only thing I know right now. But I have to go. I have to sleep."

"Of course. I love you, too. Call me tomorrow."

We hung up, and I lay down in the bed, fully clothed. Sleep would not come. I replayed every minute of the meeting with Greg, a dubbed tape on repeat.

CHAPTER 34

GOT OUT OF BED ON Sunday, my eyes burning and my head pounding. I had resolved in the middle of the night to no longer be a victim of circumstance, to take charge of my life. I could not go back down the rabbit hole of grief. The children couldn't go through that again.

I called Matt Reynolds, who had rented a room next door to mine. "Hi, Matt. I'm sorry to bother you so early. Do you know if Dr. Goodman will be at the rehab center today? Can I talk to her again?"

Matt said he didn't know, but he'd find out and call me back. I hung up and waited. He called back a couple of minutes later and said that if we left immediately, she could meet with us.

I checked the clock: nine fifteen. I threw on clothes without showering and was outside my door in five minutes.

When Matt dropped me off at the Toronto Rehabilitation Center, I said, "Matt, I want to talk to Dr. Goodman, and then I'll get back to you, okay? We can leave today, I think, but I want to make sure. And... thank you. For everything." I hugged him. "I don't know what I would do without you here."

He hugged me back awkwardly. I realized then that I knew almost nothing about his life. I told him I'd call him on his cell when I was ready to leave.

I met Dr. Goodman in the same conference room. She motioned for me to sit at any one of the chairs around the table.

"How are you doing today?" she asked, not unkindly, but professionally. Her lack of humanity grated on me, but it seemed I'd have to learn to live with it.

"I'm as well as you could expect under the circumstances. I'm better than yesterday. I wanted to meet with you to discuss Greg's treatment and my part in it. There are things you need to know, as his therapist." I took a deep breath. "We are no longer legally married."

She raised her eyebrows. "Oh?"

"I divorced him. We tried for two years to find him; he had vanished without a trace. It's not a neat, clean story, and I will tell you, not because I'm justifying myself, but because it may help you with his treatment to know as much about his previous life as possible. I believe he had an affair right before he disappeared. I didn't even know that he was in Toronto. He had left on a business trip to Rochester. I found out later that there were a number of things he lied about. I used to be angry, but I'm not anymore. I've moved on with my life. However, that being said, Greg is the father of my children. It's important to me that he become well again, as long as that takes. I may not be married to him, but I will be committed to his recovery. I just need to have a plan for how that will work."

Dr. Goodman appraised me with new eyes. Was there respect there? Or was it reproach? Some of each? I couldn't tell.

"Well, Claire, thank you for telling me. I appreciate that. We do have to consider when to tell Greg that you are divorced. You have to understand, in his mind, you are not only married, you are happy. You were just pregnant. Telling him now might derail or at least set back his recovery. He's just beginning to remember his old life. If we give him something that negative to think about, he might subconsciously choose not to remember it. Does that make sense?"

I nodded. "Yes, I think so."

"As for a recovery plan and your involvement..." She sighed. "Generally, the family is *very* involved, almost a daily involvement at this stage. But I would have to strongly recommend against moving him closer to you at this point. His doctors and therapists are here. Right now, he's comfortable here. Stress at this juncture is damning to recovery. I would plan on at least a month before he can be moved to New Jersey. Can you come on weekends? Or at least once a week for a month and we'll see how he does?"

"Can I bring the kids?"

"Yes, without a doubt. Your visits, and especially with the children, will be instrumental in helping him regain his memory." She paused. "Do they know?"

"No." I felt the tears spring to my eyes, an automatic switch when I thought about the girls. I blinked to clear them. I needed solid strength. I stood. "Can I see him now?"

She nodded. "He will be here for about another two hours. Today is his half day. He's been volunteering at the homeless shelter on Sundays, serving dinners."

I was taken aback. The Greg I knew had never been particularly charitable.

"I assure you," Dr. Goodman said, apparently catching my surprise, "your husband is a very different man from the one you knew."

⁂

Greg sat at the table in the same room where we had met the previous day. Cards were laid out in front of him in a solitaire pattern.

He looked up ruefully. "I can't remember the rules." He waved his hands at the cards. "One of the nurses tried to teach me, but I can't remember all the rules. I make up my own, I guess." He pulled all the cards together before I could stop him, making a pile. Then, he shuffled them, dealer style.

I laughed. "That's new," I said, pointing at the cards. He looked confused. "You couldn't do that. Before. Is that possible? Can you learn to shuffle cards in a coma?"

He shrugged, but grinned. "I don't know. I wonder what else I can do now?" he shook his head, still shuffling the cards. "What could I do before?" He dealt four stacks of cards and then combined them, piling one on top of the other. *Pile, pile, pile, pile, stack, stack, stack,*

222

stack. Over and over again.

I watched him, mesmerized by the rhythmic motion. "Oh. Greg," I said after a few minutes, "you could do everything. I swear, it's the truth. You were a corporate instructor. Did you know that? And just so great at it. You were so charismatic. You worked for Advent Pharmaceuticals. That's how we met." He nodded, but I couldn't tell if he remembered, or if he was just listening. "What do you remember?" I asked.

"I remember doing that. Teaching adults. I wasn't sure what I was doing until you said that, but I remember Advent. We met in a class?" He raised his hand. "Wait. You brought a book. And you came early, but you wouldn't speak to me. I thought you were the most beautiful woman I'd ever seen. I could hardly talk. It was a few days, right?" I nodded, and he smiled, proud of his memory. "You still are. Beautiful." He studied my face for so long that I shifted uncomfortably in my seat.

"Do you remember Sarah?"

He thought for a moment. "Yes! I do. She was with you the night we met. And she visits us sometimes. She's fun, and a little crazy, right?"

I laughed and nodded. Yes, that summed up Sarah pretty well.

Dr. Goodman poked her head in and asked, "How are things going in here?"

Greg nodded enthusiastically. "I remembered how we met."

"Good! That's great. Claire, this is the kind of therapy a doctor or a therapist cannot provide. Specific experience memory is so tricky. With some patients, it takes years to come back, and with others, it's like this." She snapped her fingers. "Greg, we have to move on. Dr. Welk is only here for a bit, so we have to meet him when we can. Claire, can I have a quick word with you?"

We walked down the hall a bit, and she turned to face me. "He needs this. What is your plan, exactly?"

I had been thinking about it during my visit with Greg. "I'll be back next weekend with the girls. And every weekend until he can come back to New Jersey. After that...?" I shrugged. "I haven't figured it out yet, but we'll take it one day at a time."

Dr. Goodman squeezed my arm. Her hand was warm, and I was surprised; I expected ice. We walked back to the room so I could say goodbye to Greg.

"Will you come back?" he asked anxiously.

I hugged him. "I'll always come back."

CHAPTER 35

WAS NEVER SO HAPPY TO be home. I hugged Drew with intensity.

"Well?" he asked.

"It's going to be different." I searched for words. I couldn't say the thing I knew he needed to hear, that nothing would change. We both knew everything would change.

Drew and I sat on the couch, and I leaned into his arms, relaying every detail I could remember. I had battled guilt the entire ride home, and that war continued. *How can I lie here, so comfortable with Drew, while Greg is five hundred miles away?* I pushed the thoughts away. Being with Drew was as natural as breathing. The need to share my life, my past few days, overwhelmed me.

"Do you want me to go with you next weekend?" he asked.

"Would you want to?"

He shrugged. "I would if you wanted me to. But do you think it would be confusing? To Hannah and Leah?"

"I don't know if it could possibly get more confusing. But no, they don't think of you as my boyfriend. You are an integral part of their lives now. If you came, I would want you to stay at the hotel while we visited Greg. Could you do that?"

"I don't think it could be any other way. Do you?"

I had no idea. There were no rules for our situation. "No, I doubt it."

He hugged me. "I will do whatever you think is best. For you and the girls. How and when are you going to tell them?"

I had been thinking about little else. "I think maybe Friday after school. We'll leave Saturday morning. That way there's very little time between when I tell them and when they see him. And they won't have to go to school with that in their minds. They'll have a few days."

The next four days were going to be interminably long. But I wasn't doing it alone. Guilt notwithstanding, I was very grateful to have Drew in my life.

The week passed quicker than I anticipated. I went through the motions of each day, playacting as though things were normal. We were a typical family on a typical day. *Except Daddy is five hundred miles away, recovering from a coma.* Incongruity ruled my life again, and the sensation was eerily familiar. However, at least I felt more in control of the ride.

I was mostly calm and collected. I had moments where I would be making dinner, laughing with Leah, or helping Hannah with her homework, and then I would remember. *Greg.* His name would fill the empty pit in my stomach, leaving a sour taste in my mouth. As soon as I could tell them, I knew I'd feel better. Or would I? Telling the girls would make it real. During that first week, it was almost as though our life had not been upended. Again.

Friday afternoon, I waited at the bus stop with clammy hands and a racing heart. When Hannah got off the bus, Leah ran to her, and we began our daily walk home. Once inside the front door, Hannah threw her backpack down and ran for the couch, wanting her half-hour of television to wind down from the day.

I sat next to her and pulled Leah to my lap. "Girls, I need to talk to you. No TV today, okay, Hannah?"

She sat up straighter and eyed me warily.

"Remember how the policemen were looking for Daddy?"

They both nodded solemnly. Hannah's face changed, and I knew at that moment that she knew what I was going to say. She looked at once terrified and excited.

"They found him, honey." I spoke to Hannah directly, as I knew it would have the greater impact on her.

She shook her head, her mouth open in a silent O.

"Hannah, sweetheart, Daddy is alive, and we're going to see him tomorrow."

Leah bounded up from my lap and shrieked with joy. Being only two when he had disappeared, she had few memories of Greg and none of the heartache that followed his disappearance. To Leah, getting to see her daddy was simply joyful news. She had a *daddy* again! Someone to take her to the kindergarten Daddy-Daughter dance next year!

Hannah's eyes were mistrustful, sullen, and cautious. Hannah guarded her joy, always, as though someone could easily snatch it away. "Where is he?" she asked.

"He's in Canada. Do you know where that is?"

She shook her head. "But why hasn't he come home?"

I had been weighing a response for that question that would be both truthful and age appropriate. "Daddy was sick, honey. He was in a hospital, and they didn't know who he was, so they couldn't call us. He was sleeping for a year, and that's why he didn't come home." I pulled her against me. She resisted, but eventually fell against my side. We sat like that for a few minutes, and I let her digest the news.

When she sat up and looked at me, tears were streaming down her cheeks.

"I'm happy, Mommy. I'm just scared. What if he disappears again?" And there was the crux of all things Hannah feared. What if any of us left her? She bore a permanent scar, a never-abating fear of abandonment.

I hugged her fiercely and kissed the top of her head. "Oh, Hannah, we never know how long people will be in our lives. I hate that you have to worry about this, and you're only six years old. But the best we can do is love people as much as we can while we're together." I had no idea if that was the right thing to say.

Leah had wandered into the corner and was reading books, already losing interest in the conversation. Her four-year-old mind couldn't absorb the impact of my words. Leah would be fine, though.

She welcomed change and challenge in a way that Hannah never did. I marveled at their differences—one reticent and wary, the other so tough, seeming to bravely confront life in every way. My lion and my lamb. I retrieved a globe from the playroom and I showed them Canada.

"Why is Daddy in Canada?" Hannah asked.

Good question. "I don't know exactly, Hannah." Then, I decided to tell her a small lie. "He went there for work, but made a mistake and told me the wrong place before he left. So I didn't know he was there."

"Will he come home and live here now? With you and me and Hannah and Drew?" Leah asked, and I almost laughed at the image. If it weren't such a good question, I would have.

"I don't know what will happen, Leah. We'll have to see. Daddy is going to be in Canada for a while, but we'll visit him every weekend."

"And then he'll live here?" Hannah pressed.

I sighed. "We'll see, Hannah. We'll see."

<hr />

The ride to Toronto felt significantly shorter than the one a week ago. Drew's hand rested lightly on my knee, physically connecting what emotionally divided us. I drove faster than I should have, nervously tapping the steering wheel.

I tried to talk to the girls on the way about Greg. "You guys should know that Daddy was really sick. And he doesn't look the same, okay? He feels a lot better now, so don't be worried, but he looks skinnier."

Hannah regarded me distrustfully. *What are you hiding?* she seemed to ask. Leah hummed and looked out the window, clutching Uglydoll and bouncing her feet. Drew remained silent next to me, an extra in the movie of our life. I caught his eye every so often, and he would wink or smile, making me think for the millionth time how lucky I was to have him. *I could never give this up. I won't do it.* First things first. *Get through today. Tomorrow I can worry about the rest of my life.*

My kids were about to see their father for the first time in two years.

⌘

When we got to Toronto, Drew dropped us off at the rehabilitation center and went to check into the hotel. We would call him when we were ready to leave. Before we went in, I kneeled down in front of the girls. What I was about to say made me uneasy, but I didn't know what else to do.

"Listen, girls, don't say anything to Daddy about Drew, okay?" They nodded, but I could tell from Hannah's expression that she didn't like it. Leah was agreeable; her age made her more compliant and trusting. "Daddy doesn't remember very much. His memory got hurt when he was sick, so we're going to spend today talking about all the things we did before he was gone and all the fun we had, okay?"

"Why do we have to lie?" Hannah asked.

I shook my head. "Don't lie, Hannah. If Daddy has a question, always tell the truth. But this is going to be hard for Daddy because he's missed us so much. I wanted to tell Daddy about Drew on my own. It's a grown-up thing."

Hannah finally agreed, but the mistrust in her eyes remained. I led them inside, through the hallways, and to the same room where I had spoken with Greg the last visit. I had a Disney movie tucked into my purse. If nothing else, that might help occupy Leah for the duration of our visit. I paused outside the door, holding Hannah's hand tightly.

Leah gripped Hannah's other hand, her smile brilliant and her feet tapping. "I'm so excited," she stage whispered, giggling. Little Leah saw nothing but joy in the situation, a stark contrast to Hannah, who patiently waited for the other shoe to drop. But even Hannah grinned broadly.

I opened the door and was struck by déjà vu. Greg stood at the window, then turned to face us with the same expression. But tears streamed down his cheeks. I was taken aback. I had never seen Greg cry. He approached and, with the abandonment of a child, wrapped the girls in a hug. He sobbed then, raw and guttural. I felt a lump in my throat as I knelt with them, one hand on each of the girls' backs. Hannah was crying, too.

"Why is everyone so sad, Mommy?" Leah asked.

I laughed through my own tears. "Oh, baby, everyone is so happy."

I turned to watch Greg. Realization dawned on his face, his joy replaced by regret and then anger, a spectrum of emotions I'd never seen him have.

"Claire," he said, "they're so big. Hannah is so big. I've missed everything. Why?" He sank to the floor, letting go of them, his delight turning to sorrow.

The girls scurried back to me. He put his head on the floor and cried. My heart felt ripped apart for him. For us. I reached out, and for the first time since I discovered he was alive, held Greg in earnest. Hannah stood at the door, protectively embracing Leah.

I waved her back to us. "It's okay, honey. Daddy is sad because he's missed you so much."

She reached out in a gesture beyond her years and patted Greg on the back, shushing him the way I did Leah whenever she fell or got hurt. Greg cried heaving sobs, and we waited patiently for them to subside. When he finally straightened, he didn't apologize for his outburst or try to make excuses.

It's the brain injury. He has no idea how to restrain his grief.

We all sat silently on the floor for a few moments, holding each other.

Then, Leah announced, "Daddy, I'm so glad to see you, finally!"

And we laughed.

CHAPTER 36

WE STAYED WITH GREG UNTIL four o'clock in the afternoon. By then, the girls were hungry, and we were all mentally exhausted. For three hours, we sat in the small room in the rehab facility and told the stories of our lives, randomly, all talking at once in a jumble of words, which confused Greg most of the time. We told the story of the time we went looking for a Christmas tree, and Greg wanted the biggest tree he found, which wouldn't have fit in our house. We had gotten in a fight, then, because I tried to be agreeable. We settled on a slightly smaller behemoth of a tree that still didn't fit in our house. Greg had to carve out the back of the tree to fit into the corner of the living room. On the upside, I had enough greens to make a live wreath. Hannah remembered that well, as it had happened the Christmas before Greg disappeared.

We let Hannah guide the conversation, bringing up memories at random. Some would spark Greg's memory, and some wouldn't.

She would turn to Greg, hope shining on her face, and ask, "Do you remember, Daddy?"

He would sadly shake his head and say, "Tell me what you remember, Hannah."

And she would. But I could tell she was disappointed. Leah didn't have memories to contribute, but she delighted in telling Greg all about preschool, day camp, and all the new things she could do. *Hannah showed me how to tie my own shoes! I can color a whole picture and not go outside the lines at all!*

Several times, Greg cried openly, marveling at his children—so grown, small adults with opinions he didn't help form and views of the world he didn't give them. Hannah would shrink against the back of the couch, unused to seeing grown-ups cry so candidly.

Greg's memory was spotty when it came to the year before he disappeared. He finally remembered Leah, or at least he said he did, although not specifically the day she was born. He sat on the wooden chair across from the couch, rapt as Hannah spoke. His face was alight with a joy I'd never seen. Because his baseball cap was pulled low over his eyes, I was struck frequently with the sensation of talking to a stranger. Not one expression or mannerism was recognizable as something I'd seen on my husband's face. He had never worn baseball caps; he claimed they gave him a headache.

When we stood to go, he looked crushed. "Will you come back?"

"Yes, Greg, I will come back," I promised. "Why would you think I wouldn't?"

"I don't know." His expression pierced a hole in my heart—pained, nervous, and so very sad.

I motioned for the girls to wait in the hallway for me. I kissed Greg on the cheek.

"Were we happy, Claire? As a family?" he asked.

I thought so, but you weren't. How could I say that? The answer was, simply, that I didn't. So I did what I'd gotten quite good at the last few weeks. I lied.

"Yes, we were happy, Greg." And I left.

Drew and I took the girls to Applebee's for dinner, and then we watched Cinderella in the hotel room. Hannah and Leah slept in one bed, while Drew and I slept in the other. Drew was quiet and withdrawn all night, a trait I was unused to in him. His reticence bothered me, but I let it go. I told myself that it was hard on him, too, and he had been nothing but accommodating.

The girls were fast asleep halfway through the movie, and Drew and I lay in bed, talking in whispers. I gave him an overview of the day, how the girls did, how Greg did. He pulled me to him, my head resting in the crook of his shoulder.

"How will this work?" he asked. "When Greg gets out of rehab, can he even live alone? Is he going to move back in?"

"No, he's not living at our house. We're divorced now, Drew." But I'd had the same thoughts. Could Greg ever live alone? I had no idea. "It doesn't matter right now. He has months of therapy ahead of him before he will be released anyway." I sighed. "How can I tell him? He asked me tonight if we were happy, and I got so scared, I didn't know what to say. I lied and said yes. I mean, it wasn't a total lie. I *thought* we were happy."

"Were you happy?" Drew asked.

"Yes. No. I don't know. I would have been, if I had never known what it could be like. With you, I mean. Is that crazy?"

He shook his head. "This whole situation is crazy."

He kissed my temple, then my mouth, sparking the same longing he always did. I wanted to drag him to the bathroom and make violent love to him. I wanted to erase Greg from my mind, from my heart. Instead, I lay in Drew's arms until we both fell asleep.

Sunday, we spent the morning with Greg and left around noon for the eight-hour drive home. The first half of the ride, the girls chattered excitedly about their daddy being back. They fell asleep for the second half, exhausted from the weekend roller coaster. At eight o'clock, we pulled up to our house. Cameras, spotlights, news vans, reporters, and cameramen were all over the front lawn.

I clutched Drew's arm. "Oh, my God! What the hell?"

Hannah woke up and looked out the window. "Mommy," she cried, panic in her voice. "What's going on?"

As we pulled into the driveway, reporters approached the car and knocked on Drew's window. Questions were shouted out from all directions.

"Mrs. Barnes, how do you feel now that your husband is awake?"

"Who is in the car with you?"

"Are you in another relationship?"

"How are the children doing?"

I grabbed Leah, and Drew took Hannah. We ran inside and slammed the door. Both kids were crying, and I was shocked.

Drew slammed his fist against the door. "Shit!"

"Everyone calm down!" I shouted. "This is not a surprise. Our story is extraordinary, and I'm shocked it's taken this long to spark interest."

I rummaged in the cabinets until I found an empty coffee can. Before I could lose my nerve, I opened the front door and walked outside. Within seconds, flashes were going off, and people started shouting questions. I held up my hand.

When everyone quieted, I spoke loudly and clearly. "I realize my family's story is exceptional. I will speak to one reporter, sometime later this week. I'll call you. Please don't call my house. You will win my favor by being respectful. My children are going through a lot right now, and this is scary to them. We've spent the weekend with their father, and we are exhausted. Please, go home. If you don't go home and leave us alone, I will, without a doubt, not speak to any of you. Put your business cards in the can. This will be my last public comment. Thank you."

I placed the empty coffee can on the top step, and I walked back inside to my family.

In some ways, the next few weeks were more strenuous than when Greg went missing. The dichotomy of my week against my weekend was exhausting. My weekdays were spent with Hannah, Leah, and Drew—school, homework, dance class or soccer, bath, and bed. On weekends, I made the eight-hour drive to Toronto to spend with

Greg. Mostly I travelled alone. I took the girls once, but told them we would spend a lot more time with Daddy when he came back to New Jersey. I deliberately avoided the phrase "when he comes home."

At the therapist's suggestion, we were recounting our life, chronologically and in great detail. I would haul in pictures, mementos, and things I would find around the house. When I gave him his journal, he ran his hands over the soft leather, passing the book back and forth between them. When I asked if he remembered it, he nodded. He opened the journal and read each page. He paused at the poem, *I carry your heart with me. I carry it in my heart. C!* He ran a finger over the words.

"Was C me?" I asked tentatively, not sure I wanted to know the answer.

"I don't know," he said, honestly, regretfully. "I don't remember writing it."

That stung. I had hoped it would spark a memory. Our time together was filled with so much of me talking, recounting stories, filling in blanks in Greg's memory that he might not remember minutes after I told him anyway.

That was the frustrating part. I thought that once he remembered something, it would be retained, but frequently, I found myself retelling stories over and over again.

Once, after three weeks, he forgot Leah again. I excused myself and walked into the hallway, making sure to shut the heavy latched door behind me, then kicked a chair and cursed.

"What did you expect?" a voice asked from behind me. I turned to see Dr. Goodman watching me.

"I don't know. I thought... I thought it would be easier."

"It will become easier," she replied mildly, as if my frustration was just a small part of her day. She started writing on a clipboard, all but ignoring me. When she looked up again, she smiled kindly. "Memory works like a natural tributary."

I shook my head, confused by the analogy.

Reaching into her portfolio, she pulled out a yellow legal pad and a pen. She drew two lines down the center of the page. "Memories form new memories, just like water will find water. That's how it works. Draining water will form small streams, flowing together to a larger water source. A creek. A river. Eventually, the ocean." She drew small offshoots into the larger original two-lined river. "After a heavy rainfall, smaller, temporary streams can be formed, but without a source, they'll dry up. Same thing with memory. New offshoots can be formed, but only with sufficient replenishment. With enough water, those tributaries become a permanent part of the landscape, and the earth underneath carved to accommodate the new stream. Rocks will be moved; even trees and vegetation relocate to allow for it. It's a natural, yet time consuming, effect."

I understood the concept, but I was just tired of being patient. Of being understanding.

She nonchalantly stored her notepad and pen back inside her portfolio. "The analogy works on a few different levels."

I studied her with a spark of interest. "What levels?"

"Without a sufficient source of memory, Greg will forget a lot of what he's learned. That's you. You have to feed these small creeks of knowledge, both the established ones and the new, baby ones; they're the most fragile. Feed them by telling the same stories over and over again. The people in Greg's life have to shift. New canals won't be formed without this change. You must put aside yourself, your life, your kids, everything. The landscape of your life has to change. Without it, those new memories? The small ones that he keeps forgetting? They'll be stamped out. Like a dry riverbed."

"Will he ever just remember anything? I mean, right after I tell him a story, will it ever come back fully, where he retains it?"

"It's a long process. It's not the movies, Claire, where someone wakes up from a coma and *poof!* they remember everything. Remember, Greg is extraordinary. We have rarely seen someone come so far so fast after such a long period of unconsciousness." For the first time, the cold, steely woman was helpful. I felt better.

When I told her so, she laughed. "Working with the family members has never been my strong point. I frequently find them to be a necessary evil. They are emotional and often negatively impact a patient's progress with their own way of dealing with their situation. Your situation is unique, to say the least. I have to admit I'm intrigued."

"You and everyone else it seems," I said dryly, recalling the throng of reporters on my lawn.

I thanked her and returned to Greg's room. He was sitting on the couch, staring intently at the journal.

He looked up when I came in. "Who's Karen?"

I shrugged. "I don't know." *Fuck it.* "I think you had an affair, Greg. Before the accident. I think Karen was your mistress. I don't have any proof other than that note."

He was quiet for a long time, lost in thought, searching for the memory. We were supposed to talk chronologically, and we had gotten up to Hannah's first year. I had gingerly avoided the subject of Drew. I was delaying the hard parts—the affair, the memorial service, the divorce, my new life. But we couldn't avoid them forever.

"The year before you disappeared, you were very withdrawn. Very… almost angry with me. I never knew why." I retold Rochester in detail: the empty hotel room, the Thai restaurant. I told him about San Diego, the Grand Del Mar, the golf tee, and the fake business trips. He stared at the note, *Call Karen at Omni S.D*, tracing the letters with his finger, over and over again.

"Karen Caughee," he said finally. "That's her name." Then he whispered, "Pronounced like *coffee*, the drink."

I hadn't known I was holding my breath until I expelled it, bursting out of me, relief and regret at once.

When he met my eyes, his were dry, but I'd never seen him look so sad. "She was my lover."

CHAPTER 37

When I picked up the *Hunterdon County Times* on Monday, I wasn't expecting to see my face on the front page. Then again, there was so little news in Clinton, that I supposed had I thought about it, of course, my story would be front page when it finally ran.

Weeks ago, I had pulled the business cards from the coffee can and spread them out on the dining room table. I focused on women only and, after doing some internet searching, chose the one who wrote the least scandalous and most boring stories. Rebecca Riley had reported on the inclusion of the rural outskirts of Clinton into the public sewage system and what that would mean for homeowners. I only hoped Rebecca would write my story with the same level of enthusiasm.

When Rebecca had shown up, I found her to be my age, slightly overweight, smart, and personable. I instantly felt comfortable and spoke honestly and candidly, which was my first mistake. When I got the paper after returning from my weekend with Greg, I gaped in shock. The front page displayed a close-up of my face on the night the media had been all over my lawn. My features were pinched, and my hand was up in the air. I looked *bitchy.* The use of that photo was surprising because Rebecca and I had taken a few pictures together in the house and out by the barn. I sat down to read.

Claire Barnes: Grieving Wife or Brilliant Opportunist?
By Rebecca Riley
To meet Claire, petite, mild-mannered, and cheerful, you would have no

idea of the tragedy her family has undergone in the past two years. Her husband of eight years left for a business trip two years ago and never returned home. Claire and their two children, Hannah and Leah, have remained in the home they shared with her missing husband.

In the meantime, Claire has become involved with her childhood friend, Drew Elliot. Some might say, "Good for her. She's moved on, made a life in the shadow of tragedy." Unless you know who Drew Elliot is. Semi-famous in artistic circles, he shoots compelling photographs of poverty-stricken men and women in American cities and makes a nice living doing it. Prior to his photography venture, he was a self-made millionaire when he got lucky during the Silicon Valley years. Then, one begins to think, "Lucky for her. Her troubled marriage seems to end without consequence, she has the endless sympathy of the community, and she gets to shack up with a millionaire? Seems rather convenient."

Claire is likeable. She's expressive, cheerful, funny, warm, and kind. Her home is beautiful—an old farmhouse accessorized with appropriate antiques, yet stylishly updated for modern living. She comments that the kitchen was recently redone.

"Most of the rooms in this house have been redone, actually. Since Greg left. It was a way to cleanse, to start over and regroup. You need that when you believe your husband has died, to find your own voice. I needed to make my life mine, where it was once 'ours.'"

But you can't help but notice the fine craftsmanship of the redecoration: stainless steel appliances, marble countertops, handcrafted cabinetry custom built from refurbished barn boards. You notice and wonder.

The most jarring part of the whole scene is the knowledge that Claire's husband did not leave her. Nor did he die. He was robbed at gunpoint and pushed in front of an oncoming car. He lay in a coma for a year and a half, and even after he awoke, had no idea who he was.

Detective Matt Reynolds gave a statement on Saturday. "Our investigation was sound. We never stopped searching for Greg Barnes, and we have the records to prove that."

You still have to wonder why they couldn't find him. Both Claire Barnes

239

and Detective Reynolds claim they searched tirelessly for her husband. And then, they stopped searching. A mere three months ago, Claire Barnes filed for, and was granted, a divorce from her husband. A month ago, Greg Barnes regained his memory.

Claire said, "Of course it's been hard. Greg doesn't remember our life together. He doesn't remember our youngest daughter most of the time. I travel to Toronto every weekend, and we work on what the doctors call his episodic memory, basically reconstructing his past through talking, photographs, and mementos."

Greg currently resides in Toronto, Ontario, Canada, in a community housing environment designed specifically for the brain-injured. He participates in six to eight hours of therapy every day and volunteers for the community one day a week.

But when asked what will happen after Greg can come home, Claire Barnes shrugs and appears lost in thought. "I don't know. We're all taking it one day at a time."

I was in shock. The article was so blatantly slanted. It contained no mention of Greg's lies or the reason why we had no idea he was in Toronto, several hundred miles from where he had claimed he was going. I sat dumbfounded at the kitchen island. *My newly remodeled island*, I thought bitterly.

Drew came into the kitchen, whistling, and poured himself a cup of coffee. He stopped when he saw my face and the newspaper. "Can I read it?"

Wordlessly, I handed it to him. He wasn't painted so great in the article either.

As he read, his mouth dropped open. "What did you say to her?" he asked tautly.

"What the hell is that supposed to mean? I told the truth. That was the point, remember?"

"Hey, relax. Don't get mad at me. I thought giving an interview was a bad idea to begin with." His eyes flashed and we faced off across the island.

I waved my hand, defeated. "Whatever."

Drew looked pained. The last few weeks had taken their toll on him. He smiled tentatively. "I'm sorry. That was uncalled for." He touched my hand lightly. I laced my fingers through his. He massaged my palm with his thumb and looked down at the counter thoughtfully. "One day at a time?" he asked.

"I don't know, Drew. Yes, right now, one day at a time. Will Greg move in here? No, probably not. Do I know what will happen? No, not at all. I'm so scared. He still has no idea he and I aren't married anymore." I dropped my head into my hands and stared at the counter.

Drew moved behind me and massaged my shoulders. "I'm sorry. Again, Claire. I'm sorry. I'm... I guess I'm scared." He rested his cheek against the top of my head.

I hugged his arms around me, leaning back into him. "I know. Me, too, you know? And I'm pissed. Who does Rebecca Riley think she is? I picked her because her writing was so damn boring. Why did she get all sensationalistic on me?"

We sat in silence for a few minutes, digesting the morning, another new kink in our lives.

"Do you still love Greg?" Drew asked.

I knew he'd wanted to ask that question since I had started commuting to Canada every weekend, leaving him to take care of *my* kids in *my* house. *Our house.* I considered how to answer. "Yes. I do. He's the father of my children. I'll always love him."

I saw his eyes go blank, defensively shutting down. He looked down.

Placing my hands on either side of his face, I forced him to look me in the eyes. "I will always be his family. Can you understand that? Can you live with that? Forever?"

Drew didn't respond. I didn't expect him to; it wasn't a question he could answer on the fly. I was asking him for some serious considerations. Things had been strained between us, my trips to Toronto interrupting any chance of the two of us connecting. Forging our own life together had been temporarily put on hold. I had nothing left in me to devote to our relationship.

⁓꙰⁓

My closest friends were supportive after the article was published. Robin brought me a bottle of wine one night to "drink my anger away" and then stayed to share it. Sarah ranted and raved on the phone as much as I needed her to. Mom wrote a letter to the editor. Even Melinda called to ask me if I needed anything, saying she thought Rebecca Riley was a muckraker, which I found rather humorous, considering the source.

But strangers and even acquaintances were not as kind. At my yearly checkup, the receptionist was borderline rude. A few women from church wouldn't even say hello to me when I volunteered to help with the rummage sale fundraiser. Since I wasn't going to be around to help with the event, I offered to help set up a few days early. My offer was received with cold glares and an offhand comment about it "being taken care of." I resisted the urges to grab people by the collars and yell, "Do you realize he was cheating on me? That he lied about where he was?" I doubted doing that would convince anyone of my sanity.

Since our conversation in the kitchen, Drew stayed close to my side, protective and, conversely, insecure. He frequently touched my hand or my shoulder, making sure I was still there, anchored in our life as much as I could be, with one foot in Toronto. He kissed me goodbye every Saturday morning at six o'clock, as if I were off to work or shopping with Sarah. I wondered what lengths he was willing to go to for me, and if I could ever repay him. I doubted it. I pondered the debt I owed and what a toll the situation had to be taking on him. Then, I swallowed my guilt, pushing it down, deep into the place I only acknowledge when I'm alone. And sometimes, not even then.

CHAPTER 38

THE FIFTH FRIDAY, WHILE I packed, we fought. He stood at the foot of the bed, silent and brooding, watching me fold shirts and jeans and place them carefully into my red Samsonite. Without looking up, I asked, "What?"

He sighed like a petulant child. "What's going on, Claire?" His voice held a pleading, almost panicky, note.

"I don't expect you to understand." *Socks, underwear, an extra pair of shoes.* I packed virtually the same suitcase every weekend with Dr. Goodman in the back of my mind. *Even something as simple as wearing the same shirt can help.* Greg's condition and his recovery were my only thoughts anymore. "You've never been married."

"I've only ever wanted to marry one person. Who doesn't seem to want to marry me."

I looked up from my packing, astonished at his childishness. "Really? You're going to pick this fight? This time?" *The worst time in the world.*

"I'm sorry. I shouldn't have said that. I'm so..." He ran his hand through his hair and, with his left hand, threw an imaginary baseball at the back wall, expending energy. He let out a groan, almost a half-growl. "I'm frustrated by all of this. I *know* it's selfish. I'm not an idiot."

"It's not about you," I said, turning back to my suitcase.

"It never is, Claire. You'd think I'd be used to it by now." And he left. Not in a fury, with slamming doors and yelling, but quietly, slipping out of the bedroom before I even realized he was gone, and somehow that was worse.

I came to bed late, and he was either asleep or pretending to be, and for the first time, I wondered if that fight was the beginning of the end. We'd always been honest with each other. But our conversations had become strained and halting, and I didn't know how to fix it. There was resentment there, for sure, bubbling right under the surface, like superheated water, ready to explode at the slightest disturbance. It had only been a month—*a month!*—not that long when I said it out loud. But when the days blended into each other, and the weekends came breathlessly, one on top of the other, a month was forever.

⌒⏦⏦⌒

Greg was getting better. I could see it every weekend. His strength was returning, although his body was still slight compared to his old stature. His memory was quicker; he could recall things I'd already told him, but it was still slippery, a suitcase full of silk scarves, sliding around, their fabric tumbled together in a rich heap of color. Indistinguishable. Possibly, it always would be, Dr. Goodman said.

"What will happen when I come home?" Greg asked.

We'd been sitting together, looking at pictures. I'd brought up his childhood pictures, photos of his mom and dad and some cousins.

I closed the book and ran my hand over the cover. "I don't know, Greg. Maybe a group home, like you're in now?"

"And you'll be where? In our old house? With the kids?"

It sounded so ridiculous, even to me. I nodded, not knowing what else to do. For the first time, I realized that I hadn't even glimpsed the impact Greg's return was going to have on my life. Moving would be in my future. I thought back to Friday and the fight with Drew. I wondered if Drew would stay with me. *Who would, really?* If the roles were reversed, would I stay? Could anyone blame him if he left?

That night, I lay on the bed in the dark hotel room, the television on for light, but no sound. The flickering lent a dreamlike quality

244

to the room, a vacillation that mimicked our conversation. I called Drew, and we spoke at the same time.

"Did you—"

"When are you—"

We both laughed, soft and unsure.

My mind drew comparisons to the calls with Greg, in the months before he disappeared when our halting phone conversations were heavy with silence and alternately, ill-timed starts and stops. I couldn't think of anything to say to Drew, and it was easier to make excuses to hang up.

I slept fitfully, tossing and turning with the sensation that I was failing on all accounts—as an ex-wife and caregiver, as a mother, as a girlfriend.

The next day, when I kissed Greg goodbye on the cheek, he grabbed my wrist and pulled me into a rare embrace. "I'm sorry. For everything."

I turned away because there was nothing to say and I couldn't face my anger, which still simmered under the surface. *What kind of person would still hold a grudge? Hadn't Greg paid enough?* And *yet,* in my weaker moments, when Greg would forget Leah's name, *again,* or forget, *again,* that the album we were looking at was from Maine, when we were first married, but before Hannah was born, even though I'd told him three times already, I would stare at him and think, horribly, *This is all your fucking fault.* And those were the moments that kept me awake at night, the fear of failure creeping up on me in the dark, black and wet and suffocating until I sat up, feeling for Drew on the other side of the bed and finding only the cold, empty expanse of hotel sheets.

When I returned Sunday evening, Mom had already dropped off the girls. Every other week, I arranged for them to spend the weekend with my parents instead of Drew, to mix it up and give Drew a break. A wonderful mixture of garlic and lemon hung in the air, and it smelled like home to me. I paused in the hallway, watching him stir something on the stove, laugh at something Hannah said, and take a sip of wine at the same time. He looked at ease in his kitchen, his house. When he turned and saw me, he smiled tentatively, traces of our Friday night argument still between us. I wrapped my arms around him from behind, burying my face in his back, inhaling the scent of him. I thought about how unfair things were to both of us and wondered what the future held. I rubbing my nose back and forth between his shoulder blades, saying, *I'm sorry for Friday.*

He leaned back into me and patted my hands. *You're forgiven.* He turned his head and, in profile, gave me a wry smile with one raised eyebrow. *Sort of.*

Later, I was setting the table, lost in thought, when I heard Hannah ask Drew, "When did you get home?"

Drew replied, "What do you mean, Hannah? I've been here all weekend."

As I walked to the powder room in the hallway, I stopped to listen.

"No," Hannah insisted. "There were two suitcases by the door yesterday. Remember? When we came back for our roller skates? Did you go to New York?"

Drew's reply was muffled, low and inaudible, but his tone sounded impatient.

When I came out of the bathroom, Hannah and Leah were watching TV in the living room, and Drew was putting dinner on the table.

"Did I hear Hannah say you went to the city?" I asked.

"Oh, I went to John's gallery for some paperwork." He handed me a bottle of wine and walked back into the kitchen.

That doesn't make sense. I let it go, for the moment. I had spent too much of my life blindly trusting another person, and my radar was hypersensitive, going off at the slightest signal. *I have no reason not to trust Drew.*

Yet still, all during dinner, something niggled the edges of my subconscious. I put the girls to bed and joined Drew in the living room. Sunday nights were ours. We sat on the couch in the living room, sharing a bottle of wine, sometimes talking about Greg, sometimes—more so lately—in our own private thoughts, but still together. Things felt different, though. Drew seemed quieter.

Finally, I asked, "Why would you need two suitcases to go to the gallery?"

He stumbled with his words, and then realization dawned, a horrible clenching in my stomach.

"You were leaving." I said it simply and without embellishment. He had no reply, and I knew I was right. "But you didn't. You're here. Why?"

He swirled the wine in his glass and cleared his throat. "I thought maybe you would be better off. If Greg came home, you could be a family..."

"Bullshit."

He shook his head, a small smile playing on his lips. "I was being a coward. I was scared."

We sat for a few minutes, not looking at each other. My hands shook as I sipped my wine, and I felt sick. "Are we going to make it through this?" I asked eventually, needing the answer to be yes, but ultimately unsure that it would be.

"I don't know." He pulled me to him and kissed the top of my head. "I know you're going through a lot, Claire. I try to do what I can to be here for you. But you internalize everything, and I can't sit here day after day, waiting for you to come back. Even when you're here, you're not."

"I can't help that. I have nothing left to give. Can't you understand that?"

"To some extent, yes, but all I *do* is give. And yet, I'm last. After Greg, after Hannah and Leah, even after your mom. Can't you understand that?"

We were at an impasse. I did see that, but there was nothing I could do. Ultimately, it was up to Drew to stay or go, but I couldn't make it better.

"Could you have faith?" I asked. He tilted his head, a silent question. "Could you trust me when I say that I will be able to give myself to you? In time, I mean. I just can't do it now. I'm pulled in too many directions; too many people need me. I need you to not need me."

"I think I'll always need you," he answered after a long pause. "But I'm staying, if that's what you're asking. At some point, I need to come before Greg. You do realize that. We need to come first, eventually."

I nodded because I understood what he was saying, but I knew that everything was different. Drew and I, as a couple, could never come first. My heart hurt as I thought about how close I had come to losing Drew, while I wondered if I still would. The road ahead was so long, I couldn't be sure he would stay. And what about later, when Greg came home? Could I put Drew ahead of Greg's treatments? Everything I did for Greg, I did because of the girls, so wouldn't that be akin to putting Drew before my children?

I longed for Brigantine. The idyllic summer days, too short and too few, and felt sorry for the courtship we'd been cheated out of.

We never talked about it again, daily life providing a patch, a false sense of security over the hole in our relationship. I didn't know for sure if it would get better, or if we would get stronger, but I had to believe I would eventually be able to give myself to him fully. I had to believe he would stay long enough for that to happen.

All I knew was that I had to, at least, have faith.

CHAPTER 39

I BROUGHT PHOTO ALBUMS FROM VARIOUS vacations: Maine, our Boston camping trip, the Outer Banks, North Carolina. Greg and I were paging through them, telling the stories of the trips. He was improving, but sometimes he wouldn't admit when his memory failed him. We sat close on the couch, knees touching. In some ways, I had never felt closer to Greg. We had never spent so much time just talking. Our friendship had a sibling feel to it. I didn't know if that was because of Drew or because Greg had become such a different person. Greg had become soft-spoken, quiet, and insecure. His emotions overflowed to the point where I grew impatient. He cried at every visit, sad about his new life, and frustrated with his inability to retain simple facts.

"I feel stupid all the time," he complained. "Like I can't keep up. And you look at me like I'm a child."

"Greg, I don't think you're a child. I think we need to work on this. Together, okay?" I wanted him to get better. I needed him to come back to New Jersey, so we could make decisions and move on with our lives. I reached out and touched his shoulder.

He leaned forward, and before I could stop him, he kissed me. His lips felt familiar, and I felt warmth bloom from my center. Instinctively, I kissed back, my mouth opening to his in a fleeting need to restore order to the unrelenting chaos. The kiss gained intensity, comforting only in its familiarity, and for a brief second, I closed my eyes and pretended the last two years had never happened. *But they did happen.* I pushed back, gazing into his deep brown eyes.

"I'm sorry..." Greg started, but then, he slammed his fist down on his knee and stood. "You know what? I'm not really sorry. You're my wife. I'm allowed to kiss you."

I took a deep breath to steady myself for the shock about to come, but I couldn't put it off anymore. "Greg, sit down. I need to tell you something."

He chose to sit on the opposite end.

"We aren't married anymore. The courts granted my petition for a divorce." The words rushed out of me, grateful to be free.

"What? What does that mean?" He looked incredulous. And angry.

"It means I needed to move on with my life. I didn't know where you were. We thought you were dead, but without proof, I couldn't... move on." I faltered, unsure of how much detail to divulge.

He narrowed his eyes at me. "You met someone else."

I nodded.

He paused for a moment, and then he said, "Drew."

I nodded again, and he sank back against the arm of the sofa, the anger drained, replaced with defeat. Up until that moment, I had yet to talk about Drew. I'd avoided his name in all our stories, our memories. I didn't know if Greg had any recollection of him.

"Greg, it's not what you think. We—"

"I'm pretty sure it's exactly what I think," he replied dryly. He appeared thoughtful. "Drew was always there, in the background. With me out of the way..." His voice trailed off, and he leaned back, a small self-satisfied smile playing on his lips.

I shook my head vehemently, willing him to understand, to believe. To believe what?

"No, Greg, it wasn't like that. Not for me. I wasn't in love with him when you and I were married. It's a recent development."

He sat, gazing out into the room, perfectly still. Finally, he said, "I was not a good husband to you, Claire."

I started to shake my head, tears springing to my eyes at the painful truth of his words.

He held up his hand. "Did you find out about the inheritance?

From my mother?" When I nodded, he continued, "I was so angry at that money. I watched my mother struggle. My whole life, we had *nothing.* I had the same pair of sneakers my entire four years of high school. I wore them every day, even in the summer. Even when I worked, she demanded my paychecks, saying she would put the money in an account for me. I paid for everything myself, struggled for everything. She worked two jobs, and for what? After she died, and I received that money, I couldn't figure out the point of all of it. She had the money, sure, but she was never going to spend it on her life. Never going to enjoy anything. We never went to Disney World, never took a vacation. We didn't even turn the heat on until December. My strongest memories of my childhood involve being cold and my home being dark. I put half the money into a savings account and the other half in an offshore account with a higher interest rate. There was almost a million dollars total, but I swore I would never touch it. I wanted to leave it to my kids to spend, when it wouldn't be tainted with cold, dark memories."

"By doing that, you tainted it," I interjected. He looked up, surprised. "When I found it, I was dumbfounded. And even now, knowing there's probably twice that amount somewhere that I still didn't know about, I don't understand. Why didn't you tell me? Why didn't you confide in me? Wasn't I good enough? By isolating yourself, you isolated me. I have never felt so alone in my life, being your wife." I started to cry, remembering my loneliness on nights when Greg would wander the house and snap at me if I dared to approach him.

Greg reached out and touched my knee. "I'm sorry. I don't know why. I felt like I needed to be strong for you and the kids. I had all this anger and nowhere to put it. It makes no sense now."

He put his arms around me, pulling me close. We stayed that way for a beat, but I pulled back, wiping my eyes.

He looked sad, defeated. "I ruined everything." Then softly, he added, "It's all my fault."

I placed my hand over his, and my mind flashed back to our

wedding day, our hands one on top of the other, in a simple, innocent promise. *In sickness and in health.* "It's not *all* anyone's fault. There were two of us not doing such a great job."

"Could we ever go back? Try again? Make it work?" he asked.

I tried to read his face to see what he really wanted, but I couldn't. For the first time since his accident, he seemed able to hide his emotions.

I shook my head. "I don't think so, Greg. I'm sorry."

He nodded as if he knew that would be my response. He stood up, not meeting my gaze.

I got to my feet. "Moving on was the hardest thing I've ever had to do. But I did it, and it's been over two years. I can't make myself feel something. Do you see that?"

"I think I need to be alone. Will you come back tomorrow?"

"I'll come back, Greg. We're still a family, okay? I'll always come back." And I left.

Sometimes on my visits, Greg and I would eat dinner together. Other times, when Greg had an ill-timed therapy session, I'd find a restaurant and huddle in a back booth to read a book or the newspaper. I discovered a diner a few blocks away from the rehabilitation center that made the most delicious chicken salad I could imagine, and I found solace in the isolation. No one knew where I was or expected anything from me. And most importantly, I wasn't letting anyone down. I was just... being.

On Saturday, after leaving Greg, I sought comfort in the familiarity of my diner. I sat at my booth, staring out the window at a flat gray parking lot, lost in thought. In one way, a weight had been lifted. I had finally told Greg about the divorce, about Drew. My future had some shape to it. Greg would surely be in it, but not as my husband. Alternatively, the finality made me sad. I wanted to rewind the past two years and start over, go back to a time when things were simple. But were they? Two years ago, we were barely speaking, and Greg was seeing another woman. So no, things weren't simpler. They had just appeared that way. Was that better? Surely not.

I had the sensation of time closing in on me. In a few weeks, Greg would move back to New Jersey, and Toronto would become a distant memory. The pressure was pushing *her* name up into my throat. *Karen Caughee.* Who was she? What did she look like? What did she have that I didn't? Those were the standard questions of a jilted wife, but my other questions were more complicated. Why hadn't she looked for Greg? Did she know what happened to him? *Who was she?*

I pulled out my phone and opened the web browser. After a quick search, I found an entry for Caughee, K. with a Toronto phone number, but no address. I had asked Greg a few times since the day I learned her name: *Where does she live? What does she do? How did you meet?*

I don't remember. His single, standard, infuriating answer. I assumed that was the truth, and that he hadn't learned to lie again.

I had become a little obsessed with her, a fact I couldn't reveal to Drew or anyone else. It made no sense, but the desire to answer every question was all-consuming. I'd spent two years trying to accept a life with loose ends, to move on despite uncertainty, and was *almost* there. A small part of me wanted to walk away. *What does it matter now? Just move on.* But the temptation for actual closure was too great.

I found a reverse look-up search engine and typed in the phone number. *Bingo.* 725 St. Clair Avenue West. *St. Clair.* I almost laughed. Had Greg noted the irony?

I had a thought and clicked the map application on my phone. I punched in Karen's address and expanded the screen, searching for something I knew would answer at least one question definitely. The street where Greg had been hit was Arlington Avenue. I didn't have to look very hard—it was two blocks from Karen's apartment.

A million scenarios ran through my mind. Had he just gone out for coffee and not come back? *Too many questions.*

Before I could talk myself out of it, I threw a ten-dollar bill on the table, gathered my cell phone and purse, and hurried out the front door.

CHAPTER 40

I WALKED UP ARLINGTON AVENUE, THEN crossed over to Karen's apartment. Twice. I studied the street where Greg must have been hit, and irrationally, I looked for blood on the pavement. My thoughts were so jumbled. I tried to work it out in my head. *Was this sane? Would a normal person do this?* I stood outside her apartment building with my back to the bustling street, my palms slick with sweat. A young guy in khakis and a yellow polo shirt hurried up with keys at the ready, and I knew it was my shot. I smiled at him, easy and carefree like I would have years ago, and his eyes lit up. He held the door open for me, and I followed him across the lobby. He opened his mouth to say something, but I slipped into the stairwell just as he turned the other direction.

When I heard the thunk of the elevator doors closing, I went back out into the lobby and studied the mailboxes. *Caughee, K. 4D.* To avoid Polo Shirt, I slipped back into the stairwell and took the steps two at a time. On the fourth floor, *4D* was the first door I saw.

Before I could talk myself out of it, I closed my eyes and knocked. Dinnertime on a Saturday night, what were the chances? But the door opened.

"Hi, can I help you?" A woman stood impatiently, with one hand on the door and the other held a cell phone to her shoulder. I was struck by her age, so incredibly young. *Twenty-something at the most.*

"I... do you have a minute? I'm Claire Barnes... You might not know me. Or maybe you do? I'm Greg's wife."

She held my gaze and brought the cell phone to her face. "I'm going to have to call you back." She clicked the end button, seemingly without waiting for an answer. "Greg's wife?" Her voice trembled for a second.

"Greg Barnes," I said. "He's been in an accident."

"Um... the only Greg I know is Greg Randolf. Are you sure you have the right place?"

The name knocked the wind out of me. Randolf had been Greg's mother's maiden name. *How creative.* I felt like laughing. "You're going to want to let me in."

I sat at her kitchen table and took in the sparse apartment. Newspapers were piled up on the sideboard, but the place was clean and sparingly decorated in modern, angular furniture. I watched Karen as she busied herself with the coffee pot. She had several inches on me and was naturally thin. Lithe, even. Never in my life could I have been called *lithe.* I couldn't stop comparing. She had long blond hair and moved with the assurance of a dancer.

"I travel for work, so I'm sorry for the mess." She placed two steaming mugs of coffee on the table and settled in the chair across from me. She was pretty, but not beautiful, and that made things better somehow. "You said there was an accident?"

"Two years ago, Greg was mugged and pushed into the path of an oncoming car. He was in a coma at St. Michael's until six months ago. When he woke up, he didn't remember anything, not his name, where he was from, nothing." I spoke slowly, but flat and unemotional. The drawn shades and darkened kitchen lent a surreal cast to the moment, a made-for-TV movie quality that I couldn't shake.

"Is he okay?" she asked through a hand-covered mouth, her eyebrows knitted in worry.

"Yes, sort of. He *will* be. Right now, his memory is spotty. He remembered your name, though. And mine and our children." I purposefully left out any mention of his trouble with recalling Leah;

she had no business knowing that.

"Greg was married." Her statement shocked me. She hadn't known, then? "It makes sense. I could never call him; he was always travelling, he said."

"How did you meet?"

"Where else? In a bar. He was here for work. It had to be... oh, three years ago now?" She looked up, as if the ceiling held the memory and gave a small secretive smile, which lit a quick fire in me. *Does she have the right to a private memory?*

"You didn't know about his accident, then? The nurses said it was in the paper." I stirred my coffee and fought the urge to throw my mug against the wall.

"The night he broke up with me was the last time I saw him."

"What night was that?" My voice was sharper than I'd intended, but I knew the answer before she said it.

"I don't know the date exactly. I guess it was September... late September."

"September thirtieth?"

"Maybe. It was a Thursday night. I remember because I was leaving on Friday. I had a concert in New York. I cried the entire bus ride." Her manner was cool as she appraised me over the rim of her coffee mug, her long thin fingers tapping on the ceramic.

My anger was creeping up, choking me, though it felt misplaced. "Tell me everything, please?" I didn't look at her, instead choosing to stare into my mug, stirring it slowly.

"I loved him. I think he loved me. Or at least he said he did."

"Then why did you break up? That night?" I sank to her level, willing to trade barbs. *Settle down. She has information you need, Claire.*

"His company was transferring him to China. Some executive position, a big promotion. He thought it was a great opportunity, and he wanted to go. It was a two-year assignment, but I'm a violinist in the Toronto Symphony Orchestra. At the time, I was trying for assistant principal, the youngest in the history of the TSO. There was no way I could go. We agreed to... put our relationship on hold."

I laughed in earnest. *What relationship?* I wanted to yell. *You didn't even know his name.* Advent had no foothold in China, and if they had, certainly not for a corporate trainer. Greg's *girlfriend* hadn't known him any better than I had. Questions swirled in my mind, but half of them I would never give her the satisfaction of asking.

"Karen, there was no China." I reached across the table and lightly tapped her hand. "Greg was a bored thirty-five-year-old man in a troubled marriage, with a couple of kids, in the suburbs of New Jersey."

"He said he didn't have kids, but that he'd always wanted them."

I sucked in a harsh breath. The depths of her cruelty seemed boundless. *What about Greg's dishonesty? Did that know no limits?* "Do you still love him?" My questions were primal and unplanned, and perhaps just as callous; I didn't know. I'd lost perspective in the shrinking kitchen.

She shook her head, appearing rattled for the first time. She held up her left hand, displaying a simple solitaire diamond. "I called his cell over and over until one day, after a month or so, the recording said the phone had been disconnected. It took about a year for me to move on. I knew he was American; he said he was from Syracuse, but it hadn't ever mattered because he was never home, he'd said. I stopped trying after that and met a very nice trombone player. The wedding's in May."

She pushed herself up, crossed the room, and rummaged through a drawer. When she returned, she was holding a long strip of paper. She looked at it a moment before handing it to me. Greg's face stared back at me, pushed up against Karen's, four squares, various expressions. A photo booth picture strip. I was taken aback. His face was relaxed, free of the worry lines on his forehead. Her mouth was open in a frozen laugh, wide lipsticked lips stretched across straight white teeth. In the bottom picture, they kissed through laughter, her left eye open, peeking at the camera.

"He looks so... happy." I fingered the picture. I hadn't meant to say that aloud.

"Oh, that was Greg. He was always such a goofball."

Will the real Greg please stand up?

CHAPTER 41

1 MONTH LATER

GREG CAME HOME ALMOST THREE months after we found him, which was about two months longer than Dr. Goodman had predicted. We found a group home specifically targeted for the brain-injured about twenty-five minutes away from our house. At Dr. Goodman's recommendation, Greg wouldn't be living alone for at least a year. His short-term memory was inconsistent, at best. He would undergo the same therapy in New Jersey that he had in Canada, and the group home provided for transportation to and from rehab, as well as staff therapists to aid with social transitioning.

By the time he came back to New Jersey, he functioned as well as any other adult with the exception of some minor differences. He had no filter—what was on his mind came out his mouth, much like Leah. He couldn't seem to censor himself or recognize what was socially acceptable to say and not say. The group home would help with that. He had to relearn kindness, manners, and other social skills. In other words, he'd make an interesting addition to a dinner party.

The day of his homecoming, we took the minivan and made the eight-hour trip, travelling sixteen hours in one day. Leah and Hannah were impressive, to say the least. Drew came along, and my mouth was dry with nerves because it was the first time the two men would see each other again after the accident. With Greg's newfound ability to run off at the mouth, I was dreading what he would say.

I warned Drew about that, and he had shrugged. "Anything he'll say will probably be justified."

After the weekend Drew had almost left, he seemed to accept our new life with a certain resigned grace. I had been making a real attempt to be open and honest and finally came clean about visiting Karen, the small secret eating away at my conscience.

He reacted with his usual laissez-faire. "It seems natural, I guess. Wish I could have been a fly on the wall, though."

"Oh, my God, Drew, you should have seen how young she was. What was Greg thinking? She was probably barely in her twenties at the time." We were sitting on opposite ends of the couch, my feet resting on his lap.

He trailed his hand up and down my shin. "Why do you think he broke up with her?"

I'd been thinking the same thing. Had the lies gotten to be too much? Had he missed me? Or was it something specific about Karen? "Maybe the excitement of it was gone. I mean, eventually, people just become regular folks, you know? At some point, high-powered executive Greg Randolf just became Greg, the guy who slept with his black socks on. Maybe Karen just became a regular woman? With her own demands, just like me?"

"You? Demands?"

I playfully kicked his arm with my foot.

When I told Drew about Greg kissing me, however, he flinched. "Are you sure about us, Claire? I don't want you to resent me twenty years from now for breaking up your family. You have to be sure of what you want. And be honest with yourself and with me. I want more than anything to stay with you and have you in my life. But if I've learned one thing, it's that being dishonest about your own needs never does anyone any good."

No matter what I said, or how I reassured him, he always seemed to ask the same question a million different ways. "There is no more Claire and Greg. I can't look at him the same way, not after Karen, not after his lies. If the accident had never happened, I still don't think we would have made it."

"I can't go the rest of my life waiting for the other shoe to drop," Drew said. "What about who Greg is now?"

"It doesn't matter, you know? Timing is such a huge part of life. I can't love him like that anymore. Too much has happened." I turned the tables on him. "Can you do this? Live this life? With me and the girls, the family you'd always wanted, but with Greg, too?"

"Greg doesn't matter to me. *You* matter to me. And if I have to take him to have you, then I take him. I have faith, remember?"

"You say that now, but what about a year from now or more, when you and I go through a rough spot? There will be those, you know. No marriage is all up all the time."

"What do you think this has been?" He smiled wryly. "I'm here because I want to be. Just let it go, okay?"

<hr/>

The changes in our lives affected the girls, too. Hannah started doing poorly in school and became belligerent with the teachers, refusing to do homework. She also wanted to quit dance class. Leah, as usual, fared better, but I noticed a significant jump in temper tantrums.

They would fight in the evening, screaming hateful words at each other, words I didn't even know they knew, and it scared me. I began taking Hannah back to the child psychologist once a week, then arranged for Leah to go, too. The psychologist assured me that both responses were natural and gave me ideas on how to navigate my new waters. At her instruction, I tried to keep all developments with Greg transparent, telling them in detail about my trips to Toronto and taking them whenever I could.

When the doctors decided on the date Greg would transfer to New Jersey, I had to tell the girls that Greg wouldn't be living with us. I used his therapy as an out, though it conflicted with my self-imposed honesty rule. *Some things are mine*, I justified. They reacted as expected: scared, frustrated, but still happy he would be coming home and they'd see him more.

"You'll see him all the time," I promised. For better or worse, Greg was a permanent fixture in our lives.

Greg reacted with mixed emotions when I told him about the group home I'd found. "I think it's a good thing," he said, but it sounded forced.

"Are you okay?" I asked.

"I am, Claire. I will be. I miss us as a family, I guess. I don't know what I thought would happen when it came time for me to come back. It's not realistic for us to live together. But still..." He gave me a sad smile. "I miss it. That's all. I wish things were different. I'll miss them so much. And you, I'll miss you."

I nodded because I, too, wished things were different. "You'll see more of me now than you have for the last few months. You'll get sick of me, you'll see."

He shook his head. "I don't think that could ever happen." He pulled me into an unexpected hug. Since the day I had told him of our divorce, he'd been distant, careful to not cross any lines.

I hugged him back, resting my cheek on his shoulder. He was filling out some, although nowhere near his old stature. His arms felt reassuring around my waist, and we stayed locked in a hug. For a brief moment, I wished he had been this man years ago. Would I have loved him differently? I didn't know. I pulled away, not wanting to mislead him. Was I doing the right thing? Could I love him again? Maybe. But logically, was I willing to walk away from what I'd found with Drew?

My heart hammered as we pulled up in front of Toronto rehab for the last time, I felt. Drew helped me get Leah out of the car, then hung back, deliberately fading into the background.

When we met Greg in the lobby, he carried only a duffel bag. He greeted the girls, hugging them, then kissed my cheek. He turned to Drew, and I held my breath. Greg extended his hand, almost grudgingly, and Drew shook it. Greg said, "Drew," and they nodded at each other.

Greg then turned his attention to Leah. "Your hair has gotten so long, Leah!" Leah laughed in delight, as she wanted a "ponytail that goes down my back." I expelled a breath and caught Drew's eye. He winked discreetly at me. Maybe, just maybe, everything would be okay.

<hr />

We made the trip home, stopping for dinner and to stretch our legs. Drew and Greg made casual conversation, but Drew stayed at arm's length, careful not to be overly present, not to overshadow Greg's big day home.

The next day, we had a welcome home party at the house, which was as strange as it was happy. My parents tried to put on cheerful faces. They were happy to see Greg again, but at the same time, the room felt tight with tension. We all laughed a little too loud and talked over each other, trying to make it feel normal. Greg was alternately withdrawn and excited, surely remembering his home and a time when he had a place in it.

Drew said later he'd never felt so uncomfortable in his life and that any progress toward making our house feel like his home was erased. I knew then that moving was going to be in our near future. I dreaded the impact that would have on the girls, but could foresee no other option.

As the evening wound to a close, Mom and Dad left, and I could see Greg fading. Life took its toll on him so easily. I drove him home, and the moment felt surreal. I remembered his memorial service, and the sensation of watching events unfold through Plexiglas returned. As I pulled into the parking lot of Greg's new house, we turned to face each other.

He reached out and thumbed my cheek. "I still love you, Claire."

"I know, Greg. I love you, too. I'm always here for you. But things are different now. Do you understand that?"

"Yeah. Thank you," he said. "For all you've done for me."

Guilt pierced my heart, tailed closely by ever-present anger that never seemed to abate, following me like a sinister shadow since I'd left that small, dark kitchen weeks ago. *Thank me for leaving you?* "You don't have to thank me," I replied. "We're still a family. You're Hannah and Leah's father."

I drove away, haunted by doubt. I felt selfish, choosing my happiness over Hannah's and Leah's best interests. What if Greg and I could be happy again, the new Greg, a secret-free Greg? What if I was making a choice that would scar them forever? Could I push the anger out? Counsel it away? Or would it always be there, a long-ago applied Band-Aid over a gaping wound? I had no idea.

By the time I pulled into my driveway, I was consumed with my thoughts, unsure of my choices, of my emotions. When I walked into the house, Drew sat in the living room, reading a book. A glass of wine stood on the coffee table, waiting for me.

I watched him for a second. His brow was creased in concentration, his foot gently tapping to some inner rhythm. When he looked up and met my eyes, he smiled broadly, and my breath caught. He patted the cushion next to him, and as I sat, his arm went around me.

He kissed my head and, without waiting for me to say a word, said, "Tell me."

I knew then that he understood my doubt. Because he knew me and always had. As I rested against him, telling him my fears and confusion, I realized neither loving Greg nor loving Drew had ever been a choice.

EPILOGUE

1 YEAR LATER

THERE HAVE ALWAYS BEEN TWO men in my life. This has not changed. We've all somewhat adapted to our new patchwork family.

Greg has a new job; he went back to teaching. His short-term memory was too spotty to go back to giving lectures, but he found a position as an aide at a rehabilitation center, working with people like him. Some suffer from traumatic brain injuries; some have lifelong disabilities. He's moving out of the group home and into his own apartment at the end of the month. This is no small accomplishment, and I've spent a lot of time organizing a surprise party in his honor. He's developed an enormous support system; the guest list has over seventy people. *New Greg* draws people in, and the list of people he calls friends is longer than the list of people I know.

Sarah is flying in for the party; even she has formed a new friendship with Greg. They joke and tease each other with the familiarity of siblings, and I'm always grateful for the quickness of his smile, the ease of his laugh, the lightness in the air when she's in the room. She finally decided to say yes to poor Owen, so in May, we're all going out to California for her wedding, like the big, disjointed family we've become.

Drew and Greg have forged a somewhat tenuous friendship, partly out of necessity, but partly out of mutual respect. Drew has found it in his heart to take care of not only our family, but Greg as well. On occasion, he has even driven Greg to doctor's appointments.

Drew and I sold the house and found an old farmhouse on the other side of Clinton. The new place was falling apart and needed more work than I would have liked. But Drew insisted he could fix it, even though he's never fixed more than a leaky faucet in his life. The house is a constant project, but sometimes it's a welcome distraction.

Our fixer-upper also gives Greg something to do. Somehow, in his sleep, he became adept at fixing things, when before he somewhat floundered with a hammer in his hand. I think it's a result of his newfound patience and willingness to learn, more than any real acquired knowledge. He shows up unannounced on any day of the week, tinkers with this or that, tacks up a shutter, replaces a ceiling fan, repairs a squeaky board. His therapist says it's great for him, and Drew pretends he doesn't mind.

Leah and Hannah seem to have come through the ordeal, not unaffected, but at least unscathed. They are happy to have their daddy back in their lives. Greg frequently comes over to spend time with them. They hike in the woods behind our house, and ironically, Greg, previously so stoic, has become Hannah's confidant. He now relates to her on a level I can't compete with, and I find myself jealous when she comes home from school, upset or sad, and takes the phone into her room to whisper behind a closed door. Hannah still attends dance class, and the evening fights between her and Leah have stopped.

The girls have never appeared to be resentful of Drew, but I'm not so foolish to believe they won't as teenagers. Drew is careful to love them without trying to replace Greg, and for big decisions, he defers to their father.

We have dinner together as an extended family on alternating Sundays. Generally, those gatherings are loud, raucous affairs. Deep down, I'm sure Drew wishes to have one family event without Greg's presence, but you'd never outwardly know it. He is kind and friendly toward my ex in a way I could never have been had I been in his shoes. It's on these Sundays when my heart overflows with love for Drew.

Drew and I have not married. We will someday. We would like to have a baby of our own, but I can't in good conscience do that to Greg, not yet. I see Greg watching me when he thinks no one is looking, and sometimes it is with such open longing, it hurts my heart and twists my insides. It seems my role in life has not changed, but all the players have moved around me. My feelings for Greg are mixed. I sometimes remember Greg as he was, strong and sure, but for the Greg he is now, I have a parental, fiercely protective love.

I can't help but wonder how my life would be if any of us had made just one small decision differently. If Greg hadn't gone to Toronto. If Drew had stayed with Olivia. If in the end, I had chosen Greg. But when it comes to matters of the heart, you don't always have a choice.

Sometimes, it just is.

ABOUT KATE MORETTI

Kate Moretti lives in Pennsylvania with her husband, two kids, and a dog. She's worked in the pharmaceutical industry for ten years as a scientist, and has been an avid fiction reader her entire life.

She enjoys traveling and cooking, although with two kids, a day job, and writing, she doesn't get to do those things as much as she'd like.

Her lifelong dream is to buy an old house with a secret passageway.

Facebook: http://www.facebook.com/katemorettiwriter
Blog: A Beaker's Reflection

RED ADEPT PUBLISHING

For more great books, visit Red Adept Publishing at http://RedAdeptPublishing.com.

CPSIA information can be obtained
at www.ICGtesting.com
Printed in the USA
LVOW10s1740050117
519816LV00003B/186/P